D0936291

RT 295° 300° 305° 310° 315° 320° 325° 330° 335° 340° 345°

Remarques
§ M R   Mission de Recoletz
§ M d I   Mission des Iesuittes
§ M P P   Mission de prique pied

Echelle de 100 lieues de france

de la

Terre de Laborador

Golfe

NOVVELLE

les Sept isles

Grand

FRAN

CANA

de

banc

de

Isle de Terre nœuue

S.t Laurent

GASPESIES

Tadouaç

M. d. I. du Saguenay

QVEBEC

DCA

Accadie

ANGLETER RE

Boston

Nov.

Baston

N.ouelle Yarck

Cap. Malabarre

Iroquois

pais des

La Vurginie

la Caroline

Floride C.

Riu. Spirito Santo

du Mexique

MER

DE LA

NOVVELLE

FRANCE

ou de

NORT

Partie des Isles

Isle Bermude

Plaçance M R

Cap de Raze

a Vert

Terre neuue

Ligne du Tropique Cancer

Antilles

Isle de Cuba

la Tortue

S.t Domingue

Iamaïque

P.to Rico

la Martinique

la Tortue

S.t Christophe

OVEST

Is. Andaronegua

Is. Cinquatero

Canal de bahama

50

45

40

35

30

25

20

15

L. Boulan Sculp.

250° 295° 300° 305° 310° 315° 320°

LA SALLE

165133

La Salle

A NOVEL

John Vernon

813.54
V541

VIKING

Alverno College
Library Media Center
Milwaukee, Wisconsin

VIKING
Viking Penguin Inc., 40 West 23rd Street,
New York, New York 10010, U.S.A.
Penguin Books Ltd, Harmondsworth, Middlesex, England
Penguin Books Australia Ltd, Ringwood, Victoria, Australia
Penguin Books Canada Limited, 2801 John Street,
Markham, Ontario, Canada L3R 1B4
Penguin Books (N.Z.) Ltd, 182–190 Wairau Road,
Auckland 10, New Zealand

Copyright © John Vernon, 1986
All rights reserved

First published in 1986 by Viking Penguin Inc.
Published simultaneously in Canada

LIBRARY OF CONGRESS CATALOGING IN PUBLICATION DATA
Vernon, John, 1943–
La Salle.
1. La Salle, Robert Cavelier, sieur de, 1643–1687—
Fiction. I. Title.
PS3572.E76L3   1986   813'.54   85–29616
ISBN 0–670–80083–X

Printed in the United States of America by
R. R. Donnelley & Sons Inc., Harrisonburg, Virginia

Set in CRT Garamond
Designed by David Connolly

Endpaper map: "French conception of North America in La Salle's
time" reproduced from Le Clercq, *First Establishment of the
Faith in New France*, translated with notes by John Gilmary
Shea. New York: John G. Shea, 1881 (first published in French,
Paris: Amable Auroy, 1691, with royal privilege).

Without limiting the rights under
copyright reserved above, no part of this publication
may be reproduced, stored in or introduced into a
retrieval system, or transmitted, in any form or by
any means (electronic, mechanical, photocopying,
recording or otherwise), without the prior written
permission of both the copyright owner and the
above publisher of this book.

For Charles and Patrick;
for Ann;
and in memory of
John Gardner

Ad majorem Dei gloriam.

—MOTTO OF THE JESUITS

I willingly believe the histories
whose witnesses get themselves killed.

—PASCAL, *Pensées*

Contents

LA SALLE

Preface

In 1673, Louis Jolliet and Père Jacques Marquette traveled by canoe down the Mississippi River as far as the Arkansas River, then turned back. Nine years later, René Robert Cavelier, Sieur de La Salle, and his relatively large party of forty-one people—twenty-three Frenchmen and eighteen Abenaki and Mohegan Indians from New England and Maine—became the first group containing white explorers to go all the way down the river to its mouth.

Among the Frenchmen in this party was my ancestor, Pierre Goupil. I call him my ancestor; great-uncle in the twelfth degree of descent would be more precise. For three centuries, my family has traced its lineage to him, his brother, and his brother's children, wheelwrights in Rouen, later merchants and traders, and still later wine merchants of the well-known Goupil and Sons, exporters of the finest French Bordeaux to discerning New Yorkers for more years than I have lived. Pierre Goupil was La Salle's cartographer, sometime navigator, and part-time servant; that is, La Salle seems to have regarded him as a servant when the fancy struck him. My ancestor was also accused of and hung for a crime which in all probability he did not commit, a crime which occurred five years after La Salle's Mississippi voyage, as the result of a chain of events which that voyage initiated.

I

In fact, the famous trip down the Mississippi is only half the story. La Salle's subsequent machinations to convince Louis XIV to finance a return trip to America; his inability—or refusal—to find the mouth of the Mississippi from the Gulf of Mexico; his creation of a colony in Matagorda Bay on the coast of Texas; and the fate of him and his colonists in Texas, all complete the arc of a narrative so bizarre most of us would be tempted to label it fiction if we didn't know it to be true. During all of this, Pierre Goupil was by La Salle's side. His crude but vivid and sincere account of these events forms a stark contrast to that of the master he served. In this book, I have edited the journals and letters of La Salle and Pierre Goupil in such a way as to allow the story to tell itself, through their alternating voices. Where the two men discuss the same event, I've usually included only the most interesting account, or the one most relevant to the overall narrative, though in a few cases differing versions of the same event are themselves interesting, because of the differences; the reader is therefore advised to note the dates for journal entries in order to detect when the narrative circles back.

Part I presents the 1682 voyage down the Mississippi; Part II, the correspondence of La Salle and Goupil after they returned to France, where they kept no journals. Though I've titled Part III "Texas," La Salle and his followers were unaware of such a name. One of La Salle's fatal geographical errors was not to realize—or to ignore—the fact that the area we now call Texas came between the lower Mississippi Basin and Mexico. It seems clear that he thought the mouth of the Mississippi was closer to Mexico than it was, although he didn't hesitate to move it even closer when he wanted to tempt Louis and his ministers with prospects of conquering Mexico. He could do this because the technology of navigation was such in the seventeenth century that latitudes could be calculated with a fair degree of accuracy, but longitudes could not, since the chronometer had yet to be invented.

The Mississippi empties into the Gulf of Mexico not with a roar, but by means of a delta, difficult to spot from a ship on the Gulf. Some historians think that the Sieur de La Salle deliberately sailed past the river's mouth, and that his intention from the beginning was not to establish a colony on the river (as he stated) but solely to invade Mexico. Others, including amateur scholars such as myself, smile sadly and shake our heads at one of those ironies of history which fold back on themselves; for the same inability to calculate longitudes which enabled him to push the river around on his maps also withheld crucial information regarding its location when he needed it most. He sailed past the Mississippi's mouth and landed on the coast of Texas, then spent the last two miserable years of his life looking for the fateful river whose geography he'd once treated so cavalierly.

Pierre Goupil's lengthy letter to the Governor of Quebec in Part IV completes the story, and represents the culmination of a lifetime of detective work for this writer. I will not trouble the reader with a long account of my search for all the pieces of this story. The task of fitting them together has occupied my waking hours and sleepless nights, and has driven me to a study of history untainted by professional academic affiliations. I began with Pierre Goupil's journals, which have been in my family for centuries; these were, so to speak, the fragment of an ancient treasure map I was privileged to inherit. Then, ten years ago, La Salle's journals were discovered (with much fanfare and ballyhoo) in the library of the Jesuit seminary in Quebec—another fragment. La Salle's, Goupil's, and Captain Beaujeu's letters have long been in the public domain, since the publication of Margry's *Découvertes* in 1879. But Pierre Goupil's letter to the Governor of Quebec, the last missing piece, has never been available until now, and would still lie in the graveyard of history had I not literally smuggled a Spanish translation of it out of the Archivo General de Indias in Seville, whose trustees conveniently forbid the copying of documents by any except titled scholars, preferably male. The French original of this letter has been lost.

This, then, is the first time all these materials have been

assembled and translated into English. My purpose in publishing this book is to remove the centuries-old stain from our family history. Whether it shall have this effect is perhaps another question. Professional historians to whom I have shown these documents—even some I respect—have pointed out certain internal evidence, certain inconsistencies in the description of key events by La Salle and Goupil, which appear to indicate that one of them wasn't always truthful. To them I say: I have not authored these papers, I have translated and edited them. I have changed nothing, though I have eliminated certain tedious passages in order to present the story in a popular form suited for the general reader, who may decide upon Goupil's guilt or innocence as he or she sees fit. I rest my case with the People, to whom it should have been presented three centuries ago.

I am old. When I was a child, my great-grandmother told me of a France before the railroads; her great-grandfather fought in the Revolution. When I die, I will take all this with me, as the last of the Goupils of Rouen. For fifty years, I have lived away from France, in the greatest and cruelest city in the world, surviving on the token homage it pays the past: rent control. *Après moi . . .* Yet, I feel confident of the good effect of this book, even as I write this. I may not live to see the tricentennial of La Salle's death, but should my efforts on behalf of Pierre Goupil prove successful, in 1987 we will honor more than simply a visionary but hotheaded explorer; we will also honor the man who gave him faithful service until the end.

In my capacity as editor of these documents, I have regularized and modernized the spelling of most names and places to conform with contemporary usage. Some older names have historical importance, however, and these I have retained; for example, La Salle at times referred to the Mississippi as the "Messipi" ("great river" in Algonquin) and at times as the "Colbert"—the name of Louis XIV's minister. Place names for early explorers were in an inchoate state regardless, and were bestowed usually out of homage to their patrons; had the French succeeded in colonizing the entire Mississippi Valley, as La Salle wished, we would perhaps still know the Illinois River today as the Seignelay (named for Colbert's son and successor as minister), though we may hope that the confusion entailed by giving the Red River the same name would have been cleared up by now. In all cases where confusion might arise, I've placed our more familiar names in brackets after the older usage.

I have made no effort to find English equivalents for Pierre Goupil's frequent misspellings, though most of his grammatical and punctuation errors have been translated intact. The story passed down through my family indicates that he worked as a *donné* in the kitchen garden at the Collège Henri IV at La Flèche, France, outside of Rouen, where La Salle was a Jesuit scholastic. La Salle taught him to read and write—he was one of the explorer's experiments, so to speak—and he consequently considered himself to have climbed through the ranks to become a full-fledged bourgeois. That this notion was not unfounded is demonstrated by the subsequent rise of my family, despite the blot of Pierre Goupil's presumed crime. But it will be clear from these pages that his social elevation was not accepted by the man who initiated it, La Salle, and this may very well be the source of Goupil's ambivalent feelings toward his patron. Pierre Goupil, I should add, accompanied La Salle on his first voyage to Canada in 1667, and served as cartographer and navigator on all the explorer's expeditions, although La Salle often reserved much of the latter work for himself, fearing that important information would fall into the hands of his enemies.

Enemies? Undoubtedly he had them. La Salle began as a novice Jesuit, but later left the order and turned against the Black Robes, as they were called. (His preference was for the Brown Robes: the Recollects, or Franciscans.) But whether the Jesuits actually conspired against him, or La Salle was prodigiously paranoiac, is unclear. Though the evidence of paranoia is certainly everywhere in these pages, I do not condemn La Salle. On the other hand, could I comfortably descend to the foolish hagiography of Parkman's otherwise classic study? The Sieur de La Salle is the principal of this story (I hesitate to say "hero") and the reason for its being. If it were not for him, we would never have heard of Pierre Goupil, and the burden of history would never have rested on my shoulders. But this burden is no longer mine. It is yours. Both men are here, each in his own words. Behold them, scrutinize them, judge for yourselves.

Some helpful equivalencies:
12 deniers = 1 sol
20 sols = 1 livre (or franc)
3 livres = 1 silver écu
6 livres = 1 gold écu
1 sol = 5 cents in American money;
hence, a livre or franc
is roughly equivalent
to our dollar
1 arpent = 1/28 of a mile
1 league = 3 miles

A somewhat technical note: a pirogue is a dugout canoe, used by Indians south of (roughly) the confluence of the Mississippi and the Missouri rivers, who hadn't the use of birch and elm bark, as La Salle and his men did. Pirogues were slower and less maneuverable than birch-bark canoes.

In the opening passages, the expedition is on the Seignelay River—that is, the Illinois—at roughly the location of present-day Morris, Illinois, moving southwest toward the Mississippi.

—ELIZABETH GOUPIL FOX-RECKMEYER
New York City

I

THE MISSISSIPPI

1 6 8 2

GOUPIL

up before dawn a fine day   we embarked without eating
after making ready to take advantage of the clear weather
Then comes M. Tonty to declare he must eat & all heave to
with the sleds and disembark,   after loading the canoes like
that & the Sieur de La Salle had no objection.

So we must unload again,   arms and merchandise carpenter's joiner's pit sawyer's tools food and equipment   of
course the Sieur de La Salle's trunk which he protects as
though it contained his heart or breath   no one knows what
it contains   hung with 3 hooks.   He caused André Baboeuf to make it for him in Montreal   fit tight & caulked
of tenon and mortise   oak I think   hemp stuffed along all
the corners & edges inside of it I saw when it was made back
in Montreal

Now he removes it first when we disembark   never allowing it to stray from his sight.   sits on it at camp   not
once has he ventured to open it.

ate sagamité and rabbit   my rash better
Then loaded again all the equipment in the canoes
canoes on the sleds we hauled down the ice with care,
Sanomp's rope broke it was old   Migneret fell through the
ice yesterday had to build a fire   We keep waiting for the
ice to break up but not yet   this was at nine or ten o'clock

9

& we dragged the canoes all day, I was accompanied by the savages except 3 the interpreter & his squaw, the fore part of the day cold & sunny afternoon turned hazy with a rain. Wind hard from the SW straight up the river & cold which increased until night makes the ice very treacherous the rain turned to snow after 2 hours the Sieur de LaSalle makes 39° north the river continues SW here 7 leagues

2 0 J a n u a r y 1 6 8 2

dark today all day the forests dark our four leagues today may be ascribed to the stupidity of the Sieur de La Salle who insisted the hunters pursue a herd of deer we saw on the bank who had such a start on our men they were never seen again faster than chamois. we spent the good part of the day waiting for the hunters to return emptyhanded God suffers us to court our own bondage.

the savage called Pious continues poorly today he returned from the hunt very fatigued & on his arrival drank a hearty draught of cold water & at once fell to violent retching pains writhing although he refused to cry out lay on his side clutching his stomach face perfectly composed a stranger sight I never shall see as his pulse was high the Sieur de La Salle bled him & this seemed to afford some small measure of relief

one man with a toothache two with a slight fever one has the pains in his intestines

2 2 J a n u a r y 1 6 8 2

the 21st 9 leagues SW we camped on a wide beach in pouring rain miserable

today was better made 14 leagues river continues SSW rain again tonight we prop the canoes on forked sticks & hang birch curtains for the rain & sit there pretty as a Prince with his coach and six

he sits on his trunk dripping water paring his nails with a
knife by himself   Membré confides that he seems vain
I tell him this has been so during our long acquaintance & it
hasn't changed in this abomination of earth they call *New*

Membré & I had several fine discourses tonight upon the
globes & the fixed stars as to why they do not rise & set at
the same hour all the year long, which he could not demonstrate   neither could I

L A   S A L L E

24 January 1682

The River Seignelay [Illinois] is frozen this year further
south than we had anticipated, and today we continued haul-
ing the canoes on sledges. We passed shores everywhere
confronted by towering cliffs rising out of the mist, now
appalling, now pleasing to the eye, whose walls had produced
many prodigious waterfalls of ice. It is wonderful how large
trees can find root among so many rocks, and the overall
effect of tree, rock, snow, and ice was such as to excite our
wonder.

At midday, the river narrowed and a vast wreckage of ice
loomed ahead of us. I recognized this place as near Fort
Crèvecoeur, our furthest previous penetration of this river.
Accordingly, I ordered the canoes to be brought on shore
and the sledges cached while Tonty and two of the savages
scouted a portage ahead to the fort. As I anticipated, the river
was free of ice below the jam, but our portage carried us on
cliffs above the river and as a consequence we could not reach
it again for another league, by which time we had arrived at
the fort. As everyone was fatigued, I resolved to spend the
next several days in rest here, while the hunters replenish our
stock of meat.

The fort had suffered the ravages of weather and neglect,
but we quickly repaired it sufficient for our needs. I noted
with mortification the half-completed bark I had caused to be

built for this very expedition more than a year ago, large enough to carry our entire company. Its broken shell lay tipped on a bank. Those who conspire against me would doubtless take joy in the sight of a ship whose death was the death of two; for when the *Griffon* sank on the Lake of the Hurons, the fittings, ropes, and sails for this vessel sank along with it. And the *Griffon* was sunk deliberately, as one man stabs another in the back. The crew took its furs worth twelve thousand livres and joined Du Lhut in the company of the Sioux. As for the men who deserted me at this fort, they left their mark on the hull of the half-completed bark: *Nous sommes tous savages: Ce 15—1680.* The one who wrote this, whom we nicknamed La Liberté, to mock his vanity by a swelling name, joined the Miamis and painted his face, but later died from choking upon the bones of a fish, which he ate raw.

Once the canoes were unloaded, our Illinois savage Nicanapé drew in the dirt a map of the route ahead. He said the journey from here to the River Colbert, or, as he calls it, the Messipi, is four days savage, five days French. But I've observed that the savages out of laziness tend to fall behind, unless they are sensible of danger or excited by war, in which case they paddle with such haste that no Frenchman could hope to overtake them. This Nicanapé has changed his tune since that occasion a year ago upon which he told us that our minds were diseased for wishing to descend the great river, which was impassable in places because of rapids, and guarded by monsters, Tritons, giant lizards, and barbarous nations who eat their enemies; and that even should the size and speed of our canoes protect us from these dangers, there was a final and inevitable one, that the lower part of the river was full of a series of falls and precipices with a current so violent that men and boats all go down helplessly and become drawn into a gulf or hole where the river becomes lost underground, without anyone's knowing whither it goes. These fables caused me to lose half my men and sowed doubts in the rest, but Nicanapé has since changed his story and now describes the Messipi as the most benign of great waters, navigable all the way down to its mouth. From certain details of his map I am more than ever convinced that the river discharges itself into the Gulf of Mexico, and not, as I previously thought, into the Vermillion Sea [the Gulf of California].

After everyone had taken sufficient rest, I ordered a ration of brandy to be distributed, and the rest of the day was spent in dancing and feasting, activities I normally frown upon as not conducive to discipline. But in this place and at this time of year, the temptations are few and the squaws all married. Jacques Oubidichagan's three women, who are sisters, danced all afternoon. They are fine Christian savages—those who have three women, all sisters! I reproached him gently for this. He replied that they were Christians *arech,* which is to say without resolution and solely because Father Allouez had told them that it was necessary to pray occasionally in order to be his friend. Thank God M. R. N. isn't with us.[1]

2 6 J a n u a r y   1 6 8 2

Today the hunters shot two deer, and as they were hungry, the savages, like a pack of famished dogs, tore into one of them raw. The scene was such that had I not possessed a keen appetite myself I would have forsworn venison entirely. Even little Lachine partook most ravenously, eating the kidney which her mother gave her, until her lips, chin, and fingers were smeared with blood.

In other respects, Lachine is no different from a Christian infant. Once satiated, she offered me some of her food, but I wrinkled my nose and sniffed, whereupon she did the same, then lifted her eyebrows, curved her blood-bespattered mouth in a little O, and said "Oooohhhh." One tiny drop of her upper lip hung suspended in the circle of her mouth.

---

[1]M. R. N.: Monsieur Robe Noir (Monsieur Black Robe)—that is, the Jesuits.

After the meal, she was most active, though she like her father has been unwell. In the mornings, her eyes are full of a pus which, when dried to a crust, forms a seal, thus effectively preventing her from opening the eyes. When she awakens and discovers her eyes *locked,* as it were, she screams and cries until her mother peels off this crust of dried pus. But tonight she walked around shouting and pointing, free for the time being of the confines of the basket in which she normally rides, in the center of her mother's canoe. She pointed at something on the frozen ground; bending over to touch it, she then raised her arms in an expression of triumph worthy of the Queen of England, or of our own Jeanne d'Arc. She nodded her little head and spouted a stream of nonsense, as though to mock Father Membré, who always nods and sputters when he talks. When the music and dancing have stopped, she becomes the chief source of entertainment for our company.

27 January 1682

The hunters shot three more deer this morning and we spent the better part of the day smoking the meat and mixing fat and grease with the cornmeal to make sagamité. Goupil reminds me of the French peasant who said if he were king, he would have all the grease he could eat.

Our Abenaki brave Pious continued all day sick and low-spirited. He claims to have been possessed by a manitou, which are spirits these savages perceive in the rocks and trees, and seem to be their name for both their devils and their gods. The other savages rub his body with grease, then place their hands on his head and chant some sort of dirge, and this scandalizes Father Membré, because they are supposed to be Christians. I have found that the natural stoicism of these savages enables them to bear suffering better than their supposed Christianity, which is merely skin-deep. In sickness, they revert to jugglers and witches, though Pious was a juggler himself in Montreal. When I first met

14

him, he talked for hours on end with the Devil, who lived
in a pitcher of water he carried around. But amongst savages, their jugglers (or *physicians*) are unable to heal themselves, and I've observed that they often fall into a deep
melancholy when ill, as though all their magical powers had
been sapped.

The attempts made by our priests to convert these savages
are at best amusing. They baptize infants on the point of
death, and secretly rejoice when death in fact ensues, since
the child then won't grow up to repudiate—as most of them
do—the True Faith. The savages subsequently blame the
child's death on the act of baptism, and sometimes wreak
vengeance on the priests.

In truth, life in the New World is no fun at all for the Black
Robes and Brown Robes, and were most of them not such
fools I would feel more pity for them. Some are brave to the
point of distraction, enduring as much suffering as the Lord
himself endured, but most of their sufferings are without
merit, since they could not help it.

As for the Jesuits, some of them have learned. In the Bay
of the Puans [Green Bay], the bevy of Jesuits there have
converted more iron into beaver than all the Fathers do
savages into Christians. A few have even profited by the sale
of brandy, which they condemn in others as though it were
the work of the Devil. With such money they built their
college in Quebec.

Goupil, La Métairie, and Barbier caulked the canoes with
fresh pitch this afternoon. I bled Pious again this evening,
and his daughter Lachine clapped her hands at the sight of the
blood, and formed her mouth into a circle and said
"Ooooohhhhh."

28 January 1682

A most extraordinary incident occurred this morning before
our departure. As we were packing the canoes to leave,
Pious, who had been listless for weeks, began hopping

around and screaming, claiming that the manitou which had entered his body needed to be driven out. He chased Father Membré around, who, turning as he ran, burst into a hasty series of signs of the cross and shouted with extreme distress, *"Vade retro, Satanas"* several times. Finally, Pious collapsed and insisted he be given a canoe to make his way back to his own people. I was reluctant to give up one of our vessels, but Tonty thought it best; we could always construct another. No one expects Pious to be capable of returning all the way to Montreal, but the savages have their own ways of dying. His squaw made no protest.

At last we started out and the canoes sat like perfect corks in the water. With one less canoe, the added weight, distributed evenly, caused the water to come up within several fingers' width of the gunwales. This felt like we were kneeling in the river. We ride the high river in places the savages must portage during the summer, according to Nicanapé. The water continually appears to be rising, and carries us swiftly, to our greater glory.

In her canoe, Lachine refuses to be confined by her basket any longer. Her mother is forced to watch her carefully. She trails an intestine from one of our deer in the river, allowing the water to rush through it.

GOUPIL

30 January 1682

SW 12 leagues a good day   we paddle with ease the river does the work,   some ice trailing behind us nudged my canoe Paddle faster Pierre!

the water appears to increase in velocity

31 January 1682

we continued SW about 3 leagues when we noticed more ice,   the level of the river having dropped.   all the pieces

of ice of every description is small and appeared to be broken
by Some Convulsion

then close to midday larger chunks of ice making navigation perilous,   the water rose all at once & flooded & we
scarcely had time to decamp as fast as possible & attain high
ground   putting our goods in the trees.

but I was less fortunate than the others,   with Migneret
the carpenter who scarcely knew how to avoid the ice   our
canoe tips over and we receive a frigid dunking   Migneret
who can't swim screaming carried down the river,   but he
snares a tree and pulls himself up.

most of the equipment we were able to retrieve and build
a fire to dry the men & goods   but I haven't told the Sieur
de La Salle that the water carried off our only compass even
though I felt for it along the bank until my arms were
numb.   Without said compass I find it more difficult than
ever to   calculate our longitude as I've been charged,
moreover the Sieur de La Salle keeps the astrolabe himself
on a chain around his neck with which to astound the savages   he makes his own calculations   sometimes conde-
scending to share them with me

I make 43 leagues difference east & west from Quebec to
Montreal   from Montreal to Fort Frontenac 61 leagues
from the fort to Niagara 65   from Niagara to the end of
Lake Erie 122   from there to the mouth of the river of the
Miamis 117   thence to the Illinois 52   thence to fort
Crèvecoeur 27   from Crèvecoeur to here 15 leagues but
the river ahead appears to swing directly south.   all this
about 500 which makes about 24° of longitude on a great
circle on which I ought to take an east-west line from here
to Quebec with 17 1/2 leagues for a degree of the equinoc-
tial,   as I've been taught

without the compass I can guess by the sun but overcast
skies will make this difficult   also excessive windings and
twists of the river   God follows an ordinary & common
way but rivers twist and bend like the Master of Darkness
himself   my map to reflect this

we spent the greater part of the day drying off goods while the river fell   my leg hurting from having struck it on the gunwales when we tipped over.

in the late afternoon we were surprised when the sick savage the Sieur de La Salle had sent back to Canada came paddling down on abated waters,   he disembarked & warmed himself at the fire without a word which appeared to infuriate the master who made unflattering gestures & pointings & expressions behind his back   Pious looks to be cured of his illness but the Sieur de La Salle thought he should be bled

he bleeds the father but dotes on the daughter   who the men took to calling Lachine because of her seeming oriental features   but as well out of some mockery for the Sieur de La Salle's former fancy to find a passage to China and also out of suspicion for the excessive fondness he shows her   : For it seems unnatural to these men Barbier Prud'homme Migneret   that a Frenchman should be so enamored of a savage infant not of his blood, or so it appears   this can be accounted for by the Sieur de La Salle's lonely temperament   which requires itself to be entertained by a little pet

her name corrupted by the savages to Lakeen   with their inability to master our tongue.   Her oriental appearance make some of us wonder whether these savages is all in some way related to the race of Chinese across the South Sea eons ago finding a way to cross unknown waters in their canoes   they might have come to the shores of this continent   where afterwards they reverted to savagery

2 F e b r u a r y   1 6 8 2

as the Sieur de La Salle who never takes anyone's advice likes to follow along the banks sometimes in order to hunt,   & seeking to make some profitable discovery   he insisted I accompany him 2 days ago for which my gratitude overflows to be treated like a servant   having no choice I followed lame leg & all.

but the snow began to fall & I could hardly keep up
noticing we'd somehow strayed from the river,   moreover
the marshes we met obliged us to make a wide sweep & we
unable to find the banks of the river   his temper mounting
all the while.   We shot off volleys but heard nothing in
return

after marching in this way for more than three hours we
saw some fire on a mound   ascended it brusquely calling all
the while   instead of finding our party it was but a little fire
among some brush and under a tree   the spot where a man
had been lying down on dry herbs but now he was gone.

in the midst of our terror & misery this excited the Sieur
de La Salle's curiosity no little bit, as we had not seen another
person since leaving the Miamis though savages are known
to live by these shores.   the Sieur de La Salle called out in
some of the gibberish these savages speak   at last to show
that we did not fear him he cries out that we will sleep in this
place   renewing the fire & making ready to sleep among
boughs in this bitter cold,   while I find myself trembling in
every limb   I prostrate myself in the snow more from fear
than cold   but the Sieur de La Salle took steps to guarantee
us against surprise   he cut down around us a quantity of
bushes,   falling across those that remained standing this
blocked the way & no one could approach without making
considerable noise   then he lay by the fire & slept.

but I continued trembling & shivering   I must have slept
at last   snowing all night   the next morning we went to
seek trails & found that someone had approached 2 or 3 times
this rampart of brushwood,   daring not to cross it for fear
of being discovered.

at last that day we found the river bank & following it
discovered our party,   who expressed the greatest dismay
and consternation   but of course they could not censure the
Sieur de La Salle, master of us all

For ten years now I have followed this man, three years
since I've lived in a house   pursuing for five years his
rumor of a river   we have lived in canoes bark cabins on

the ground in rain & snow   a fort was like the Louvre by
comparison   we have starved have eaten putrid meat and
tasteless cornmeal   for three years I have not had a bite of
bread,   nor slept on a bed or pillow   we have subjected
ourselves to the hazards of heathen savages wolves and
bears   suffered the desertion of his men   & I prevented
one from shooting him in the back   suffered the loss of his
supplies and finances   the treachery of his enemies who
have instigated the ferocious Iroquois against him

we have suffered ourselves to be blamed by these savages
for the diseases they bring upon themselves by their filthy
habits   one going so far as to blame me for the disease
of his people by means of a poisoned cloak I sent among
them

we have lived among these savages and been forced to
smell them   contracted their lice   in a bark house you
can't stand up in the winter you lie or sit all day like a prison
or dungeon   the winds come in you can't move right or left
can't stretch out because your feet would be burned by the
fire   you freeze on one side roast on the other   and the
smoke!   eyes watering constantly   I have had to lie down
for hours on end with my mouth to the earth in order to
breathe,   while the savages around me jabbering away all
the time I thought they would cut off my head   then wake
up with five or six dogs sleeping on my shoulders and feet
& eat deer meat hard as dry wood and become sick to go
outside every 2 hours in snow up to my waist and empty my
bowels   return to find a snag-toothed squaw gathering up
handfuls of grease in the kettle and offering it   meat covered with moosehairs or sand.

would you be a famous adventurer and chart unknown
lands for the glory of God & the King?   never to set foot
in a civilized house or smell decent cooking & see French
women and children or listen to their conversation   I've
gnawed at the tips of branches in the woods and the tender
bark underneath the outer covering   with an eel skin for all
three meals I considered myself well fed   & for what?

now we are off again on this man's chimerical pursuits & who knows where it will lead us?

LA SALLE

2 February 1682

Yesterday out hunting with Pierre Goupil I came across the live coals of a fire on a hill, still smoldering, and in order to tempt the savages living in these parts to come forward and trade with us and bring us information about the countryside and its resources, I chose to spend the night in this camp, much to Goupil's dismay; for we have not yet seen any of those natives who Nicanapé claims populate these lands, though some of the men imagine they watch us continually and are ready to attack at any minute.

It appears that the absence of these natives creates more apprehension in my men than their presence would provoke caution; for they aver that the savages who live here are afraid of us and consider us cursed for going down the river to parts unknown. But the coals in this fire were proof that these savages have not all run off; and though this one failed to return that night, we saw the next morning by signs that he had approached the camp several times, without however making himself known.

All of this contributed to Goupil's unease. He complained we were lost; I assured him we weren't; but assurances for the ignorant work as thorns. Even when our little digression was over and we had rejoined our party, his glum behavior persisted, much to my annoyance; for such public displays are cankerous as to the spirit of the men, and make it doubly difficult to perform the great task before us.

For the rest of the day we made good progress, and should soon attain the River Colbert. When the ice broke up the river rose, but now it seems to have dropped a small measure. In places along the banks lie honeycombed patches of snow, but some signs of winter are beginning to abate.

3 February 1682

The land about these parts is all flooded, and the weather continues cold and damp, making complainers of even some capable men. To assuage Goupil, who still mopes about like a gloomy dog as a consequence of yesterday's adventure, I have decided to name a tributary we passed today for him. Thus, his immortality is assured; he will give it prominence on his maps, and transform Goupil's ditch into a torrent.

As for those who reproach me with rash deviations from our course, or with all manner of things, with ostentation or foolish outlays, I could name a few swamps for them. Let my accusers explain what they mean; I am busy charting unknown lands. Since arriving in this country, I have had neither servants nor clothes nor fare which did not savor more of meanness than display. They see my box and imagine it contains all the comforts which they themselves abandoned in coming to this place, whereas all they need do is regard my clothes to know that I am just as ragged as they are. They charge me with love for the appurtenances of a life the very abhorrence of which drove me to this wilderness in the first place. I may reserve some small comforts and accessories to myself, by prerogative of rank, but I would never have voyaged to the New World had I not been willing to give anything up, with the exception of my honor; and the more danger and difficulty there is in undertakings of this sort, the more worthy of honor I think they are.

I fear I may have been poisoned again. This morning we ate some fish from the river; then at noon before the meal was cooked I was taken with such a violent pain in the intestines that I couldn't partake. Nika and the other savages prepared for me a concoction of black and viscous liquid boiled from sticks, moss, and bark, which tasted bitter; by evening I was relieved from pain, and the fever I had contracted abated. These savages may be the only ones I can trust; I speak more openly to them than to the rest, who are generally spies of my enemies. Deserters and thieves await any pretext to commit their crimes; then lie through their teeth once caught.

GOUPIL

5 February 1682

I make 13 leagues today in flooded land   the river's banks sunken hard to find

before we embarked this morning a commotion drew our attention Pious the Abenaki brave with an unexpected surge of energy   attacking Father Membré threw him to the ground,   then approached the Sieur de La Salle with hatchet upraised   M. Tonty forced to shoot him   shot him in the hand   immediately he collapsed   the Sieur de La Salle who acts as our physician dressing the wound as best he could.   but the savage broke into a paroxysm trembling like a leaf   then lapsed into sleep from which he hasn't woke yet.   we laid him in Tonty's canoe & proceeded

decamped after dark as dry land difficult to find we must sleep all damp   Pious still sleeping   a controversy has arose over giving this savage the last rites of the church Membré points out he was baptized   I say once a pagan always a pagan   as to morals the savages are lascivious & revert to their heathenish ways the first chance they get they have among them many such fools as Pious or rather lunatics & insane people   they dwell in the darkness of paganism.

6 February 1682

slept poorly last night   how I longed for a bed which to me now would prove Paradise   I wished with all my heart I had stayed in France   all night just above me two owls with their horrid hooting   chased them off 3 times but after a minute they were back again   finally I let them howl

expert hunter that he is the Sieur de La Salle says he flushed a deer wounded it but it escaped   I knocked it down but it ran off he said   That does not mean anything my dear You must bring home the liver   the liver!

Pious slept all this day   12 leagues SW

7 February 1682

in the morning we woke up Pious was stiff and cold.   this didn't seem to bother anybody,   Father Membré said some prayers over the wretch they wrapped his body in a blanket and threw it in the trees   I think the Sieur de La Salle was happy to see him dead, some of the men smile behind his back

miserable sinner so are we all   I meditated on the corpse to remind me of our earthly state and the corruptions of the flesh,   which worms shall eat

this is the second one of our party who died   the ship's carpenter having taken ill last November   died after horrible fevers convulsions

8 leagues SW   river not as fast now

LA SALLE

7 February 1682

By this morning our Abenaki savage, Pious, was dead. Father Membré sprinkled some holy water on his corpse, and as is customary with these savages, we carried him into the woods, to a clearing, and lay him on the ground covered with a blanket. It was snowing lightly, and another blanket soon covered him. Membré said a few prayers and one or two savages (including his daughter, little Lachine) mimed the sign of the cross.

Normally, these savages are rarely sick; nor gouty, dropsical, or fever-vexed. They are extremely robust and vigorous and may go for whole days without eating; yet paddle a canoe vigorously from dawn until several hours after sunset, then rise the next morning and do the same. As for Pious, his choleric temperament burned him up from within; and I would like to be able to see his spleen, which I fancy by now would be an organ self-consumed, a piece of scorched leather.

8 February 1682

The River Seignelay is about the size of the Seine at Paris, and in two or three places wider. Prairies beside the river give way to hills, whose sides are covered with trees, which in turn give way to prairies again. Between the hills lie long marshy strips, flooded at this time of year, with naked trees standing in the water. Tonty and I climbed one of the hills and discovered beautiful prairies farther than the eye can reach, interrupted at intervals by groves of tall trees. These trees would make excellent building timber, especially some very fine oaks, full like those in France and very different from the oaks of Canada. These trees are prodigious of girth and height, and you could find there the finest pieces in the world for such shipbuilding as could be carried out upon the spot. All the vessels of France could be built in this place, which would give the trees in our exhausted forests time to grow again.

Tonty and his men shot sixteen partridges, which are exactly like those of France except they have two ruffs of three or four feathers each as long as a finger near the head, covering the two sides of the neck. Their flavor is the same.

My diarrhea continues; tonight it turned into a bloody flux. Membré has it too. The Sieur de Boisrondel has a strained back caused by slipping and falling in the canoe.

9 February 1682

Before departing this morning, I stood on the bank staring at the river, and a miraculous, strange bird came out of nowhere and shrieked in my face.

At midmorning, we found an enormous buffalo mired in the banks of the river; Tonty shot it in the brain and twelve of our men dragged it with difficulty to solid ground with a rope. We spent the rest of the morning cutting it up, eating the best parts, and smoking some of the meat.

At last we arrived at the River Colbert [Mississippi] with a joy in my heart which I can scarcely express. The river was high and swift, with great floes of ice, and we were forced to disembark before entering. I see now that we shall be obliged to camp here for a while until the ice this majestic river carries down from its unknown reaches in the north has diminished.

On sounding, Goupil found fourteen brasses of water. The width of the Colbert here varies from as much as a league to four or five arpents. I make the latitude as between 36° and 37° north. Goupil, who has a large jaw and face like a mule and always looks morose, pretends to calculate the longitude, but I know he is lost. Three islets at the juncture of the rivers form several large sandbars which trap the ice and trees and other debris floating down the Colbert from the north. Approaching this confluence, I noted a flat precipitous rock on the south bank of the Seignelay well suited for building a fort. Across from it, on the north bank, are fields of black earth stretching as far as the eye can see. They look as though they have been freshly turned, although of course this is impossible. But I could not fail to observe what a suitable location for a colony this would be. At this location, one could attract trade from the north and east and channel it not through Canada, but south on this river, if it proves to be navigable all the way to its mouth. Moreover, the soil is so rich and fertile that a substantial colony would easily begin to support itself within a year or two; and trees suitable for ships and houses are well within reach. From here, the flow of ships and goods back to France might double that of Quebec.

But this says nothing of the beauty of the land, which now appears terrifying, now so temperate and calm, with hills and groves of woods scattered here and there, that one would think that the ancient Romans with all their princes and nobles would have made them as many villas as they could with a prospect of these rivers.

Then night falls and the land grows vast in the dark. The men become quiet. We hear wolves and other creatures crashing through the brush, and the ceaseless rush of the water, with its sounds like broken *tongues* or *choruses* carried off by the immeasurable length of the river.

1 0 F e b r u a r y   1 6 8 2

I am beginning to feel better today and have regained my strength, in gratitude for which I said a prayer. Among the men, Bassard's fever has abated, but Goupil still pretends to be lame. We celebrated Mass and received Communion for the last time this year, as Father Membré has no more wine. The thought of confessing to him turns my stomach; I meditate upon my transgressions alone. I reminded him today of the Roman courtesan, mistress to one of the Popes, who confessed her sins to this Pope as well; so that the same ears which heard the confession in the morning had also heard her cries of love the night before. This failed to rattle our good Membré, who treats everything as the deepest matter of theology, and preached to me upon the Donatists, in order to prove that the whore's confession was valid.

I asked him, Is the Holy Presence evenly distributed throughout every crumb or atom of the wafer; or does it withdraw itself from the Part in order to more fully adhere to the Whole? This he could not answer. Then he grew angry, in suspicion that I was teasing him. Our discussions prove vexatious to him because he doesn't know whether I am treating them as a game. The slow fish takes an unbaited hook.

Our men grow restless because of their eagerness to be off and share in the glory of discovery. The rain and mud inhibit our hunters, who managed to kill today only a single porcupine, which served to season the last of the Indian corn we had. We still have seen no signs of savages or any other humans, except for the prairies burned for miles around by savage hunters, and the bones and horns and skulls of buffaloes on all sides. According to Nicanapé, when the savages see a herd of buffaloes, they set fire to the grass everywhere around them except for some narrow passage, which they leave on purpose and beside which they take post with their bows and arrows. Seeking to escape the fire, the buffaloes are thus compelled to pass near these hunters, who sometimes kill as many as a hundred in a day.

But we have seen no savage hunters, and no buffaloes; and from our eminence above the river, with its endless debris, as well as from the prospect around us of miles of burned prairies, it seems to our fancies as though the rest of the world has been destroyed by a cataclysm, and we are the only ones left alive.

11 February 1682

The hunters returned again today empty-handed, and the men continue to complain. I could feed them Membré, but the meat would be stringy. As is usually the case, our savages, better able to endure hunger, and ashamed of complaining, act as though nothing disturbs them. I've observed that their obtundity, or insensitivity to pain, is a characteristic whose further study might well prove profitable to us; for even while undergoing the most excruciating tortures, they refuse to cry out, unless it be to sing. One Huron tortured by the Iroquois was said to have told them, "You have no sense, you do not know the way to torture, you are cowards; if I had you in my country, I would make you suffer much more." Before he said this, the Iroquois had bitten his fingertips, rolling them in their teeth, until splinters of bones showed through the skin; they had cut off slices of flesh from his back and put live coals in the wounds; they had hung a collar of red-hot hatchets around his neck, a torture which to my mind is the most excruciating a human being could endure; for, bound naked to a post, what posture could he take? If he leaned forward, the hatchets on his shoulders would weigh the more on him; if he leaned back, those on his chest would make him suffer the more; and if he kept erect, without leaning forward or back, the burning hatchets, applied equally on both sides, would give him a double torture.

But still this savage refused to complain or beg mercy until a woman heated an iron skewer in the fire and ran it into his private parts, upon which he finally uttered a cry and said, "You have sense, you know how, that is the way to do it."

I've also observed that the savages can run for a long time altogether, and carry burdens that two or three of us would find it difficult to raise. And their women bring forth children without pain, a characteristic which makes Perrot and others suspect they are born without Original Sin.

One would like to be able to take a savage child, such as Lachine, and raise her from infancy in a French home. Would her blood render her hopelessly savage, or would she think and act and speak exactly as French children do? Lachine's antics now seem no different to me from children I've observed in Rouen or Quebec. Yet, Raymbault and some others suspect that the constitution of their blood and inner organs is different from ours, having more natural spirits in the blood, and their brains more vapor, as well as a smaller liver, two stomachs, and thicker intestines, in order to digest the bark and roots and the foulest of offal they eat, such as our stomachs reject. If this is correct, then the joke is on the priests, who may as well be baptizing dogs. Those who don't regard them as animals regard them as devils, but in any case it might be wiser for us instead to place the humanity of such philosophers under suspicion; for men who have expressed dismay to learn that their ancestors resembled the savages of America—as Acosta and others aver—would be far more dismayed to learn that they themselves bear this resemblance.

In fine, if we are to champion the stability of the laws of nature and rigorous standards of proof, we must either dis-

cover the evidence to support such assertions (that the savages are *animals*) or regard them as just as spurious as those
accounts of tribes whose members have only one leg or no
heads, or who give their excrement through the mouth and
urinate under the shoulder, as some writers have described.

Colin Crevel failed to return this morning with the hunters, after following a path in the forest southeast of this place;
he told them he was going to shoot a bear. Three of the men
set out in search, but found no signs of him. We fired our
guns in the camp all evening at intervals of an hour, and plan
to do the same in the morning.

1 2   F e b r u a r y   1 6 8 2

[Entry crossed out.]

B., you were correct. If I allow it to happen again, even you
may require me to prove I'm not a madman. The usual penance. Most of the time

1 2   F e b r u a r y   1 6 8 2

Paid to M. Bazire for the repayment
   which I was obliged to make   10,000 livres

Further to said Sieur, for supplies,
   clothes, and canoes furnished to
   carry provisions   6300

To M. Petit, for so much as he provided for the acquittal of the debts of
   the men who went to Catarakouy,
   for victuals and clothes furnished
   them   6000

For the supply and maintenance of 41
   men and savages at the rate of 200
   livres each   8200

For the pay of M. Tonty	700
For the wages of the ship's carpenter, dead two months ago	240
For 150 minots of wheat bought from M. Ravier, steward of the clergy of the Montreal Seminary, at 4 livres the minot	600
	32,040 livres

Furs lost on the *Griffon* worth 12,000 livres. Those cached at Fort Miami worth between 10,000 and 20,000 livres. Mme. d'Allonne may still be good for the rest, if she hasn't found a new husband. Those few furs cached in the attic at Michillimackinac I have given up to the avarice of the Jesuits.

Still no sign of our lost hunter, Crevel.

13 February 1682

Today our hunters struck an inexhaustible supply of meat in the shape of a migrating herd of buffaloes. Surfeited, the men are in better spirits, though impatient like myself to be off, as the season is now wasting apace. I've resolved not to prolong the search for Crevel beyond the time the river clears. Nearly three months have elapsed since we left New France, and we have yet to embark on the River Colbert, whose length is unknown. Making allowances for the return trip, even if the estimate of Jolliet is correct (and I doubt that it is), I am fully persuaded that unless we leave soon, we won't reach Quebec again this season, and may even be forced to winter in unfamiliar territory.

In our camp, Lachine walks around swinging her arms like a prosperous Montreal merchant. The death of her father seems to have had little effect upon her spirits. She climbs every boulder in sight, even though her legs are short and stubby, like her mother's. Her mother plays at slapping her buttocks, to make her laugh, and to help her forget the abscess in her eyes, which causes her to rub them with her fists. Slapped in this manner, she can't stop laughing, but one slap follows another until at last it appears that her mother is beating her and the laughter has turned to tears. Then Orakwi stops and cradles her daughter, and presses her full lips to the girl's swollen eyes. The tears are good: they drain the abscess. For the most part, the child bears her affliction with admirable fortitude.

GOUPIL

11 February 1682

A fine mess! still no food & today one of our hunters Colin Crevel a person of capacity and courage walked off by himself and never returned   we were hunting south along the bank of the River Messipi then inclined toward some forests camped at noon at the edge of this woods when Crevel jumps up and announces his intention to go and shoot a bear

our Illinois savage tells us there are no bear near this place. If Crevel saw one why didn't he cry out   we fired a volley to guide him back and hunted along the edge of those trees leaving Barbier to intercept Crevel upon his return, Barbier his friend.   as there was no sign of Colin Crevel several hours later Migneret Baron & Sanomp searched along the path where he disappeared, the rest of us continued the hunt   both parties unlucky

Barbier thinks he was killed by savages, we are surrounded every day by a hundred savages   without knowing it who knows if this is true   Barbier says he feels them watching

the Sieur de La Salle discussed with me this evening his thoughts upon the River Messipi   it circles all our lakes where it rises in the north   this I doubt   downriver he said the savages burn excrement dried in the sun because they lack forests   these savages who talked with Jolliet live

only 5 days from a tribe which trades with the natives of
California   so even if the Messipi debouches into the Sea
of Florida [the Gulf of Mexico] it gives to an outlet from the
sea toward Japan and China he said   he showed me Jolliet's
maps but I could see their mistakes   when his stomach is
empty the Sieur de La Salle tends to rave about fables
touching his northwest passage it slipped southwest the same
fable   he can't be content with savages of the New World
having to seek those of the Old World as well inventors of
gunpowder and spices.   no wonder the men fall silent
when he approaches

12 February 1682

weather good food bad   we are forced to accustom ourselves to eat a certain moss growing upon the rocks.   being
a sort of shell-shaped leaf always covered with caterpillars
and spiders   this we boiled, it furnishes an insipid soup that
wards off death more than it imparts life

when a savage wants food he says my belly is small

the men complain because of lack of food which they
blame upon the Sieur de La Salle for lack of foresight in
seeing to the provisions   in my view the provisions were
adequate but we took too many people to share them
especially savages

heard some men say they would break into the Sieur de La
Salle's trunk which they say contains smoked meat and dried
fruit   but I dissuaded them from this

hunted all day and searched for Crevel   both parties
found nothing   our little group found a stag dead 4 or 5
days but the offensive odor prevented us from trying to eat
it   I can still smell the putrid thing

we are all miserable but our sorrows have a grand di-
mension   boundless in this waste.   our sufferings link
us with our beginnings in Adam   his first sin and the
world's corruption

we continued the hunt today this time along the river Seignelay and were blessed by God in the most unusual manner   this is how it happened

we took our canoes as the hunting near our camp had
proven so poor   paddling up the Seignelay whence we had
come 4 days before   along the way Membré & I looked for
turtles along the bank, we found a large one thin shell fatter
meat.   while I was trying to cut off his head he all but cut
off one of my fingers

we had drawn one end of our canoe up on the bank when
a violent gust of wind drove it back into the river   it was
cold but Membré pulled off his habit & threw it on the turtle
with some stones to keep it from escaping & we both swam
after the canoe in the frigid water   having reached it with
much difficulty an eighth of a league away   Barbier found
Membré's habit and not seeing the canoe concluded some
savages had killed us   meanwhile so shivering and numb
that our limbs could hardly move we pulled the canoe up on
shore when a rumbling shook the earth like something we
never heard in our lives   we looked up and saw more than
sixty buffaloes crossing the river to reach the south lands
I jumped up on the bank and pursued the animals calling
Barbier with all my might waving my arms to try to get
around the beasts & drive them down to the hunters   for
my arquebus was back on the bank with the turtle   they
started crossing back but Barbier ran up & shot 3 with such
swift dispatch that I jumped in the air & shouted huzzah
despite all my shivering   Membré who looked such a sorry
sight like a half naked savage was jumping up and down for
joy too   Pierre You ran up with his habit and the turtle
one of the animals fell in the water and we could get it ashore
only in pieces being obliged to cut the best morsels   La
Violette later shooting one more   & with turtle soup back
at camp everyone ate so much some of us were sick

these *buffalo* have fine wool instead of hair   horns all

black thicker than European cattle   but not so long   their
head is of monstrous size   neck short and thick and sometimes six hands broad   with a hump or slight elevation
between the two shoulders   legs very thick and short covered with wool.   on the head and between the horns their
long black hair falls over their eyes   giving them a fearsome look   the meat of these animals is very succulent
  later it began to rain   no sign of Crevel today again
we all fear he's been abducted by some savages   the Sieur
de La Salle better tempered today   the 3 of them beneath
his canoe in the rain the daughter the mother the Sieur de
La Salle   very cozy   the river brown and ugly still perilous filled with ice

14 February 1682

this evening the Sieur de La Salle announced he was calling
off the search for Crevel, the men so livid about this that
should we leave tomorrow without Crevel a rebellion will
surely ensue   of the kind which occurred two years ago
when I prevented Duplessis from shooting the Sieur de La
Salle in the back
  he complains about the time left for our voyage   but
here it is only the beginning of February.   we could make
two trips down his abomination of a river & still be back in
Quebec before the winter next
  the camp is filthy   the savages scarcely ever wash their
platter they leave their garbage where they ate   their
clothes rot on their backs   these savages eat in a snuffling
growling way puffing like animals, when they eat fat they
grease their whole faces with it   and these are the Christians!   they make water before anyone   break wind too
the women too
  Membré and I scrupulously said our evening prayers   a
few of the savages joined us   adding some paraphrases on
the Response of Saint Bonaventure Cardinal in honor of
Saint Anthony of Padua   we begged of God to meet the

savages we shall encounter only by day   for when they
discover people at night they murder them

L A   S A L L E

15 February 1682

Today the waters of the river rose and a great torrent of ice
came down, after which there was little ice and the level of
the water fell, which led us to conclude that an ice jam had
broken upriver and it was safe now to proceed. We embark
tomorrow morning.

And now, as seems fit, I commend my soul to the Lord,
who may dispose of it as he wishes. Whatever use he makes
of me, his vessel, may it be for the greater glory of our family,
King, and country. We are about to enter a wilderness whose
depth we possess no method of calculating beforehand, penetrated by a river which no civilized men have before traversed the length of. The good or evil it holds for us has
perhaps already been charted out, in God's inscrutable signa-
ture, which we are not permitted to view. To His grace we
submit, may it meet with my purpose. In these vast, barbarous, and unknown countries, He may blink at our exploits;
for we are but motes in His eye. His face is toward Europe
and the Church, and if there could be said to be a world
without God, this rumor of a country would be it. But as our
mental state generally colors events, I confess that though the
future is something to be feared, it is also something to be
welcomed, and I welcome it warmly as the fruition of a
project dear to me for almost ten years' time; nor is it possible
to describe my confidence that we shall succeed to the glory
of us all, or the feelings that encourage me to esteem this
evening of our embarkation upon the River Colbert as the
most happy of my life.

Before setting off this morning, I gathered the men about me and delivered a speech concerning our grand enterprise, and caused a *Te Deum* to be sung (led by Membré) and several volleys to be shot in celebration, then inspirited them each one as they entered the canoes until we all were gliding for the first time upon this majestic, wide river in a flotilla of handsome canoes with Tonty and myself in the rear. This river is so large it appears to curve in the middle, like the ocean; we are but water spiders on it.

A commotion ensued when Barbier's men set their canoe on shore and announced they would search for M. Crevel before proceeding any further, but Tonty and I persuaded them to continue. I made Membré lead some more singing. M. Tonty thinks Crevel by now has most likely been served up for a meal by some savages, but I suspect that he is rather serving such a meal; having become a savage himself.

Below its confluence with the Seignelay, the River Colbert is almost everywhere a league and three or four arpents in width, and divided repeatedly by islands covered with trees interlaced by such a tight webbing of vines as to render them nearly impassable. For the first league or so, the chains of hills on either side of the river are set pretty far back from the banks, so that between the mountains and the river there are large prairies with some herds of wild cattle; perhaps the same ones we intercepted on the Seignelay several days ago. As our supply of meat is ample, kept fresh by trailing behind us from the canoes in nets devised by Nika and Sanomp, we declined to stop and hunt.

The river was high and brown; the current, after the agitation of the past week, surprisingly mild. Once a monstrous fish struck our canoe with such violence I thought it was about to rupture or split the bark.

In the afternoon, as we rounded a bend, Nicanapé, our Illinois savage, became visibly nervous and distracted in his canoe; we soon perceived why. Upon some rocks whose height and length inspired awe were painted two enormous monsters. All our savages talked restlessly among themselves and dared not to look upon these pictures. They were large as wolves, possessed horns like a deer, horrible red eyes, human faces, a body covered with scales, and a long tail winding round the body, passing over the head, and going back between the legs, ending in a fish's tail. They were green, red, and black.

While we were marveling at the ingenuity of the savages who painted these pictures; for nowhere did there appear to be a purchase or ledge upon which they could have safely stood; a great quaking and roaring as of a cataract rose up around us. As the day was fine and clear, we hardly knew what to make of such an inconceivable wonder, and thought for a moment as our savages did that the monsters on the rock had come to life, and were parting the waters in pursuit of our canoes. The current had become very strong and it was only with difficulty that we paddled to the shore to avoid the dreadful maelstrom, upon which we saw the source of all the commotion. This turned out to be that place of which Marquette makes note in his letter, where the River Pekistanoui, or Osage [the Missouri], discharges itself into the Colbert, with a dreadful churning and frothing of the muddy water, and a tangled accumulation of trees, branches, logs, and floating islands. This river pours in so much mud, that from its mouth the water of the Colbert, whose bed is also slimy, is more like clear mud than river water. We were fortunate to have been able to gain the shore before the torrent of mud overwhelmed us.

At this point, we portaged a league or so south of this juncture, and made camp, as the hour was late.

The River Pekistanoui discharges from the northwest with such considerable force that we are inclined to believe the report of those savages who claim that by means of it one can gain another river which empties into a large lake and from thence proceed to the Vermillion, or California, Sea. The journey is five or six days up the Pekistanoui, five more days to said lake, and two to the sea. The portage is not great. With good health and the blessings of our King, I hope someday to make this portage and reach at last a passage to China and Japan.

This river and its tributary waters are said to be rich in the peltries of the beaver. According to report, the savages on its bank hunt with horses. A good location for a fort or trading post exists on a slight eminence below the juncture of these two rivers.

GOUPIL

1 7   F e b r u a r y   1 6 8 2

we camped last night below some rapids made by the tributary river Pekistanoui   the Sieur de La Salle raving all the while about his northwest passage   of which I'm heartily sick

he accosted me tonight about the layout of this country   Hudson's Bay a 10 day journey north from Lake Superior,   making a hundred leagues   the Gulf of Mexico 300 leagues south   this we shall have accurate measures of in good time   200 leagues NW to a lake which enters into the Vermillion Sea   SW the same

according to the report of Father Druillettes the whole of North America is surrounded by sea on the east south north and west   it must therefore be separated from Groeslande [Greenland] by some strait   which may be the lake one reaches by means of the Pekistanoui   my map to reflect this

if we could locate some savages near to this place we might have better report   Quivira said to be west of here where long canoes ply the waters with 20 rowers huge eagles of solid gold mounted on the prow   the men want to go there

he speaks of erecting a fort on this place   the Sieur de La

Salle builds forts the way other men make shoes   when
they come to someplace new the Spanish build a church,
the English a tavern   but we French build a fort or trading
post.

I make 6 leagues today due south   1 league portage

1 8 F e b r u a r y   1 6 8 2

6 leagues today   weather mild   now the river swings
southeast   how am I to calculate this with accuracy   hills
and plains half flooded empty and wasteful earth   I find it
ugly   a vast confusion

2 0 F e b r u a r y   1 6 8 2

12 leagues today   still SE   we found an empty village of
one hundred bark cabins   called the Tamaroas   the Sieur
de La Salle hung cloth and trade goods beads knives on
posts   and signs of our route downriver.

outside this village some platforms where they lay out their
dead   made by boards & pieces of canoes set on poles
Great numbers of bones around this place a putrid smell
the skeletons of several dogs as well.   these animals must
be sacrificed when their owners die

one corpse very recent   half decayed and partially ate by
bears or wolves   a war calumet beside the platform, which
was caved in   earthen pot upset some other articles   in
the pot the savages leave a quantity of buffalo meat to assist
the departed on his voyage to the land of souls

as we made our way back to the canoes La Violette turning
around spotted a figure moving in the trees behind this burial
ground   he shouted and several men gave chase   it was
clearly human not a deer   or bear but he vanished beyond
our reach with great speed

LA SALLE

21 February 1682

After a day on this river I begin to doubt the evidence of my own senses and become convinced that nature is not a *thing,* but a shadow of our mind, or spirit; and our thoughts are not copies of things, but the other way around; things are but the shadows thrown by our thoughts; at least, so it seems to me when, after paddling on this river all day, at last we decamp, and from the trees and hills still appearing to glide past us, though we are stationary, I conclude that such things are mere *froth* and *foam;* and the objects we see but shadows, which even little Lachine's finger could penetrate, like a reflection on the skin of the water.

But to clear up this darkness in our minds by reminding us of the idea of solidity would be like trying to cure a deaf man by shouting.

GOUPIL

22 February 1682

we set out early   the weather much warmer   misty this morning fog on the river   11 leagues south   we passed the Ouabache River [Ohio] which the Sieur de La Salle claims extends northeast all the way to Iroquois country, they never venture down this river.

assuming a mask of unconcern Nicanapé told us we were approaching the place of the manitou or demon who devours travelers on this river   I could see he was distracted   we found the demon to be a cove or narrow canyon   surrounded by cliffs twenty feet or more in height   here the whole current of the river contracts & backs up makes a tremendous roar.   at one point an island compels the waters to pass through a kind of trough   all the various waters conspiring in a violent struggle to throw each other

4 1

back   the savages howled with terror   so did some of the
French   the Sieur de La Salle grinning all the way

noticed below here an iron mine which the Sieur de La
Salle considered very rich   several veins of ore   bed a
foot thick   water bloody in appearance from the iron

23 February 1682

last night we were compelled to sleep in the canoes   no
way to make such a bed soft   or dry   the banks low and
marshy full of thick foam rushes walnut trees etc.   no place
to land for a full 42 leagues   exhausted   south ever
south   I take this river to be the will of God   unsearch-
able his judgments and his ways past finding out

we paddled after dark   here the river knotted with such
twistings & windings & devious ways I threw up my hands
at making accurate calculations

at night we heard some frogs coming from the marshes
their bellowing loud as the lowing of cows, my canoe drew
several inches of water.   we should stop to caulk them.
meat running low

L A   S A L L E

26 February 1682

Once again one of our hunters is lost, Pierre Prud'homme,
an able and worthy man hired as armorer, but new to such
a wilderness as this. This time I am resolved to remain here
until we find him, to forestall any further complaints by those
men who were disturbed when we made no greater effort to
find Crevel, though we searched every day for almost a week,
and fired volleys each morning and evening, wasting valu-
able gunpowder.

As some of the men saw footprints nearby, there is fear that
Prud'homme has been captured by savages, and that we will

soon be attacked; for Nicanapé says that the Chickasaws live near this place.

Of course, my enemies will accuse me of illegal trading; and of making profit from peltries that ought to go through Montreal; but I have decided to build a fort here, to protect us from attack as well as to cache the furs we brought with us from the Illinois country, and to serve as a base for future trade. Tonty thinks we should name the fort after the lost man, Prud'homme, to assuage the men; in this I concurred, knowing nevertheless that any of the men to whom I remain in debt might appreciate the flattery better, especially if they receive nothing else from me.

27 February 1682

Still no sign of Prud'homme. Construction on the fort proceeds apace. I felt myself unwell again this morning and took some salts, from which I now feel some relief; but the men delight in irritating me, knowing I am ill; and they fell and drag their trees as though they had all the leisure in the world to construct a Versailles.

Fort Prud'homme we have situated very advantageously upon an eminence overlooking the river; the bluffs here fall dramatically to the river, whose width at this spot is nearly two leagues. Here, the trees have begun to display their foliage, and flowers are opening; we have passed into the kingdom of spring. The fort I directed to be constructed in the following manner: on a cleared spot 15 toises long by 10 wide [90 by 60 feet], without any bastions, we shall erect standing palisades formed of stakes as thick as a leg; in the interior, roofed with bark, we shall construct a *corps de garde,* a powder magazine, and some barracks, merely huts, but sufficient for our purposes. This fort may be entered flat-footed from all sides; already the half-completed palisades afford us some protection; the savages prefer to camp outside them.

Several men are somewhat disabled now, one with an arm dislocated but well replaced, several with bruises from falls, and two or three with bad boils or blisters on their feet. Goupil has had another fit, his first attack of the falling sickness since we left Montreal. I heard a cry and came upon him behind the fort in the midst of *le grand mal,* lying on his back and flapping his arms as though to fly; froth and spittle dribbled from his mouth; his eyes had rolled up into his head, and his entire body had been thrown into a violent agitation. With his hands cramped, legs feebly kicking, and with that red and swollen face, he reminded me of an ox whose throat had been cut. I called Nika and directed the savage to prevent the poor man from swallowing his tongue, then retired to the fort, out of severe distaste for such displays. The contents of his bowels and bladder had been ejected.

This falling sickness has no cure or known cause, and I fear may lead to insanity. When this fit was over, I directed Goupil to take some peony, which sometimes prevents immediate recurrence. He spent the evening praying with Membré. They mouth prayers together designed to induce a kind of stupor: breathe in, "Lord Jesus Christ"; breathe out, "Have mercy upon us." This goes on for hours at a time. The savages make a wide berth around the two men, assuming they are engaged in driving out through incantations the manitou which had possessed Goupil; and not wanting to catch it when it escapes.

Lachine continues unwell, though her spirit is undaunted. The discharge from her eyes appears worse. She opens and closes her mouth as if to say "pa pa pa pa pa," and nothing comes out. But this is a game, not a spur of her affliction. She opens her mouth and invites me by gesture to tap her teeth with my fingernail; apparently the sensation pleases her. But I have to take care that she doesn't bite.

G O U P I L

2 7 F e b r u a r y   1 6 8 2

I felt myself stupidly grinning and squinting   having suddenly turned aside and walking abruptly past the men I was
with   then I dropped a log on my foot   standing there I
could do nothing   all at once a sensation as of a breath
of air blowing across my body and passing upwards to my
head   after that oblivion

    this my first fit in almost a year   convinced the noxious
moisture rising from the river makes me unwell   now the
air turns warmer   it may happen again   such is the power
of the Devil over us all   Blessed be God

2 8 F e b r u a r y   1 6 8 2

Blessed be God I am better today   I could work with the
men who nonetheless avoid me,   most of them didn't know
before this

    all this morning spent felling more trees for the construc-
tion of Fort Prud'homme   our search party heard a volley
deep in the woods to the east   must be Prud'homme
they fired a response and shouted   all the woods quiet after
that.

    the Sieur de La Salle thrashed Jacques Oubidichagan today
for sleeping when he should have been dragging trees   no
good will come of this   in front of his squaws   he treats
the men like children   but surely there is no men in the
world of more insolent spirit than these   and the master
morose all day   he spoke to no one

    this evening in a sudden inspiration I cut all my beard in
order to rid myself of some vermin   will do my chin with
a pumice stone hereafter,   note the savages regard facial
hair as ugly   Sanomp embraced me   everyone has their
own idea of this   some think it fine and pretty to paint their
face all manner of gaudy colors and grease.

    I feel much better this evening except for a blister or issue

on my neck very sore   chafed by the stiff collar of my shirt
stiff with dirt and sweat   which I never wash

1 March 1682

the hunters killed some turkeys today which we all dined
upon,   Pierre You spotted some savages in the forest but
they ran off   tonight the Sieur de La Salle commanded the
company to sing some songs   so we had to sing   Membré
preached a sermon   the pesky child distracting him   with
the disrespect of the savages this made a mockery of the
Lord's day   but I prayed again with Membré after that
and so to bed

LA SALLE

1 March 1682

She bends over upon the earth and peers back through her
legs at Membré, whom she enjoys teasing. She runs to him
and touches his large crucifix, which always hangs from his
waist. Attaching herself, she swings from it until he is
forced to shoo her off like a little chicken. Then she comes
to me and raises her arms to be lifted; her laugh is free and
open and bubbles up like water from a spring. She enjoys
playing with my astrolabe, which I wear upon a chain
around my neck. It distracts her and holds her fixed in
trance.

Tonight Membré preached to the company upon Original
Sin. But Lachine spoiled his sermon by wrapping a blanket
around herself and lifting it as she walked back and forth,
exactly as the priest does, and mouthing her gobbledygook
all the way. Mistaking disdain for dignity, the priest refused
to acknowledge her, thus making himself appear all the more
foolish; while the savages, who never chastise their children,
believing that it makes them weak or timid, laughed openly
at the spectacle.

2 March 1682

Upon the completion of our fort, I organized a party to make a reconnaissance and see if we might find Prud'homme or the Chickasaw savages, whose villages are said to be east of this spot. The fort I left in charge of sixteen men under Tonty's direction. Membré asked to go with us in case the harvest of savage souls should prove abundant; I think he hopes to improve the manners of the savages, and teach them the courtesy natural to us French; otherwise, they might be tempted to remove his head and set it upon a stake.

We were told this river was populated up and down its banks with savage nations of all variety, but until today we had not seen even one. This is how it happened; observe the courtesy natural to our French: we followed for most of the day a path through the forests and came upon a valley in a clearing. There below us a savage sat beside a fire. Barbier, who had gone on ahead, approached him slowly; Membré beside me began to tremble; our main party was coming up behind, but I was apprehensive of making any signal to them lest the savage, who had stood up to face us, should suspect some unfriendly designs upon him. Suddenly, out of the bushes to our left burst a second savage, and Membré let out a cry, then prostrated himself before the confused man and shouted out (in French, of course), while trembling in every limb: "Oh my Father, God be blessed, He has permitted it, He has willed it, His holy will be done. I love it, I desire it, I cherish it, I embrace it with all the strength of my heart." When I asked him later what he *desired* and *embraced* so fervently, he replied, martyrdom. But his hopes were disappointed as the savage stood there laughing at the spectacle. Then I held out the calumet the Illinois savages had given us, and he took it as though recognizing its design, and raised it to the sun. By this time, Barbier had seized the other man, but I signaled him to let him go. Nicanapé walked up and we conversed with these men as best we could, using the common language of gesticulation or signs, and the Chickasaw tongue, which Nicanapé knows imperfectly. I've observed that even among the adept, this sign language is liable to error, for only the strong parts of ideas are communicated by it; or perhaps I should say, only the *clear* and *distinct* parts; therefore, our first question concerned the location of their village, as I hoped someone there would know the Illinois tongue. They gave us to understand that their village was back in the direction we had come from, and several leagues south on the river. I made them presents of knives, awls, glass beads, and needles, and urged them to take us there. Accordingly, we all turned back with our two new friends, and managed to arrive at the fort before sunset.

These Chickasaws are robust and healthy; dressed in skins and a kind of skirt and leggings. They were taken with Membré, whom they regarded as a juggler or clown, no doubt due to his behavior at their meeting. When he held out his great cross for them to see, Providence must have moved them to sense its power, for they threw tobacco upon it as an offering. Tobacco is their most precious possession. Now and then they touched the cross, which, hanging from the rope about his waist, must have reminded them of a scalp, or weapon; and touching it, they then rubbed their hands upon their bodies, taking special care to include the private parts, in order to absorb some of its power.

Upon returning to Fort Prud'homme, we found that its namesake had been located, none the worse for his ordeal, though famished; not having eaten in five complete days. The men were celebrating Prud'homme's return with song, under Tonty's firm guidance; and our arrival, as well as our discovery of these savages, gave further occasion for celebration; so that for the first time since Fort Crèvecoeur I allowed a ration of brandy to be distributed. Everyone appeared excited by the news of the Chickasaw village nearby, and by the prospect of trading with these savages and replenishing our supply of cornmeal; but during the celebration one of the Chickasaws disappeared; undoubtedly in order to warn his people of our coming. Therefore I have resolved to take every precaution I can upon the morrow to forestall a possible violent reception.

GOUPIL

3 March 1682

leaving 10 men behind in charge of Fort Prud'homme, the Sieur de La Salle boarded our men & equipment in the canoes & embarked for the village of the *Chicaza* savage we caught,   the other one having escaped.

with Tonty and the master in front   Baboeuf La Violette Jean Pignabel & some others in several canoes just behind   weapons loaded & ready   the Sieur de La Salle with the *Chicaza*   Tonty holding up the calumet

this calumet of great value says Membré   I believe it you can walk safely through the midst of enemies who in the hottest fight lays down their arms upon viewing it   made from polished stone like marble   having a bowl for tobacco a wooden stem 2 feet long thick as a cane decorated with the heads necks feet of colorful birds   you hold it to the sun   then everyone smokes

at a signal all disembarked on the eastern shore   about 3 leagues down from our fort   then marched along a path which this savage pointed out for several hours until we attained an eminence   and there below us sat the village

now the Sieur de La Salle had directed Nika and Sanomp to carry his trunk,   which excited my curiosity no great deal   for what does he have in it amongst all the clothing but a robe of the finest Chinese damask embroidered with birds and flowers,   I discovered from Membré this was in case we found a passage to the South Sea or the Sea of China   or found some Mandarins who making use of such a passage to trade with the Indians,   might trade with us.

so there he stands by himself on the hill having sent ahead the savage to announce his coming   long damask robe with birds and flowers red blue especially green   holding up a

pistol in each hand   while Tonty a little way off holds up
the calumet   the rest of us waiting back by the woods
when all at once a commotion goes up in the village all the
savages running around   moaning & screaming   they
think it is a manitou   they flee they run they hide in the
trees   making sounds like birds or geese in confusion

but the Sieur de La Salle holds his ground   pistols in
hand alone and silent   until the chiefs making shouts and
gestures to drive him off   accompanied by the savage we
caught   pretty soon they come bearing gifts they lay at his
feet   belts garters sashes made of hair of bears and buffaloes dyed red yellow gray   as these were of no great
value the Sieur de La Salle instructed us to bury them   out
of sight of the savages   so as not to burden ourselves unduly   then they bring a warrior to give to the Sieur de La
Salle as a present   who turns out to be the savage that
escaped, called *Chukafala* or *Chuka*   and he never leaves
the Sieur de La Salle's side   when all smoke the calumet
offering it to the sun   and we march to the village in grand
procession   the rest of the savages skulking about   they
come back one by one gazing upon us in awe, they touch our
knives guns hatchets the Sieur de La Salle's astrolabe equally
and Tonty's artificial hand   rubbing their bodies all the
while

these *Chicaza* have some 2000 warriors   the greatest
number of whom have flat heads which they consider to be
a beauty   they look like newborn children, the head is
flattened in the following manner   : the women bind a
cushion or bag of sand to the child's forehead fastening it by
means of a band to the cradle   thus making the head take
this form   which resembles a large soup plate.

some of the warriors shaves the sides of their heads
leaving a roach or crest such as the Spanish wear on their
helmets   this is smeared with bear grease   they paint
their faces   the women are very beautiful & clean, very
unusual for savages   but some have pieces of their nose or
ears cut off   : which signifies they were caught in adultery

the men wear ornaments in their ears & nose   their nose split like a swine or malefactor   one of them tried to steal my knife, I think they are vindictive and ferocious   but the Sieur de La Salle wants to stay here several days   they crowd into our cabin and place morsels of meat in our mouths,   the Sieur de La Salle made a grand speech   now they all want to see Louis our king.   but I wonder if they understood much, Nicanapé put the words into gestures and sounds   they all nodded their heads murmuring approval

these are handsome savages but slaves of the Devil   the women think nothing of baring their breasts   with all this fine fertile lands around them only the women plant a little corn,   the men too proud to till the earth   revelation says to man thou shalt till the ground   but what use do these streaked spotted & speckled cattle make of the soil?   ah but we are all miserable sinners infinitely destitute of the merits of the apostles   & the Sieur de La Salle has all he can manage to prevent our men from succumbing to the wiles of these half naked squaws   who oil their skin with bear grease till they gleam

4 March 1682

today spent all day in feasting & dancing   music made from log drums flutes etc.   they danced in circles singing hey! ey! ah! hem! oh! oh! & so forth stamping their feet as they danced

gave us to eat sagamité fish a piece of deer meat a whole dog   the dog we refused   plates very dirty

we have to visit each cabin   which are bark cabins covered with mud   more gifts belts garters sashes a very fine calumet for Tonty   we gave them knives hatchets cloth but they refused our offer of a gun   which frightened them in the demonstration the chief however remaining placid

one cabin is full of slaves which they abuse, the slaves look like them but come from a different tribe they call *Chacta* [Choctaw]

they showed us skins of the buffalo they sell to other sav-

ages & M. Tonty told them we would come back and buy
such skins & build a house to keep them in & pay them with
knives and other things if they would supply us with said
skins,   at this they seemed pleased and made gestures to
build the house now   M. Tonty said we already built the
house up the river   not far from there   they seemed
amazed.

M. Tonty says that their vices and superstitions are so
fondly held that conversion would be difficult.   but father
Membré hardly despairs of trying   he distributed little copper crucifixes   his steadfast faith an inspiration to us all

Membré says the Chicaza believe that in ancient times a
flood covered the world   this made a great excitement
among the men   some of them wishes they had their
Bibles   and the savages showed us shells larger and thicker
than oysters in the mud on their cabins   these came from
the hills around this place, they were left over from the flood
in ancient times

the Sieur de La Salle showed us one of their ingenious
calendars which are knotted thongs   when each day passes
they untie the knot

L A   S A L L E

5 M a r c h   1 6 8 2

In the cabin where I sit, Chuka, my Chickasaw servant,
watches as I write by the light of the fire, entranced with what
he deems a form of magic; for these savages have no knowledge of writing. Across the cabin, a squaw who might be a
daughter of Eve—before she was clothed—sits weaving a
mat of rushes. The smoke in here brings water to my eyes,
as much of it fails to escape through the smoke hole. Next
to the squaw are several warriors, each equally naked; one
sleeps, one stares in vacancy, a few eat some grease from a
bowl, one binds a stone arrowhead to a shaft by means of the
sinews of some animal. They have no steel implements,

which proves we are the first Europeans to come here; but they did aver they have seen men like us to the east and west, or other *spirits* as they style us, because our skin is white, saying that savages are only *men,* but we are *spirits;* these must be the English and the Spanish, who have nevertheless failed to reach this place.

These savages sleep on beds or platforms piled high with skins and furs, several hands' breadths off the earth; that is, just beyond the reach of fleas. The mud and clay with which they plaster this cabin keeps it as warm inside by means of one fire as a Dutch oven; therefore, once inside with the door safely chinked, they freely shed their clothes, male and female both, which scandalizes Membré. I've observed that all priests congratulate themselves at the good effect they've produced when they make the savages a little ashamed of their nakedness. This nakedness really is a practical problem; it has little to do with sin. Each night I can't forbear speaking to my men with some degree of asperity, to prevent them from succumbing to the attractions of these women; for it weakens discipline, as regards executing the work I am commissioned to do; and debaucheries become a source of endless delays and frequent thieving. But as to guarding each and every one of them in the darkness, this I cannot do. Anything can happen in the dark.

Some men claim these savages are no better than monkeys or cattle, and deserve to be used as such. Others assert they are veritable Adams and Eves, and America is really Eden rediscovered. But did Adam and Eve eat their own lice, wear their clothes until they rotted off their backs, smell of smoke and fish and putrid meat (and worse)? Just as after the Fall the original worship of the true God in the First Times became confused and weakened by idolatry, so customs declined, races dispersed, languages multiplied (for America is a very *Babel* of tongues), and men separated from their origins by distance and time reverted to *savagery,* which is nothing more than a corruption of life in the Garden. The only advantages we French possess over the savages are due not to our greater proximity to the First Times, but rather to our Christian religion and the accidents of climate and soil, which enabled us to develop polished customs and habits, such as writing, rather than spending all our time in the necessity to hunt for survival.

But how do I tell this to Chuka, who, equally naked (except for his moccasins), watches the lines I make on this paper, unable to decipher them, or even to suspect them of conspiring to mean something? That writing is a magic of which his gods could be ignorant perhaps sends his mind a-reeling; but to know it as the formation of propositions; as the arrangement of the *subject* and the *predicate* and their *copulation;* and to know furthermore that every science has its name, every notion within a science has a name, and that everything known in nature is designated, as is everything invented in the arts, as well as all phenomena, manual tasks, and tools; this would be so far beyond the reach of his understanding as to remind us of the inconceivable sun for those who live in caves, in Plato's parable.

Of course these Chickasaws have names for things, but their names and our names despair of correspondence. In my efforts to construct a vocabulary of their language, to aid our attempts at communication, I made Goupil run across the ground this morning, and asked the savages their word for *run.* I pointed to various parts of my body and asked Chuka their names, while Goupil wrote them down. Preoccupied as he was with the marks Goupil made, Chuka urged him to put all the parts of the human body on a page, touching them as he said them. As Goupil hesitated before writing certain indelicate words, about which these savages have no scruples, this afforded Chuka and his fellow braves a great deal of chattering laughter amongst themselves.

When they speak, the Chickasaw sound like birds; their words are very agreeable to the ear, courteous, gentle, and musical. The letter *r* is not sounded in one word of their language, so far as I can discern.

Chuka calls the paper we write on a spirit because it tells

us what to say. The paper is white; perhaps this accounts for such a curious identification. As it was raining lightly this morning, he thought I could stop the rain if I wrote it down on the spirit, but I pointed to the clouds and folded my arms, as if to say *that* is the true spirit, the Great Chief of heaven who makes everything happen and won't do my bidding. But he failed to understand this; or refused to. Tonight Chuka concluded that if I wrote my words upon his skin, the word for *shoulder* upon his shoulder, and so forth, then he would become a spirit too; accordingly, after he had begged me for some time to do this, I finally agreed, and taking a piece of charcoal from the fire, wrote such words as appeared to please him—*hand, arm, shoulder, chest, back,* and so forth—upon his body, while he sang all the while beautiful songs of ecstasy, like those of a bird; rolling his eyes into his head and raising his arms. Shortly thereafter, however, he rubbed the words off, and he was normal again. I asked him why he did this, but he merely smiled; compared to the others, he is a most laconic savage. I imagine it was enough for him to become a spirit for just a brief time, before returning to our common condition.

This Chuka, like many of the Chickasaws, is a handsome savage, about eighteen or nineteen years old; tall, well built, with reddish-brown skin, hair black as the raven's feathers, and large black eyes. The Chickasaws are proud and superior savages, but I've observed that they show no reluctance to take whatever in our equipment they want; and I've been forced to keep a close eye on my trunk, which though locked, could still disappear in a twinkling; for these savages, like most, have no idea of personal property.

7 M a r c h   1 6 8 2

This morning the usual penance [Entry crossed out.]

When the savages woke up, we ate some fish and dried fruit they prepared for us; the fish cooked with oil rendered from bear's grease and mixed with sassafras and wild cinnamon. Dried persimmons and raisins pressed into cakes, quite good, and tea made from the roots of the sassafras. The best cooks of Paris would have envied our fare!

Some of the Chickasaw warriors paint their faces; these resemble the maskers who run around France during carnival time. All of these savages are healthy; I have seen no sickness among them, and they appear to be frightened by our little Lachine, whose suppuration of the eyes strikes them as the manifestation of a manitou.

Some men among these Chickasaws dress like women all their lives and glory in demeaning themselves to do everything the women do. They never marry, and are treated as women, but nothing can be decided at councils without their advice; in short, they pass for persons, or spirits, of consequence.

Membré walks around wringing his hands and says, how much dust there is in their eyes; and how much trouble there will be to remove it, that they may see the beautiful and terrible light of Truth. He plots an invasion of Brown Robes next year to harvest these savage souls. With Nicanapé acting as his interpreter, he questioned one of the chiefs upon where souls go when men die, etc. They go, replied the chief, very far away, to a large village situated where the sun sets. But how can they cross the great ocean? asked Membré. They go on foot, replied the chief, fording the water in some places. But Membré, attempting to demonstrate the impossibility of this, showed him a round stone which he said was the earth, and told him that the French have been all around the earth in great boats, but have never seen this village of souls. But the chief said Membré was an ignoramus and had no sense; for the souls of two of their countrymen had once returned from this great village, and explained to them everything concerning it.

What do these poor souls eat, making so long a journey? asked Membré. They eat bark, said the chief. And what do they do when they arrive at the village? During the daytime they sit with their two elbows on their knees, and their heads between their hands; but at night they hunt. Oh, but they can't see at night, said Membré. Be silent, you have no sense, said the chief; souls are not like us; they do not see at all during the day, and they see very clearly at night; for their day is in the darkness of the night, and their night is the light of the day.

What do they hunt? asked Membré. They hunt the souls of buffalo, deer, and turtles, using the souls of arrows to shoot them. Then Membré smiled, nodding his head, and screwed up his eyes and leaned close to both the chief and Nicanapé, whose faces nonetheless remained placid. But what happens, he asked, when they have killed the soul of a buffalo; does that soul die entirely, or has it another soul which goes to some other great village? But at this the chief grew visibly angry and with gestures and shouts ushered Membré and the interpreter out of his cabin, telling him he had no sense, that he had never been in the great village himself, but he would like to send Membré there right now.

But apparently Membré's efforts proved somewhat fruitful, as one of the savages approached him later and told him that the Chickasaws do not act right, and he wanted to come with us. This makes two; Chuka, who never leaves my side, and this savage named Mingatuska.

We traded some rings and colored beads for cornmeal. I spoke again with their chief about their buffalo skins, and traded for two of them to carry with us. With these Chickasaws as our allies, and with a sufficient string of forts and trading posts along the River Colbert, I am convinced that France could eventually control the trade of this entire continent; for the river drives a wedge between the Spanish and English (who are sometime allies), and with the lakes, the River St. Lawrence, and eventually the Gulf of Mexico under our control, we can encircle the English by means of a continent-wide commercial base; and this noose once in place, we can then tighten it; and thence turn west.

Today we made ready to leave the Chickasaws, much to the dismay of my men, who have done their best to avail themselves of the hospitality of the savage squaws. I gathered the entire village around me and gave more presents to their chief, including a lodestone, whose use I demonstrated; but they looked all around it to see whether any paste or glue was upon it.

Then I attempted by means of a harangue in their style to make them sensible of their dependence upon our King and government for every species of merchandise they may wish, as well as for their defense against their enemies; and I impressed upon them once more the strength of our government by discharging a few of our weapons and showing them a picture of our King Louis; whom I characterized as the most powerful man in the world, more powerful even than these sticks that spit fire; but who would nevertheless love them if they helped him. I told them that the reason we wished to penetrate their country as far as the big waters was to find the best way to bring merchandise to them to trade for their skins, which in good time we would carry away down the river in huge boats that resemble giant buffaloes. This trade, I told them, depended upon their good will and their willingness to assist us and form a league with us against their enemies and ours; for which purpose, in good time, we would even supply them with weapons such as they had seen me fire. At this, they were much pleased; my whole speech excited their astonishment and admiration, so that there was no end to their murmurs and cries and their touching of our bodies and articles, especially the weapons.

Their chiefs then made speeches, most of which we could not understand, but which ended with phrases meaning, "See what is good, my brother, you have honored us with your visit." They informed us about the villages and nations we could expect to meet downriver, and about the lack of Europeans on this river, which greatly pleased us; for we had

feared the Spanish might have established an outpost somewhere on the Colbert by now. Then they accompanied us to
the outskirts of their village, singing and embracing us as they
sang, so that tears nearly appeared in the eyes of several of
our men.

But what was our astonishment several hours later upon
arriving at the river where we had pulled up our canoes on
land and stored most of our supplies and equipment to find
all of this plundered? The canoes were intact, because these
savages disdain canoes made of bark; preferring their own
pirogues, or dugouts. But all our boxes and skins had been
opened, and the contents stolen or strewn about: breeches,
shirts, mittens, several livres of wool, shoes, thread, pins,
bullets, kettles, plates, awls, gun flints, and so forth; all we
had not taken with us to the village. I was so mortified to
realize that we should have left a guard at this place, and to
know that we had been so manifestly deceived, that in my
extreme anger I kicked a hole in one of our canoes.

But the baleful effects of that vexation were yet to be felt.
Leaving the Sieur de Boisrondel in charge of salvaging our
equipment and repairing the canoe, I took Tonty and a dozen
men with our weapons to return to the Chickasaws and seek
out our goods and punish these savages; accordingly, we set
out on the path to their village, which is several leagues long;
but when we arrived, the village was empty. We attempted
to set fire to their cabins, but, being made of mud and clay,
they wouldn't burn; so we forced ourselves to be content
with strewing their own possessions around, and breaking as
many as we could find; though they had been careful not to
leave much behind, and these undoubtedly their most useless
items. Chuka joined us in this feeble revenge, but Mingatuska held back; though to tell the truth I felt like throttling
both men, and pushed Chuka roughly aside while I swung
the large limb of a tree at the chief's cabin, which, however,
it failed to damage.

Then we returned to the canoes and embarked once more
upon the river.

GOUPIL

9 March 1682

a fine day everyone angry   2 leagues down the river this
morning the canoe the Sieur de Boisrondel repaired after our
master kicked it split open the bottom filling with water
immediately it sunk   Louis Baron which could not swim
hung on to the canoe, the Sieur de La Salle had one of the
other canoes unloaded on the bank & went to assist the man
in the water

  some of our food and merchandise lost   we are reduced
to the stock of poor cornmeal the *Chicaza* gave us,   half of
it rotted.

  finally we had to abandon this canoe, with the others
loaded we embarked again.   made 8 more leagues,
stopped early to send out the hunters but a ferocious storm
drove them back at once   we taking shelter beneath the
canoes.   one bolt of lightning large as a tree trunk burst
from the bank across the river.

10 March 1682

once more we are carried south,   endless voyage   What
if this river passed through Florida?   it would not surprise
me   the river being divided into small channels by a number of islands   no one knows where we are

  the Sieur de La Salle did speak many severe words to me
this day concerning my calculations   & the loss of the compass which I confessed,   so that I think for a great while
there cannot be any right peace between us   & maybe he
should teach his new servant the Chicaza who never complains or speaks his mind how to make maps and take read-
ings from the sun.   but I must look about me and mind my
business   because of his temper.

  all we have is cornmeal   the men complain   a fight
broke out between d'Autray and Barbier over some toilet
articles tonight,   Barbier's face all bloody   the Sieur de

60

La Salle too distracted by his own melancholy to punish them.

the Sieur de La Salle has contracted a catarrh caused by sitting in the damp grass after being heated all day long paddling

I had another fit not as bad   no one knew

this place where we camp full of lofty cottonwood trees admirable for their height and girth   all prairies hereabouts ready to receive the plow   no forests   the cottonwood trees by the river nowhere else   these trees gives off huge tufts of cotton to the wind   hence the name   warm to-day   I make 14 leagues

12 March 1682

fog so thick this morning we could not see the river   set off anyway

I'd rather eat grass and bark as the savages do than one more portion of cornmeal

the weather bad all day   much fog   through swamp and canebrake the river stinks   one man saw a huge fish or serpent in the water   shot at it but missed

the sound drew the attention of some savages we heard on the western bank   their drums and outcries a possible war dance   but the fog so thick we could see nothing, so we crossed to the opposite shore & threw up a fort from drift-wood & logs   the fog lifting after that   the astonished savages saw us and ran off   giving yips and cries   we embarked again

then a storm rose sending waves across the river pushing our canoes toward the bank   where the villages of these savages was,   they flocked to the bank to receive us & haul us in from the waves which rose to an extraordinary height   but the Sieur de La Salle fearing the designs of these savages   & afraid some of his men would desert, pushed on, & we were obliged to follow him notwithstanding the evident peril of the storm.   all of us soaked and the men disheartened

after 2 more leagues he saw no other course but to land
so he leaps into the water with his 3 canoemen and all together take hold of the canoe & its load & drag it ashore
in spite of the waves which sometimes covered them over
their heads.

then they came to meet each of the canoes in the same
manner   waist high in the water   I made a powerful
effort & carried Father Membré on my shoulders who isn't
strong   he knelt & kissed the bank

But what was our astonishment to look up & find ourselves
surrounded by these same savages   who we thought to
outdistance   some two or three hundred of them, they
built fires to dry our clothing   and appeared to show great
joy at our coming

these are the *Arkansas* whose villages we passed   the
Sieur de La Salle fired his weapon to impress them with his
power   suspicious of their intentions.   but they brought
us food, their chief invited us to visit their village,   which
with reluctance the Sieur de La Salle consented to   sharing
the calumet after the storm had abated and all of us dry,
this time leaving 10 men to guard the canoes in a little hasty
fort of driftwood.

then we followed these savages to their village   who
greeted us with every manner of courtesy and kindness
inviting us to sit on mats outside their skin tents   while the
chief to our amazement took a basin of water and washed
with a soft skin the Sieur de La Salle's face   then they
rubbed our legs down to the soles of the feet with bear's oil
buffalo grease to relieve our fatigue   then their chief made
a speech pacing back & forth, no one understood it   Nicanapé understands their tongue imperfectly   he said the
chief welcomed us

then the Sieur de La Salle stood up and pacing back and
forth in the manner of these savages made a speech too he
gave them a few gifts   he said Louis his master was called
the King of France who is the mightiest chief beyond the
great water   his goodness reaches to them and even to their

dead,   his subjects come among you to raise up your dead,
he said   but they must obey all his laws   and preserve the
life he has given   then he said we shall assume all the names
of their dead people   and give support to their squaws and
children by our gifts   and by the love of our King.
Nicanapé and Chuka labored to translate these words with
signs and incoherent grunts   but the Arkansas seemed favorably impressed & feasted us with all manner of food
on large wooden platters sagamité whole corn dog's flesh
which we ate this time with relish being hungry
     they cook their corn in great earthen jars which are won-
derfully made, they offer their guests large dishes   from
which all eat at discretion & offer what is left to each
other.   the Sieur de La Salle caused some of this food to be
taken to the men guarding the canoes.
     then all smoked again the calumets offering them to the sky
as though the sun would smoke them   behind the clouds
     and the Sieur de La Salle and M. Tonty then erected a cross
in the middle of the village bearing the arms of France   the
Sieur de La Salle in the king's name taking possession of this
country   & drawing forth from the chief an oath of fealty
to Louis XIV   I wonder if he knew
     then all the men shouted *Vive le Roi* and Membré sang a
hymn   then these savages sang too and it sounded to my
ears like plainsong   Membré said this too
     they erected skin tents for us   but the Sieur de La Salle
set a guard in each one   still suspicious

LA   SALLE

1 4   M a r c h   1 6 8 2

Membré finally approached me this evening and apologized
for calling me a pedant last night. On his lips the word found
its perfect shape; a pedant he is, an ill-polished savant, as the
gentlemen of Port Royal define it. He blanched upon learning that I myself had been amongst the Black Robes for ten

years, though I'd since turned against them. He must know that he wouldn't be here if I hadn't pressed Frontenac to supply us with Recollects instead of Jesuits.

He upbraids me for my stiff manner and excessive caution among these Arkansas, which only proves that his memory is short. I will grant him this, however: so far we have not lost the value of a pin to these savages. They brought us poles and skins to make our tents, they supply us with firewood each morning, and they take turns all day in feasting us. In truth, their civility and kindness seem genuine, and had we not been so roundly deceived by the Chickasaws I would warm more to the good qualities of these Arkansas, who appear to be gay, civil, and free-hearted. Though more alert and spirited than the Chickasaw braves, the young men are nevertheless so modest that not one of them will take the liberty to enter our tent unless invited in; rather, they stand quietly at the entrance.

They take great pains to relieve the sufferings of little Lachine, who is much worse these days; packing mud on her eyes, which have swollen up, and bathing her in a great earthen jar to lessen the effects of her fever. They have even attempted to make a gift to me of a little girl, signaling that I should keep her until Lachine is better; I refused, but they pressed me, insisting that I take the girl without condition, as a gift; I must say I was tempted! I offered her to Chuka, who disdained the thought. Among the Arkansas, children of parents who die are quickly adopted by a relative or a childless member of the tribe.

1 5   M a r c h   1 6 8 2

Lachine continues dangerously ill; she was very restless last night. The swelling has passed into her jaw and throat, and, this morning, to the back of her neck. The Arkansas show every manner of attention to her. I would bleed her if not for the risk of this procedure applied to children. She is listless, yet uncomfortable. We applied a poultice of wild onions, which we repeat every several hours; and give her a small dose of salts. Orakwi is always with her. One Arkansas who carries around the bones of a dead man in a skin bag began a chant over her, but Membré chased him off, saying this was a Christian savage. This appeared to astonish the Arkansas, and, I believe, after hearing Membré's stories, they were waiting for her to die so that they might witness us raising her from the dead.

16 March 1682

Lachine still very ill, but we make preparations to leave on the morrow nevertheless, as the river calls us. Her neck is much more swollen today, and her fever still high. We continue to apply the onion poultice. The Arkansas think we should take her to the sweathouse; which is a hole in the earth with hot stones heated by a fire, and covered with willow poles and skins.

The Arkansas continue to prove themselves the most civil and kind of barbarians. Our canoes and supplies remain untouched, and yesterday I reduced the guard upon them. These savages must be proof against those thinkers who assert the natural superiority of the Europeans, saying that we are better endowed for the conquest and subjugation of nature; and that savages such as these have never developed a higher civilization because they have little time to think, they have unrefined passions, and they tend to live like the animals they hunt. I say, on the contrary, they have much to teach us; for how can we conquer nature if we cannot live in it? Those of us who miss our polished lives, our forks, wigs, and coaches and sixes, will be doomed in our attempts to establish such luxuries here unless we first adopt some of the ways of the savages. We call them barbarians, but indeed all men term barbaric that which is not their own custom. True, we don't eat the flesh of our enemies; but we often treat strangers or beggars with contempt, whereas these Arkansas treat us according to the most ancient rules of hospitality. In this, perhaps Acosta is correct in saying that New World savages are descendants of the Biblical Hebrews. Like the Hebrews, they anoint their bodies with oil, they attach superstitions to dreams, they bewail the dead with horrible moaning, and they have no fixed and settled abode. Yet, in physiognomy and language they are also similar to the Tartar tribes of the northern parts of Asia. Horn thought he could trace the origin of the Iroquois to the Turks. Others see all these savages as Welshmen.

In truth, they are probably less different from us than we think. Proof of this is that sooner or later they welcome our corruptions with open arms. In New France, the Jesuits condemn traders for selling liquor to the savages, who will do anything to obtain it. As merchants and traders know, no cheaper way may be found of buying furs. For this and other reasons, the New World will never yield its abundance to men of spirit as long as the Jesuits rule in Quebec.

Perhaps we French are the *Tartars* or *Welshmen,* or possibly even the cattle or monkeys; I know some Frenchmen with four stomachs; and the savages, fabled to have animal souls and animal organs, are in reality the true children of Adam.

GOUPIL

17 March 1682

this morning we returned to the place where our equipment and canoes was under guard, we found that 2 of the men had deserted   the Sieur de La Salle attempted to keep this knowledge from the Arkansas who accompanied us singing all the way,   for it would appear to signify that we French are less than happy with our lot.

but where would these men go in such a country   it was Buret and André Hénault   maybe they missed their Chicaza squaws

I know some Frenchmen who joined the savages, Jean Lalemant became a Sioux   within a year he forgot the

French language   no thank you I'll stay a Christian   their
happiness springs from ignorance   like little children
   we embarked on the river and made 12 leagues on a fine
warm day   the river winds a lot here   strange country
how I miss France and my little house   saw large herds of
buffalo
   the child very sick and helpless carried by her mother
wrapped in a skin   her face neck chest all inflamed   the
Sieur de La Salle very melancholy about this

                                    1 8   M a r c h   1 6 8 2

fog this morning   Lachine very poorly   I saw her mouth
puckered & dry   face all swollen   then at noon her
mother sends up a wail   howling and wailing in the utmost
distress because the child is still in her arms   no one knew
when she died   Orakwi in her distracted state almost
dropped the child in the river
   so we disembarked & unloaded the canoes,   to set up
camp this early in the day   the savages sent up mournful
wails   Membré blessed the dead child with holy water
at the edge of some woods   the hunters went out
   later we carried her into the woods   set her upon the
ground in a clearing   laid on a blanket   the trees all adrip
from the fog   Membré and the rest of us singing   the
savages howling I cried too   the Sieur de La Salle made a
little speech, saying we are all of us sprung from one head
and made in one image   and if we regret this brotherhood
now we shall nevertheless be forced to join hands hereafter   & a child shall lead us   he was very stoical but the
lineaments of melancholy were writ deep in his face
   then Membré held the crucifix before her face & repeated
the names of Jesus & Mary   when all jumped back in
amazement   because she sat up her eyes flew open   her
face beaming   the savages even Orakwi ran off howling
we fell to our knees   and prayed incessantly repeating the
names of Jesus and Mary   then the Sieur de La Salle sat-

isfied himself that the child was still dead   completely still
he laid her back but no one could doubt the hand of God in
this wondrous occurrence, through her he touched our
hearts,   for having found Jesus on his cross this precious
infant found the rose in the thorns sweetness in bitterness all
in nothing
    we composed her body   covering her with another blan-
ket   walked back to camp praying all the way
    and so to bed our hearts full of sorrow and wonder   6
leagues before we stopped   the river S   all twists & turns.

LA SALLE

1 9 M a r c h   1 6 8 2

Rising at dawn, I walked into the forest to the place where
we had laid Lachine in a clearing, and knelt beside the still
figure and uncovered her; her eyes were still open. Her head
and neck remained puffed and swollen; in my distraction, the
face resembled a small bruised fruit. I observed that savages
appear to turn darker when they die, rather than, as we do,
more pale.

Removing her clothes, I made one continuous cut from the
clavicle to the pecten pubis, severing the muscles of the chest
and abdomen, then removed the tissues over the sternum and
split the sternum down to the xiphoid cartilage, as Galen
advises. Separating the membranes, I drew asunder and bent
back the two halves of the sternum, affording me partial
access to the heart and lungs, enough to note and affirm their
position, exactly as described by Vesalius.

Then I carefully opened the peritoneum as best I could,
beginning at the navel and slicing underneath where it at-
taches to the diaphragm, and lower across the stomach and
intestines, and pulled it to the sides, freeing the natural
members. Here, I noted that contrary to the description of
Mondino, the stomach is not spherical, but shaped like a
pear or squash, and the liver does not have five lobes but is

gibbous above and hollow beneath, and this is as it should be in the *Fabrica* of Vesalius and his other works. As for the viscera, these are the same as in us; from the fundus of the stomach, food and drink pass into the interior, and thence, by means of bile poured into the stomach from the gallbladder, they arrive at the caecum of the large intestine and are forced through the remainder of the intestines. I noted the additamentum of the large intestine in the caecum, which might be deemed a second stomach, but only by the ignorant; in fact, humans possess this, but cows, monkeys, and pigs do not.

For a moment I knelt there regarding this spectacle; I may have even mouthed a prayer. Then I closed her up as best I could, covered her with the blanket again, and walked back to camp, where Tonty and his men were already preparing breakfast. Shortly thereafter, we embarked upon the river.

GOUPIL

21 March 1682

14 leagues today in perfect sunshine   saw an otter on the bank eating a large ugly fish which had a kind of paddle or beak five fingers broad running from its head   it looked like a devil   but this didn't prevent us from eating this monstrous fish,   for it tasted very good.

I find this country very strange convinced we have passed into Florida   though this couldn't be.   here we find great forests hung with moss   swamps & crescent lakes   the river grows narrow and deep   bright green banks   large birds standing in the water   vines already out of blossom,

today we saw several large alligators which are the giant lizards Nicanapé warned us of   these monsters equally created by God with the birds & fish   I was very frightened   ferocious of mien with large sharp teeth   Tonty shot one   their young born of eggs like chickens   this surprised us very much

69

22 March 1682

my sleep disturbed all night by thoughts of the ferocious alligators hereabouts   dreamed of my mother weeping at her bedside   she was dying but what was strange her hair covered her face   which I couldn't see   God have mercy on her soul

the mosquitoes plague us eye gnats too equal to any plague God visited upon the Egyptians

made 16 leagues the river more swift   everything strange and frightening here

23 March 1682

today after we had made 10 leagues M. Tonty spotted a pirogue ahead and gave chase   being full of savages then as he overtakes it a hundred savages appear on the shore   pointing their bows at Tonty and his men   the Sieur de La Salle signals Tonty to withdraw   and we all encamp on the opposite bank

the Sieur de La Salle whose word is law sent Tonty across the river calumet held high   standing in his canoe but these savages were still shouting and gesturing with menace   so that I thought we would find ourselves at last drawn into a bloody battle and began to tremble   a few arrows falling about Tonty in the water   until they perceived the calumet and murmured amongst themselves   then received M. Tonty warmly at last, these savages signify friendship by joining their hands   but Tonty being unable to do this as one hand is made of metal,   he signaled his men to perform this rite in his stead.

then the rest of us crossed the river   greeted by these savages called Natchez   and we all went to their village leaving some men to guard the canoes.

these Natchez live like kings   we were astounded by their houses   better than any peasant dwelling of

France   four square walls and a kind of dome   they resemble mushrooms sprung from the earth   temples M.
Tonty called them   all plastered and whitewashed

their chief made a speech   his wives howled to do him
honor   Chuka who knows their tongue tried to translate
Nicanapé translating Chuka,   why can't everyone be born
speaking French?

but we found this was not their principal village   which
is two leagues off   where their great chief or Sun of their
nation lives, he wished to meet us,   so we go there arriving
for a feast they prepared   having heard of our coming
all singing and dancing

this principal village has about 20 dwellings of mud plastered & whitewashed very strong   & several large temples
of the sun   the chief came out of his cabin to greet us
and the Sieur de La Salle surprised everyone, he washed the
chief's face with a cloth   as a sign we may never see sadness
on his brow,   this appeared to shock all the chief's retainers
who set up a howl & his wives were wailing   but the chief
did the same to the Sieur de La Salle, washing his face   then
the Sieur de La Salle made presents to the chief   and made
a grand speech, he presented the chief with a pair of scissors   but first he cuts a lock of his own hair, reaching forward to the dismay of all these savages the Sieur de La Salle
cuts a lock of this chief's hair too,   then mingles the hairs
in his hand to indicate the French and the Natchez are one.
this is the first word, he said   he has nine words to give
them,   the first word is that the French and the Natchez are
one   & as he said this they burst into applause & song
though I doubt they knew the meaning of his words   but
the Sieur de La Salle spoke like a man possessed, which
stunned all these savages   he paced back and forth waving
his arms   the second word that Louis our King loved
them   and so on through nine words a most impressive
speech   all we French applauded too,   Chuka pretended
to read them a speech

with each new word the Sieur de La Salle made them
gifts   hatchets knives scissors needles beads   when it was
over the chief approached the Sieur de La Salle,   with a
grave countenance   and throws himself upon his neck in a
warm embrace   whereupon everyone cheered French and
Natchez both, then set forth to feasting and dancing to all
hours of the night   we slept in one of their cabins,   warm
as muffins

LA SALLE

23 March 1682

The whole country here is covered with palm trees, laurels
of several kinds, plums, peaches, mulberry, apple and pear
trees of every kind. There are also five or six kinds of nut
trees, some of which bear nuts of prodigious size. The savages gave us dried fruit to taste, which we found quite large
and good. They have many other kinds of fruit trees which
I never saw in Europe, but the season was too early to allow
us to see the fruit.

In every respect, the Natchez possess the most extraordinary degree of civilization I've chanced to observe among
savages. Their principal village, or City of the Sun, is laid out
like a small French town, with streets and lanes and as many
large square houses of ingenious construction; a far cry from
the wretched bark cabins of our northern savages. These are
square dwellings in each of which twenty or more savages
live, built of sun-baked mud mixed with straw, arched over
with a dome-shaped roof of canes, and whitewashed and
placed in regular order around open areas or plazas. The
insides are commodious, and furnished with genteel couches
upon which to sit, raised on four forks of timber of a proper
height.

The chief, a marvelously grave and dignified man, clothed
in a white robe and accompanied by two servants bearing

fans, invited myself, Tonty, and a few of our principal men
into his residence, where I made a speech and gave them
presents of knives, scissors, beads, and so forth. At each of
my presents all in this house uttered loud shouts of applause
from the depths of their chests, though the chief maintained
a becoming silence. The rest of this large village and the
remainder of our men were crowded outside the door, listening, and they all shouted too. I was occupied fully two hours
in delivering my speech, which I pronounced in the tone of
a savage chief, walking back and forth, as is their custom, like
an actor on stage. I must confess I was in quite a sweat by the
end. I delivered the entire speech in French, which Nicanapé
and Chuka labored to translate.

But what was my consternation, when I had finally
finished, to find my Chickasaw servant Chuka standing up,
and having scribbled some incoherent lines upon a piece of
paper, pretending to read this in a deep, official voice,
while pacing back and forth, exactly as I had done. The
people in this dwelling oohed and ahhed and stared at each
other, but I noticed some of them wore smiles upon their
faces. With great and ceremonious dignity, Chuka read his
speech, then sat down while they applauded politely. Later,
one of them made known to me by signs that they considered Chuka a *juggler* or *crazy person,* and in their society
such people have the privilege at certain times to perform
such mocking displays.

When all was finished, the chief took me outside and embraced me warmly before the assembled village. Then we
spent the remainder of the day feasting and dancing. The
women prepared flour for us to take upon our journey,
mixed with a kind of fruit mash which they call *paquimina.*
The chief was served by slaves. Their dishes are made of clay;
their knives and hatchets of cane and stone.

Then we visited all the houses of their village, stopping to
admire each one; for some are decorated with fine ornaments
and carvings made of wood and turtle shells; but to tell the

truth, we were all much fatigued by this time, and welcomed with relief the offer of a large dwelling at the edge of the village in which all we French might sleep; the chief having ordered its residents out. I have set up a watch, for I know now it is better to err on the side of caution, though I feel confident these Natchez have no ill designs upon us.

2 5 M a r c h 1 6 8 2

The usual penance [Entry crossed out.]

This much I have been able to learn about the Natchez, by signs and with the help of Nicanapé and Chuka: The sun is the principal object of veneration to these people; as they cannot conceive of anything above this heavenly body, nothing else appears to them more worthy of their homage. For the same reason, the chief takes upon himself the title of Brother to the Sun, for he cannot conceive of anything upon the earth more dignified than himself. In this, he resembles our own King Louis, whose bearing and manner are no less lofty, and whose kinship with the sun is well known.

Every morning the chief, whose door faces the east, honors the rising of his elder brother with many howlings and with a ceremonial lighting of his calumet, the first three puffs of which he offers to the sun; then raising the calumet above his head and turning from the east to the west, he demonstrates to his brother the direction he must take in his course that day.

Those who enter the chief's house salute him with a howl, but avert their eyes from the place where the chief is, as though he were too bright to look upon. They never venture into the space between the cane torch in the middle of the house and the camp bed where the chief sits; always, they must make a circuit of this torch. If the visitor be anyone whom the chief holds in consideration, he answers with a weary sigh, then the visitor may be seated and speak, always howling before he says anything; and, when he takes his leave, he prolongs a single howl until out of the house.

These people obey the slightest wish of their great chief, who is held to be the master not only of their property but their lives. When he dies, all his servants are strangled in order that they may go to serve him in the spirit world. Their bones are placed with his in the temple of the sun.

Only this habit of subordination to their chief appears to us as a mark of weakness among the Natchez. M. Tonty expressed the interesting idea that if articles of trade might be found which especially attracted them—copper items, for example, which to them represent the sun—then they might be obliged to engage in some sort of industry which their habits of subordination would effectively prevent them from rebelling against. In this climate, the silkworm could be introduced, for the forests here are full of mulberry trees; and these savages might very well be induced through their chief to make silk to trade with the French, a profitable commerce which could be conducted by way of the Gulf of Mexico and the mouth of the River Colbert.

Or we could trade with them for pearls; for their chief made to me a gift of a fine string of sixteen pearls, tarnished but large as peas. Having ordered the interpreters to inquire where they came from, I was told the sea, in shells; and that there were many more where these were found. Upon this, I inquired how far the sea was from here; and they said only seven days' journey, and further that the river is placid and negotiable all the way to its mouth. At this news all our men cheered, and expressed their desire to be on their way once more in order to complete our grand purpose. Accordingly, we leave on the morrow, though it will be difficult to part with these noble Natchez.

26 March 1682

The continual light rain today, combined with the warmth and fog, swelled up all my joints, making it difficult to paddle.

This morning, we left the Natchez on foot and passed through several more of their villages on our way to the river, trading for pearls in each one. Our canoes and guards we found unmolested, and by midday we had embarked once more and were being carried along once again by the river, stopping now and then to trade with other villages of peoples related to the Natchez; all of whom received us warmly, through the intercession of two Natchez braves whom the chief sent to accompany us through his kingdom.

And now I must declare that of all the savages I've lived among, these Natchez alone may be described as happier than Christians. They live guided only by the light of Nature, void of care, which torments the minds of so many Christians. Their natural drink is the crystal fountain, and this they take up in the hands by joining them close together and drinking at the wrist, the sight of which in ancient Greece caused Diogenes to hurl away his dish. *Natura paucis contentat.* Their eloquence and oratory are signs of an original genius lost to Europeans. Nor will they be troubled with superfluous commodities or the infinite artificial wants which we find no less craving than those of nature; indeed, they might wonder at our anxious precautions and unceasing industry in providing for future wants, for by means of such preposterous folly, we thus increase the troubles and the labor of life.

But our destiny beckons to us, and we can't but heed its call. The Natchez will never engage in great enterprises and, for all their ingenuity and intelligence, have never crossed the great ocean; indeed, they seldom venture beyond the borders of their kingdom. Only we French can knit together this world of savages of every manner and color, and unite it under the benevolent rule of reason, in the person of our great King; for if these savages have a common fault, it is their love of war and ferocity, which leads their tribes into continually bloody conflict against each other. But if we could but turn this to our advantage, and make them all our allies, they would enjoy the benefits of mutual accommodation by uniting for a common purpose; and we would enjoy the advantages, with their help, of at last driving the Spanish and the English from this continent, forever.

GOUPIL

27 March 1682

Good Friday   we stopped at noon and spent the three hours of His agony in quiet prayer and contemplation   a soul very thirsty for the son of God I mean for his suffering,   would find plenty here in this world of savages and alligators to satisfy it   *misere nobis*

our two Natchez guides turned back at this point   also the Chicaza brave Mingatuska   but the other Chicaza Chuka remains   declaring he will serve the Sieur de La Salle all his life

at this point the river divides into two channels with an island in the middle some 60 leagues long,   we took the west channel in heavy fog   passed a river from the west said to lead into the heart of New Spain   made 14 leagues today

Easter Sunday
29 March 1682

Why do you seek one who is alive here among the dead
we greeted the glorious sunrise with songs of celebration and love the Sieur de La Salle singing loudest of all   Membré preached a fine sermon on the triumph of Christ his earthly & his heavenly realm   the city of man & the city of God

the Sieur de La Salle enspirits the men urges them to our task   soon we shall arrive at the sea   Nicanapé claims he can smell it ahead but this I doubt

some of our men somewhat disabled   2 or 3 with bad boils or blisters   Baron's infected ankle continues to bother him   Membré has a toothache Prud'homme a slight fever   my evening's physic did work & give me a good stool this morning   10 leagues today the river veers east

3 0 M a r c h   1 6 8 2

fog today cooler   passed a town of the Oumas   at midday
saw some fishermen in their pirogues in a marsh   who fled
at the sight of our party into the canebrake   moments later
we heard drums & whoops,   the Sieur de La Salle sent
Tonty and his men to meet these savages   a shower of
arrows came from the fog
   anxious to keep the peace the Sieur de La Salle recalled the
men & we pursued our voyage.   we were warned about
these savages the Quinipissas.   16 leagues,   the river
continues SSE   all surprised by this eastern swing.

1 A p r i l   1 6 8 2

rain today more fog   our joy inseparable from the melancholy of flesh   for all of us grow weary of paddling
anxious to meet the sea
   distant thunder a sound as of enormous footsteps   saw
no lightning
   discoursing tonight of thunder and lightning Membré told
me of ships he saw masts all shivered   lightning struck the
mast of a Spanish galley shattering it   melted the shackle of
one of the slaves right off his leg only singed the leg,   I
expressed amazement at this miracle.
   I make eleven leagues today   direction hard to determine in the fog.

LA   SALLE

3 A p r i l   1 6 8 2

This morning we passed a village of the Tangibao savages,
and disembarked in order to inspect it. This village had been
abandoned, and several of the cabins burned to the ground.
A putrid smell told us what to expect, but we searched each

cabin until we found its source in a sight which filled some of the men with horror; but which they nevertheless could not forbear gazing upon: a pile of nine or ten corpses dead perhaps a week, puffed up and swarming with flies. Their scalps had been taken.

But this only serves to confirm my suspicion that these savages will never prove useful to themselves or to anyone else so long as they continue in their murderous ways; for their education serves not to correct the extreme violence of the passions by the improvements of reason, but on the contrary to give them full and unbridled scope.

Two leagues below this place the water turned brackish, and the men plied the river with redoubled effort. Goupil said we made nearly twenty leagues. The mosquitoes very troublesome tonight.

7 April 1682

Last night, we reached the place of which the Natchez had informed us, where the River Colbert divides into three channels. We saw gulls in the air; the current grew turbid. The breeze here carried the smell of the ocean and of salt flats whose mud is habitually exposed.

Accordingly, after we had eaten this morning, I directed Tonty to follow the middle passage and d'Autray the eastern one, while I took the one to the west. We were all much surprised at the strong eastern swing of this river; but there could be no doubt that the Gulf of Mexico was near.

In our channel, the current soon grew sluggish and the brackish water changed to brine. Everything here was marshland and feathered birds of all description. At last the Gulf of Mexico opened up before us, as far as the eye could see, and I lifted my heart in thankfulness, such was the flood of joy in my breast. The men with me sent up a cheer, and we fired off a volley, expecting to hear a response from one of the other parties; but they must have been farther off than we thought.

With the astrolabe, I determined the elevation of the north pole here to be about 27°.[1] For the last fifty leagues or so, I had been apprehensive of meeting a Spanish settlement or vessel, but to my gratification not a sail was in sight on these vast waters. The tide was out, and we walked about on the sandy shore; almost at a loss, however, as to what to do now, or how to express our ecstasy now that our long voyage had found its end. But at last I fell down and kissed the ground, with the realization that I had been nearly ten years in coming to this place, and finally had fulfilled the terms of the license of our beloved King, granted four years ago. *Vive le Roi!*

Then we paddled back up this same channel to search out some dry land upon which to spend the night, in anticipation of reuniting with the rest of our party, as we had agreed, upon the morrow.

GOUPIL

7 April 1682

The Sieur de La Salle fell to his knees & kissed the beach I could not help it I did too   throwing sand into the air some of the men wades into the water and douses each other with water from the Gulf

Membré says this is proof of the Hand of God governing the world,   searching out its furthermost corners   for he brought us here to our destination safe

we all shouted into the vast ocean   not knowing what to do   imagining our voices could be heard in France across the waters   mother did you hear me   I called your name   Barbier shouted to his whore

---

[1] In this and the following La Salle entry, the figure 30° was crossed out, and 27° inserted, apparently at a later date.

LA SALLE

9 April 1682

In the name of the most high, mighty, invincible, and victorious Prince, Louis the Great, by the grace of God King of France and Navarre, fourteenth of that name, this ninth day of April, one thousand six hundred and eighty-two, I, in virtue of the commission of His Majesty, which I hold in my hand, and which may be seen by all whom it may concern, have taken, and do now take, in the name of His Majesty, and of his successors to the crown, possession of this country of Louisiana, the seas, harbors, ports, bays, adjacent straits, and all the nations, peoples, provinces, cities, towns, villages, mines, minerals, fisheries, streams, and rivers comprised in the extent of said Louisiana, from the mouth of the great river St. Louis, on the eastern side, otherwise called the Ohio, Ouabache, Alighin, or Siporé, and this with the consent of the Chouanons, Chickasaws, and other people dwelling therein, with whom we have made alliance; as also along the River Colbert, or Messipi, and rivers which discharge themselves therein, from its source beyond the country of the Kious or Nadouessious, and this with their consent, and with consent of the Motantees, Illinois, Mesigameas, Arkansas, and Natchez, which are the most considerable nations dwelling therein, with whom we also have made alliance, either by ourselves, or by others in our behalf, as far as its mouth at the Sea or Gulf of Mexico, about the 27th degree of the elevation of the North Pole, and also to the mouth of the River of the Palms; upon the assurance which we have received from all these nations, that we are the first Europeans who have descended or ascended the said River Colbert, hereby protesting against all those who may in the future undertake to invade any or all of these countries, people, or lands above described, to the prejudice of the right of His Majesty, acquired by the consent of the nations herein named. Of which, and of all that can be ceded, I hereby take

to witness those who hear me, and demand the act of notary
as required by law.

[signed: —*La Métairie, Notary*

    de La Salle   *Jean Pignabel*
    Pierre Goupil   *Jean Michel*
    Henry de Tonty   *Gabriel Barbier*
    Louis Baron   *Pierre Migneret*
    Père Zénobe Membré   *François de Boisrondel*
    Jacques Cochois   *Sieur d'Autray*
    Antoine Bassard   *Pierre You*
    Jean du Lignon   *Jean Masse*]

G O U P I L

9 April 1 6 8 2

the Sieur de La Salle ardent all morning about trade on this
river & the colonies we will establish   saying access to this
river from now on must be from the south from the Gulf of
Mexico   & all the buffalo hides   20,000 écus worth each
year   the iron copper wood beaver furs pearls   a profitable silk trade might be established on this river   everyone
excited by the prospects

    I make the length of the river to be some 800 leagues 300
from the mouth of the Seignelay   and giving him these
numbers   he seemed surprisingly mild at my failure to find
the longitude,   saying we shall return to this place.

    on a hill above the place where the river makes three
channels we then assembled mustered under arms,   and
the Sieur de La Salle erected a cross and a post bearing the
arms of France,   it said *Louis le Grand, Roy de France et de
Navarre, règne le 9e Avril, 1682.*

    then what to our amazement   out of his trunk he pro-
duces this time not a Chinese robe but a scarlet cloak   such
as nobles wear at court   trimmed with gold lace.   &
knickerbockers of the finest Rouen linen   silk stockings

from Lyons   & fine buckled shoes.   we who never knew
he had these things dressed in our wretched skins   but we
sent up a cheer invigored by the sight   at last he put on a
long powdered wig

then we fired many volleys shouted *Vive le Roi*   we
chanted the *te Deum* the *Exoudiat* the *Domine salvum fac
Regem*   and the Sieur de La Salle made a grand speech, he
claimed this country for the king reading from his book.

I signed the proclamation, we embraced each other   while
the savages looked on in astonishment   some had tears in
their eyes   Chuka grinned   then we all cheered and
shouted once more gratified with all we had accomplished
and Membré exclaimed I did too   that this is the best company we ever was in   and we hope we can live and die in
it both.

II

PARIS

1684

LA SALLE
TO THE ABBÉ CLAUDE BERNOU [1]

Paris
29 January 1684

I have just had your letter; it is disconcerting the way you subject my modesty to so severe a strain. I repudiate all you say, but thank you for it nevertheless.

You asked when the propitious meeting at court was to take place, and I may tell you now: it happened yesterday. I hope you are prepared for this account. My savage friend retained his dignity and bearing throughout the entire ceremony, but the King and the Dauphin behaved like the children our savages are sometimes accused of being.

First, Chuka was allowed to observe the King at prayer, in his chapel. As you know, he is being instructed in the articles of our faith. This seemed to make a great impression upon him; that is, the esteem with which our King holds the same

---

[1]Claude Bernou was one of La Salle's friends and sponsors; his ambition was to become Bishop of all the territories La Salle had discovered, and thus circumvent the Jesuits, who ruled in Canada and considered the spiritual jurisdiction of Louisiana to be under the Bishop of Quebec. La Salle's discovery of the mouth of the Mississippi meant to Bernou that the entire territory drained by the great river could now communicate with Europe by means of the Gulf of Mexico instead of by the St. Lawrence, thus increasing the likelihood of a separate bishopric for it. During the time of La Salle's stay in Paris in 1684, Bernou was living in Rome.

doctrine we teach him. Then the entire court was assembled in the Gallery, and I presented Chuka in his native costume to His Majesty. Chuka appeared astonishingly unimpressed by the wall of looking glasses which I have seen disconcert other savages in his place.

The King, who has been through this sort of ceremony before, asked the usual questions. His purple coat was buttoned so as to conceal his shirt, and his sleeves fastened; purple crepe hung to his calves. Chuka's feathers and bones and skins and pierced nose seemed hardly a novelty to me, in a world in which mourning is so subject to fashion.[1] But of course the ladies were amazed by the savage, and their eyes glittered. Have you been baptized? asked the King. I answered that he was being instructed in the faith. Between you and me, Monsieur, my knowledge of his tongue is still imperfect, and I was obliged to swell up his answers a bit. How many meals did his people take each day? What sort of things did they eat? Did they have one or many wives? Chuka became confused by the question about the number of meals, and I answered the King that they eat when they are hungry, like a cat or dog. They eat venison, buffalo meat, fish, roots, fruit, and cornmeal; and they have one wife whom they can divorce by a mere declaration; but their chief or king is allowed to have several wives. At this Louis sagely nodded his head.

Then His Majesty invited Mme. de Maintenon to step forward, and she questioned the savage as to matters of ferocity; how many wars he had been in and how many men he had killed and scalps he had taken, and so forth. On her lips these questions sounded innocent enough, for she was searching for the means by which to pity his savagery; but I saw many smiles behind fans. I must admit my friend's answer surprised me as much as the others, for he claimed to have killed upwards of twenty men, as well as a large number of women and children. But he had taken only six

---

[1]The Queen, Marie-Thérèse, had recently died.

scalps, of warriors whose valor he could be proud to have bettered. He smiled at the stir his answer produced. The Dauphin's face lit up at finding himself in the presence of a murderer, and one could sense his burning desire to learn the details of this carnage: whether it was by hatchet, by his bare hands, by bow and arrow, by means of his teeth, or whatever. But he restrained himself and the topic passed, not without a collective shudder.

We were soon to know what was really on his mind, however; for, when Mme. de Maintenon had finished, the Dauphin stepped forward and asked Chuka whether he had ever eaten a slain enemy. On his lips, the question seemed highly appropriate; you have seen his girth; perhaps he was searching for a new delicacy! Chuka's answer stunned the court; although, since it came through my lips, the astonishment appeared to be directed at me. Many times, said he, he had dined upon slain warriors; his sinews and muscles were those of his enemies, for they have nourished his flesh. At this, the men stared in stupefaction, the Bishop blessed himself, and several women left the room.

Then the Bishop stepped forward and questioned Chuka about religious matters; whether he had a name for that being we call God; whether his people believed in an afterlife or *spirit world,* to which the soul travels when the body dies; how they treated their dead, the manner of their burial, and so forth. As he was speaking, a life seemed to go out of the court, and I noticed that the King and the Dauphin were nowhere to be seen. We continued the interview, but even Chuka appeared conscious of the missing ears and eyes for whom all this was on display. But what was our astonishment when, in the midst of these questions and answers, His Majesty and the Prince returned, divested of their mourning, and dressed from head to foot like savages, in skins and leggings and feathers! Behind them came servants bearing on pillows the King's collection of bows and arrows, headdresses, beaded costumes, native furs, and so forth. You would have been delighted, my friend, at the struggle of the court to compliment Louis and his son. Even Chuka seemed amazed; I explained to him that other savages from across the waters had visited France, and in the course of time our King had collected specimens of their costumes. But I refrained from telling him that as a boy Louis had often dressed up as a savage, and once had even evinced a desire to scalp the Cardinal and roast him alive! This seemed to Chuka the best time to present the King with his gift, a crown of porcelain beads and shells which I had fabricated for this occasion, and which the savage laid at Louis's feet as a sign that this great chief was the true and lawful monarch of his people. Then Louis presented him with some splendid robes of gold, velvet, satin, and scarlet, and a basket to carry them in; in truth, they haven't left his side since. Mme. de Maintenon gave him an ornamented snuffbox.

His Majesty signaled the end of this ceremony by pretending to puff upon a calumet, which he held out to Chuka for his admiration. The King suggested to his ministers that the entire court adopt savage costumes and savage ways; we shall live in caves, he said, and eat our enemies; that way, the English may be able to distinguish us from the Flemings. Wouldn't you like it, my dear, he asked Mme. de Maintenon, if we were not to wear breeches at court? With other such bons mots and witticisms, the sort of thing I've told you makes me abhor court life, he retired with his Ministers, and the ceremony was over.

Apparently, however, he did wear this savage costume the rest of the day, for he made his appearance still dressed in it during our private audience later in the afternoon. His wig was back on his head, and Chuka's crown sat beside him on the floor. I must say he looked foolish: a savage chief in powdered wig. Nor can I satisfy you that all went well, but Louis did appear to be receptive to our plans. My enemies have gained his ears, that is clear; but he was astonished to hear that Fort Frontenac was not abandoned, as La Barre had written him; and that La Barre had driven away my men, suffered my land to run to waste, and even told the Iroquois that they should seize me as an enemy of the colony. Louis may restore my property, and if this occurs, my heart will surely warm more easily to another expedition. But the King cannot dissolve my debts, Monsieur; you know this as well as I do. Therefore, a great deal remains to be done.

Yes, I have seen Hennepin's book. It is all a fabrication; or perhaps I should say, there is nothing improbable in the adventures he describes save their occurrence to himself. He was not with us on the voyage down the River Colbert; ask Du Lhut. While we sought the Gulf of Mexico, Hennepin was a captive of savages near the Ouscousin [Wisconsin] River, where he was rescued by Du Lhut. His account of the discovery of the Colbert, or Messipi, is taken word for word from my report to the minister; Hennepin has simply insinuated himself into the expedition, and even tries to imply that he was its leader! Everyone here knows better, however, and the book has had the unexpected result of making me a celebrity in this city, a position I cannot say affords me any comfort, due to that timidity I suffer from, which you and I have discussed before. I am ill fitted for society, but the invitations mount up. I suppose if I am to embark upon more explorations, I had best do it soon, as that life is more suited to my solitary disposition, even if living amongst savages makes me less polished and complaisant than the atmosphere of Paris requires. I well believe that there is self-love in this; and that, knowing how little I am accustomed to a more polite life, the fear of making mistakes makes me more reserved than I like to be. So I rarely expose myself to conversation with those in whose company I am afraid of making blunders, and can hardly help making them. Abbé Renaudot can tell you with what repugnance I had the honor to appear before the King yesterday, even if I joke about it here. I paced in my quarters all the day before, and thought it best to turn them into a Trappist house, and live instead entirely in solitude and meditation; in short, to pace up and down and become bored to death for the love of God. But you are the only one with whom I can safely discuss these feelings. Yes,

I confess it: I am anxious to be off again to the New World, whose savages are more courteous than those at court or in society, with their loose tongues and looser morals.

But to return to Hennepin's book. You can imagine how uncomfortable I am when people approach me on the street and ask me about it. They expect my face to be painted, and want to know how I survived a world of hairy monsters, giant lizards, terrible insects, huge birds, and putrid food no Frenchman could possibly eat. To say nothing of the lack of Frenchwomen, though I tell them this is the easiest deprivation of all to endure. By the way, two men from our expedition have been ennobled. Plain Michel Accault has become the Sieur d'Accault, and honest Pierre You has blossomed into Pierre You d'Youville de la Découverte. Thus is the lead gilded.

The winter continues severe; the wine freezes in the glasses at Versailles. Take heart you are in Rome. The bustle and noise of this city are overwhelming, and added to this the Seine has frozen over. The people dying of cold and starvation in the provinces deceive themselves that Paris will offer relief. Here is the relief: they serve dog in the sausage shops, and cooked rat in the streets—to those who can afford it. And the hangman is in constant demand, what with the influx of beggars, thieves, highwaymen, and other such vagabonds into the city.

Good-bye, my friend. Your kindness has been a great consolation to me. When the spring comes, we shall talk of expeditions.

de La Salle

GOUPIL

TO FATHER ZÉNOBE MEMBRÉ

Paris

12 February 1684

Are you well my friend?   you asked me to write to you and
now I am doing it, I live in wretched quarters in the Rue de
la Truanderie   the Sieur de La Salle lives upstairs he lodges
me with the savage on the first floor, in this house I lay down
on the mat to sleep but am prevented from doing so by the
mice and vermin with which this house abounds and which
are very troublesome to me,   but Chuka sleeps like the
dead not bothered,   here I have my table my instruments
the Sieur de La Salle helps me when he can   & in this I take
consolation having only made rude sketches before   but
my measurements are faulty, I would have the river pour into
Florida the Sieur de La Salle wants it closer to Mexico so we
split the difference   we draw pictures of the animals in
places where they roam, a picture of the monsters painted on
rocks above the river, he says the King will publish this map,
I have a parchment 6 feet long 4 feet wide ink pens a compass
etc.   but in this cold the ink freezes in the pen I have to
thaw it every morning at the fire,   our purpose is to show the
extent of his conquest & the new dominions of the King
being larger than all of France and Spain together,   already
he talks about another voyage I say between you and me for
one who lives as narrow as he does this is out of the question.
with his foul temperament   yesterday cursing the landlord
and calling him every foul name he could think of for pretending to charge more than the terms they agreed upon for
these rooms which are worth nothing,   having agreed
upon 2 livres a week for the two floors   now M. Armand
the landlord says we owe him 10 livres though we've been
in these quarters but 4 weeks   & this makes the Sieur de La
Salle livid at being so barbarously used   he swears up &
down Chuka merely smiles, I try to teach Chuka the French
tongue but his mouth is not suited for forming our words,

he makes progress in learning the articles of our faith being instructed in pictures and signs by Father Noyrot at St. Eustache   Sometimes I accompany him there   as you know my dear friend to cause the blood of Jesus Christ to be applied to the souls for whom it was shed,   is a glory little known among men.

I have had more fits   of the manner you saw on the ship coming back   the apothecary gives me purges which are very strong and vinegar & honey too, he says if I feel a fit coming by means of a breeze or cold pouring of air across an extremity,   such as my hand this extremity I should tie tightly with a cord meanwhile wrapping myself in warm blankets.   but I find this doesn't work.   the moon he says has the same cold temperament as the brain & therefore may inflict epilepsy,   for Satan operating by means of the full moon exerts his influence when the body is weakened,   the humors being stirred up & the brain affected   he tells me to spit when I feel it coming   & to fix a nail to the spot where my head strikes the ground the lizard he says swallows his discarded skin because he begrudges this remedy for my illness to mankind having been cursed,   so he gave me the skin of a lizard to swallow but this I could not compass, the body if not supported by the soul is overcome of its own weight and falls down, with a sudden clouding of the mind the body falls down the soul standing idly by

sometimes now I merely lean against a wall seized by a confusion in my head & a darkness of sight,   & feeling it come on like this I say an Ave Maria & the paroxysm has passed then I spit.   or I will evacuate my bladder of the sudden & look around as though stunned & move something from one place to another such as a pen   I pray to St. Valentine 3 Paternosters & 3 Ave Marias daily for the souls of the fathers & mothers of the 3 wise men each day   whose names I must whisper upon wakening from a fit Jasper Melchior Balthazar   and carry them in writing on my body once I saw a little man digging into my eye   have I ever spoken any strange languages   the apothecary said I should

ask this of those who had witnessed my fits   such as have
I ever spoken Latin or Greek or did I say the angels were
taking me away or speak of seeing anyone in Paradise or sing
divers songs & hymns or tell of the future or of secrets
possessed by those around me,   none of these things could
I recall doing but I thought perhaps you might have some
knowledge I could not have of these things I mention if any
of them happened on our passage   for it may determine his
remedy.

    sometimes I know it is coming when I see a black woman
approaching me, she fills my heart with fear & when she
comes near I fall down   M. Danceny the apothecary says
this woman is a thunderstorm   it is my illness I mean which
he likens to a thunderstorm,   for when a thunderstorm
comes near the animals feel it & become restless just as I
become terrified when a fit approaches, the sky darkens in a
thunderstorm just as my sight darkens & I grow sleepy
next comes the wind sweeping everything away & I feel a
wind inside me making me swell   then the thunder shakes
heaven & earth & I become convulsed in all my limbs, the
thunder sheds rain & I froth at the mouth, hail & lightning
strikes everything & breaks objects & my limbs are bent and
broken by the storm in my body, thus he compares a thunderstorm to the falling sickness,   after a storm the wetness of
the rain and the mud takes time to dry, in like manner the
reason & senses of the epileptic take time to recover,   what
think you of this?   it is an ingenious comparison & deter-
mines the remedies & concoctions he makes   I met him in
the Place Dauphine   selling medicines on the street

    I hope you are happy in your convent   and have not the
itch of these wanderers and unsettled people   you know
who I mean,   to be off on discoveries each new day   but
resolve to lead a more settled life as God so arranged it.
I am your friend,

Pierre Goupil

L A   S A L L E
T O   T H E   M A R Q U I S   D E   S E I G N E L A Y [1]

Paris
18 February 1684

Monseigneur,

In 1678, I offered to undertake the discovery, at my own expense, of a port for the vessels of the King in the Gulf of Mexico, if it should please His Majesty in return to grant to me the seigniory of the government of the forts which I should erect on my route, together with certain privileges and an indemnification for the great outlay which the expedition would impose upon me. Such grant was made to me by letters patent on the twelfth of May, 1678. Accordingly, in order to execute this commission, I abandoned all my own pursuits which did not relate to it. I did not omit anything necessary for success, notwithstanding dangerous sickness, considerable losses, and other misfortunes which I suffered. I made five voyages under extraordinary hardships, extending over more than five thousand leagues, most commonly on foot or by canoe, through snow and water, almost without rest, traversing more than six hundred leagues of unknown country, among many barbarous and cannibal nations, among whom I was obliged to fight almost daily, although I was accompanied by only thirty-six men, having no other consolation before me than a hope of bringing to fruition an enterprise which I believed would be agreeable to His Majesty. On the last of these voyages, I did descend the great River Colbert, or Messipi, and did discover the place where it empties into the Gulf of Mexico, along three mouths which are as many harbors, capable of receiving every description of ships; where those of His Majesty will always find a secure

---

[1]The Marquis de Seignelay, Louis XIV's Minister, was the son of the previous Minister, Colbert, who had died the year before. Seignelay had been an early supporter of La Salle at Louis's court.

retreat and all that may be necessary to refit and revictual them.

I believe that I have sufficiently established the truth of this discovery by the official instrument signed by all my companions, which was placed last year in the hands of the Minister your late father by the Count de Frontenac, as also by a report drawn up by the Reverend Father Zénobe Membré, missionary, who accompanied me during this voyage and who at this time resides in the Recollect Convent at Béthune in the province of Artois, and by the construction of a *map,* to be drawn in the most accurate and scientific manner by my cartographer, Pierre Goupil, and to be forwarded to Monseigneur upon its completion. These proofs are sufficient to contradict whatever may have been written to the contrary by persons who have no knowledge whatsoever of the country where the discovery was made, never having been there.

Now, Monseigneur, I hope to remove all debt and prejudice by the design I entertain, under the favor of Monseigneur, of returning to the country of my discovery, this time by the mouth of the River Colbert in the Gulf of Mexico, since I must have lost my senses if without being certain of the knowledge whereby to arrive where I propose, I were to expose not only my own fortune and that of my friends to manifest destruction, but my own honor and reputation to the unavoidable disgrace of having imposed on the confidence of His Majesty and of his Minister. Of this there can be no likelihood, because I have no interest to disguise the truth, since, if Monseigneur does not think it convenient to undertake any enterprise in that direction, I will not ask anything more from His Majesty until my return from the Gulf of Mexico confirms the truth of what I have alleged. With reference to the assertion that my voyage would produce no profit to France, I can reply that I have observed great advantages which both France and Canada may derive from my discovery, to the glory of the King, the welfare of the kingdom, the honor of the ministry of Monseigneur, and the memory of him who employed me upon this expedition.

Firstly, the service of God may be established there by the preaching of the gospel to numerous docile and sedentary nations, who will be found more willing to receive it than those of other parts of America upon account of their great civilization. These savages, the Natchez, already have temples and a form of worship.

Secondly, we should obtain there everything which has enriched New England and Virginia, and which constitutes the foundation of their commerce and of their great wealth —timber of every kind, salted meat, tallow, corn, sugar, tobacco, honey, wax, resin and other gums, immense pasturages, hemp, and other articles with which more than two hundred vessels are every year freighted in New England to carry elsewhere. There are also pearls in this place as large as peas, and the savages are of such docile temperament that a profitable industry of silk weaving might be introduced. There are mines of coal, slate, and iron, and the lumps of pure red copper found in various places indicate that there are mines of copper too. Close to this place are the silver mines of New Biscay, which are open everywhere on all sides and are defended only by a small number of Spanish so sunk in effeminacy and indolence as to be incapable of enduring the fatigue of wars.

While other colonies are open and exposed to the approach of foreigners by as many points as their coasts are washed by the sea, whereby they are placed under the constant necessity of having many persons to guard these points of access, on this river one single post, established toward the lower part, would be sufficient to protect a territory extending for more than eight hundred leagues from north to south, and still farther from east to west, because its banks are accessible only from the Gulf of Mexico through the mouth of the river, the remainder of the coast being impenetrable inland for more than twenty leagues, in consequence of woods, bogs, reeds and marshes, through which it is impossible to march; and this may be the reason why the exploration of this river has been neglected by the Spanish; if they have had any knowledge of it. It is true that this country is more open toward the southwest, where it borders upon Mexico; but this place is protected from the insults of the Spanish by a great number of warlike savages, who block their way to the river by engaging them in cruel wars, which would certainly inflict greater evil when assisted by some French, whose more mild and more humane mode of governing would prove a great means for the preservation of the peace.

To maintain this establishment, which is the only one required in order to obtain all the advantages mentioned, two hundred men only are needed, who would also construct the fortifications and buildings and effect the clearings necessary for the sustenance of the colony, after which there would be no further expenditure. The goodness of the country and the soil will induce the settlers to remain there willingly, and the ease and happiness in which they live will make them attend to the cultivation of the soil and the production of articles of commerce, and will remove all desire to imitate the inhabitants of Canada, who are obliged to seek subsistence in the woods, under great fatigue, in hunting for peltries.

It may be said by some that this colony might injure the commerce of Quebec and cause the desertion of its inhabitants, but the answer is that Quebec has its peltries and Louisiana has other articles of commerce, such as I have already described, which could in no way compete with those of Quebec.

If foreigners anticipate us, Monseigneur, they will deprive France of all the advantages to be expected from the success of this enterprise. They have already made several attempts to discover this passage, and they will not neglect it now that the whole world knows I have discovered it, since the Dutch have published it in their newspapers upwards of a year ago, and a scurrilous book about it has lately appeared in France. Nothing more is required than to maintain the possession of this country I took in the name of His Majesty, who will probably derive the greatest benefit from the duties he will levy there, as in our other colonies, and to whom I remain eager to give those marks of zeal and of the most profound respect with which I am also,

Monseigneur,

your most humble, most obedient,
and most faithful servant.

de La Salle

LA SALLE

TO THE ABBÉ CLAUDE BERNOU

Paris

24 February 1684

I have met your Penalosa and must tell you bluntly: I do not like him. He is old, he spits when he talks, and his willingness to betray his own country stains his character in ways that make me shudder. Yes, we can make use of him; he begs to be made use of. But I will do nothing in league with this creature. If he has turned the King's head with tales of invading Mexico, we can take advantage of this without him; we can move my river into Mexico, if you wish. The good thing is that the King's ears are softened, and the Jesuits have fallen out of favor. My guess is that Louis is distracted by thoughts of the silver mines in New Biscay, which are not far from the River Colbert; a tributary of this river, navigable along its length, leads directly to them. By establishing a colony on the River Colbert, we can claim a foothold in Mexico, or at the very least a port from which we might harass the Spaniards in those regions from whence they derive their wealth. There is no problem in altering the course of my river for the better, as we were not able to determine its longitude, and its latitude is variable—the day was cloudy. As I told you, for the last ten leagues or so the river swings east, and appears to debouch at a coast running north and south rather than east and west, although this may be simply a large bay. At any

rate, anything is possible; America's face has yet to be
formed; and for our purposes, the war with Spain may be all
that we require to colonize this vast dominion.

I beg you to thank our friend for the kind letter he wrote
to me; when he returns, I shall speak with him.

By the way, M. Giffar plans to transfer his regiment to the
King for 250,000 livres; this should relieve all his debts. As
you know, he lost a ship last year off the coast of Labrador,
to the value of 1000 écus' worth of pelts.

I shall continue to go into society, as you suggest, as long as
it helps our cause; but I am anxious for this business to be
resolved. We visited M. de Ménars, whose collections of ancient coins, oriental manuscripts, and maps he bored us with
all evening. On Thursdays, we go to the Arsenal, to see *les
Divines;* they never tire of Chuka, and as a consequence this
salon has become the most frequented in Paris. When we go
there, she receives us with her hand. Many things are said and
replied to. Good food sits there uneaten, for this is apparently
the polite way to treat it; Chuka, however, helps himself, observing most of the niceties I've taught him. But the crumbs
prove unmanageable, and the wine defeats him. It widens his
grin a league, and this unnerves visitors, who think he knows
something. Then we perform the usual charade, whereby
Chuka answers questions through me; that is, he grunts and
squawks and I make up the answers. Yes, he finds this city
astonishing; so many people grouped together under one
chief! And they stack their cabins on top of each other, drive
around in leather cabins pulled by huge dogs, etc. But why is it
—our savage wants to know—that those who are hungry or ill
clothed do not take the others by the throat and demand their
share of the food and clothing? For it is evident that in passing
out the goods, someone had erred by neglecting certain people, a mistake which the chiefs of his own tribe would correct
the moment it was pointed out. Accompanied by Chuka's une-
ffaceable smile, this statement produces such a stir that twice as
many people show up the following week, wishing to be subjected to the same kinds of dangerous sentiments. The salon

becomes a battlefield; for example, Mme. de Frontenac and Mlle. d'Outrelaise both slip off their gloves at the same moment to offer the serviette, but Mme. de Frontenac gets there first, thus subjecting our pet to the most humiliating defeat; but such is the way of the world.

To speak more seriously, I come away feeling that I shall never be suited for this sort of life. Having peeked behind the scenes more than contributes to my ease, and having examined the wires and mechanisms of the show, I find the entertainment has long since ceased to exhibit any appeal to me. Chuka grows weary of it too; he speaks less and less, in public as well as in private, except to inquire when we shall return to his people; his sole consolation is the basket of sumptuous robes given him by the King, which he pores over like a miser poring over his gold. I think he has some of the ice in my composition; this is why he follows me. Society with its thousand endearments has no appeal for him.

As for this Penalosa, let us speak no more of him, as his name carries the smallpox.

de La Salle

GOUPIL
TO FATHER ZÉNOBE MEMBRÉ

Paris
2 March 1684

my friend I need your advice again, what should I do, he tore up the parchment & abused & kicked me when it was almost completed saying failure to determine the longitude of the river was all my fault,   because I lost the compass though he knows it would have been of no assistance,   and whereas before he was mild upon this loss now I must make a new map & move the river a hundred leagues west   & make it empty into the western extremity of the Gulf but this it doesn't do,   and as this brings the Messipi River nigh

upon the Rio Bravo [Rio Grande] he avers we may as well
join them together   giving them a common mouth   but
this is a sinful deception & he insists I must do it   after
having delivered himself so favorably of the other map, and
proving himself so mild upon it,   I need not add that this
mortifies me so much I may leave his service, his changes of
mood are a mystery to me   but perhaps we have 2 souls,
as M. Pascal mentions   one for the good and one for evil
for after abusing me so the next day he was sweet and docile
& apologized for the blows he had given me & paid me for
the first time since we have been here then spoke persua-
sively for an hour or more upon the course of the River
Colbert   how its twisting course veered west as demonstrated by the changing vegetation   how his log noted all
the compass changes he approximated by observations of the
sun   and the eastward course of the river's mouth proved
it emptied into the western extremity of the Gulf of Mexico
then he asked me about my mother & our family   reminding me in subtle ways of all he had done for my family & for
me how he had found me with the Jesuits and taken me into
his confidence teaching me how to read & write & take
measurements of the sun use an astrolabe & compass & draw
upon parchment   then returning to speak of the river &
proving to me by certain Spanish books he pretended to read
from   that the 2 rivers joined & formed a common mouth
until he nearly convinced me & we drew a rough cartoon of
the map but now I'm no longer sure my friend   I'm afraid
it is a cruel deception & he has treated me cruelly   he
frightens me his vanity and temper are monstrous,   he is
gone all day & walks his room all night & Chuka sits in his
corner with his head in his hands the way savages mourn.

    after he beat me I had a fit   he won't pay me until I fin-
ish the map   I can't bring myself to finish it I suppose I
must   when I am paid I can serve a more honest man
next   I am your friend,

Pierre Goupil

L A   S A L L E
T O   T H E   M A R Q U I S   D E   S E I G N E L A Y

Paris
9 March 1684

Monseigneur,

The principal utility which I expected from the great perils and labors which I underwent in the discovery of the River Colbert, or Messipi, was to satisfy the wish expressed to me by the late Monseigneur Colbert of finding a port where the French might establish themselves and succeed in driving the Spaniards from those regions whence they obtain more than six million écus a year in silver. The place which I propose to fortify lies twenty leagues above the mouth of the River Colbert, in the Gulf of Mexico, and possesses all the advantages for such a purpose which can be wished for, both upon account of its excellent position and the favorable disposition of the savages who live in that part of the country. The right of the King to this territory is the common right of all nations to lands which they have discovered, a right which cannot be disputed after the possession already taken in the name of His Majesty, by me, with the consent of its inhabitants. As the river called by the Spaniards the Rio Bravo [Rio Grande] luckily happens to be the same as that the savages call the Messipi, the undertaking of Comte Penalosa and that of myself will serve to support each other, the former proceeding west from the river, and myself north, in order to surprise the Spaniards in that part of their territories where their forces are weakest. The savages along this river, having been so conciliated by the gentleness of my men, have offered to accompany me anywhere, and I have no doubt that they would favor my enterprise as much as they would oppose themselves to the enemies of France. This any person may judge by the offerings which were made at the posts upon which the arms of France were attached, and by the assembly of more than eighteen thousand savages of various nations, some of whom had come from a distance of more than two thousand leagues, who met together in a single camp, and who, forgetting their own old disputes, threw themselves into my arms and made me master of their different interests. By the union of these forces it would be possible to form an army of more than fifteen thousand savages, who, with the aid of the arms which I shall give them, would not find any resistance in the province which I intend to attack, where there are not more than four hundred native Spaniards, all of whom are officers or artisans living in indolence, better able to explore mines than to fight wars.

Upon account of these considerations I propose, with the approbation of Monseigneur, to undertake this enterprise, and, if peace should prevent the execution of it, to establish a very profitable station for commercial purposes, very easy to be maintained, and from whence, at the commencement of hostilities, the Spaniards might be harassed, since peace is the most proper time to prepare for war when it shall become necessary.

It is certain that France would draw from the mines of New Biscay greater benefits than Spain, owing to the facility of transport. We might also, perhaps, open a passage to the South Sea, which is not more distant than the breadth of the province of Culiacán, not to mention the possibility of meeting with some rivers near to the River Seignelay [Red River], which may discharge themselves on that side.

I would not think this affair so easy if, in addition to my knowledge of their language, I was not familiar with the manner of the savages, through which I may obtain as much confidence by a behavior in accordance with their practices, as I have impressed on them a feeling of respect in consequence of all that I have yet done in passing with a small number of followers through so many nations and punishing those who broke their word with me. After this, I have no doubt that in a short time they will become good French subjects.

It may be objected that, peace being concluded, no advantage could be taken of this post. The answer to this is that even peace should not prevent us from insulting, *en passant,* some of their maritime places, the pillage of which may well repay the entire expenses of the expedition; and peace could never prevent us from entering into that commerce respecting which I have already written to Monseigneur. Respecting this, I will oblige myself, in case the peace should continue for three years, to repay to His Majesty all that may be advanced, or to forfeit the property and government which I shall have created. Awaiting your favorable receipt of these proposals, I remain,

Monseigneur,
your most humble, most obedient,
and most faithful servant.

de La Salle

*Note of What Is Requisite
for the Expedition*

1. A vessel of thirty guns, armed and provided with everything necessary, and the crew paid and victualed during the expedition.

2. Twelve other pieces of cannon for the two forts, of five or six pounds to the ball, and eight cannon of ten or twelve, with the gun carriages and train; two hundred balls for each cannon, and powder in proportion.

3. Two hundred men, levied at the expense of His Majesty, but selected by me. Their pay for one year to be one hundred and twenty livres a man; as the money would be of no avail to them in the colony, it shall be converted at the place of embarkation into goods proper for them.

4. Six hundred muskets for arming four hundred savages, in addition to sixteen hundred who are already armed, and the others for two hundred Frenchmen.

5. A hundred pair of pistols proper to be worn in the girdle; one hundred and fifty swords, and as many sabers, twenty-five pikes, twenty-five halberds, twenty thousand pounds of gunpowder.

6. Musket balls of the proper caliber in proportion; gun flints, powder horns, rifle flints; pickaxes, hoes, shovels, axes, hatchets, and cramp irons for the fortifications and buildings; five thousand to six thousand pounds of iron and four hundred pounds of steel of all sorts. A forge, with its appurtenances, besides the tools necessary for armorers, joiners, coopers, wheelwrights, carpenters, and masons.

7. Two boxes of surgery provided with medicine and instruments.

8. Two chapels and the ornaments for the almoners.

9. Refreshments for the sick.

LA SALLE
TO THE ABBÉ CLAUDE BERNOU

Paris
12 March 1684

Enclosed you will find a copy of my letter to the Minister, dated 9 March; Renaudot has his ear; all we can do now is wait.

You tell me that the Pope will refuse to issue a bull of institution for the new Bishop; this has been expected here. Louis will decline to demand it in return; only one above the law can pretend it doesn't exist.

The sitting began the first thing this morning; I am doing this upon your recommendation, such things being distasteful to me.

I have a new valet, and the manner of his coming to my employment was extraordinary. I think you will be amused to learn it. On Saturday last, near St. Eustache in search of a hackney coach to take me to Renaudot, I passed the usual Saturday market, such as it exists in this poor quarter; consisting of stalls of old shoes and crockery, wooden cages of pigeons, vendors hawking turnips, chestnuts, bonnets, blacking, sponges, and other such articles, as well as a puppet show and one old woman selling stuffed rats decked out like dolls. As coaches weren't to be found, I was forced to walk through this commotion, in which the line between selling and begging is very thin indeed. At the entrance to an alley, some girls and an old woman were dancing obscenely while a crowd expressed its appreciation in coarse terms. Several other similar displays were in progress in various corners of the square; in one, a man dressed up as a woman and a country clown danced a ballet which represented disgusting attitudes and immoral acts with their gestures and postures; and I couldn't forbear from thinking that such were the wretched lives of these people that only displays of this kind could make them happy. There were also the usual jugglers, tumblers, singers, and fiddlers, and, near the steps of the church, beggars and cripples with withered limbs and hands shrunken and twisted inward like birds' claws, some of them walking on leather braces attached to their knees. A group of clubfeet exhibited their naked feet and held out their hands to receive coins. Besides these beggars there were some *convulsionists,* that is to say, people seized by all manner of fits and attacks, trembling in every limb, foaming at the mouth, and dropping to the pavement; but the police had already begun to put a stop to this display, and were engaged in chasing them away and burning their flea-ridden bundles; for it is well known that these convulsionists are fakers, and only feign their paroxysms in order to elicit sympathy, or to distract the crowd while their accomplices sneak around picking pockets and stealing purses. Whilst the police were herding them together, one broke free and, stopping to taunt his pursuers, did a brief dance on the street to the immense delight of the crowd, a nightmarish parody of an epileptic's fit. I can testify to the accuracy of the counterfeit because my servant, Pierre Goupil, shows me the real article enough times a day to drive me mad. This taunter's epileptic dance was accompanied by obscene gestures of his hips and hands, and a violent trembling and shaking of his body; he thrust his tongue out and rolled his head around, before running off in the direction of Les Innocents with several police in pursuit. I thought that this man would surely be caught, as his hair was the color of an orange, but I had found my coach at last, which proceeded to thread its way with some difficulty through the crowd toward the Rue St. Denis, and I naturally assumed that my observation of these amusing distractions was at an end.

What was my surprise, then, when rounding the corner of the Rue de la Verrerie, I saw this same orange-haired beggar transformed into a vendor and hawking his wares on a corner with another man. They were selling birds' nests, which they held out in baskets before them. You understand, my friend, that he had become a vendor so instantly in order to avoid detection, for these street vendors, I've since learned, serve as scouts for the beggars, and warn them of approaching authority, as well as helping them to disguise themselves if necessary. My curiosity got the upper hand, and, pretending to take an interest in birds' nests, I stopped the coach in order to talk with the man from my window. The creature must have recognized me from the market, for he appeared to wink as we spoke, as though I were in upon his secret and must not betray him. In one arm he held a basket of nests, with eggs of different colors, all emptied of their contents by small holes drilled in the bottom, and in the other hand he squeezed the neck of a live snake, which twisted and un-twisted itself around his arm. While describing these nests to me, which he priced at five sols each, and one sol apiece for the eggs, insisting that gentlemen could use them to decorate their apartments, of a sudden he broke off and began offering his services as a valet with such vehement insistence and distress that I was forced to order the coach to proceed. But this man was not to be gainsaid, and he was so officious about me that I could not get rid of him, for as the coach went forward, he dropped his wares and jumped up behind it with such evident violence that one of the doors flew open and allowed my case to fall into the street. Upon calling out to the driver to stop, I saw our friend running up behind with my case as though returning it for a reward. In short, there was no saying him no. I gave him a coin and the driver chased him off, yet he followed us by running down the street and waving his arms all the way down the Rue de la Verrerie, until it appeared that we had finally lost him on the Rue St. Antoine.

This was Saturday morning; I spent the day with Renaudot, during which we composed the letter to the Minister which you now have in your possession. I suppose you have found nothing so much extraordinary as unusual in any of this, but now hear the rest: at 3:00 a.m. that night I was roused from a deep sleep by the slightest sound from my balcony window. The window swung open and in stepped a darkened figure whom I immediately recognized as this same man, owing to his negligible stature, and perhaps even to a certain glow his hair appeared to give off, in the meager light from the night candle on my bureau across the room. I pretended to sleep, in order to see what this person would do next; of course, he went straight to the wardrobe, and proceeded to search through my pockets for my purse—which nevertheless was under my pillow—when I leapt from the bed and, seizing him by the neck, threw him to the floor with such violence that I thought for a moment I had killed him; for he lay there in a lifeless heap at my feet. This turned out to be another feigned fit, however, for he regained his legs once I had kicked him several times, and begged me not to call the landlord, and once more, with the utmost extravagance of manner, requested me to engage him as my valet, for he had observed in my coach that I had none with me. I answered him that I did not take my valet everywhere I went, that indeed I had two valets already, in a room downstairs, and

had no need of a third, but he replied that I evidently had
no personal valet who attended to my toilet and other immediate needs, as there was none in this room; whereupon I
reminded him that twice that day he had accosted me, this
time with the intention of robbing me; that I intended to call
the landlord and have him arrested, and that the punishment
for what he had done was death by hanging, preceded by
breaking on the wheel, the news of which threw him into a
fit of weeping and moaning and thrashing on the floor, until
I was forced to quiet him down, for fear he should wake
everyone in the house.

To tell the truth, my friend, I had no intention of arresting
this man, as he piqued my curiosity not a little bit; and once
I had calmed him, I asked him to tell me about himself, while
I lit some candles, put on a dressing gown, and exchanged
my nightcap for a wig, the better to conduct this interview
with a dignity that was certainly lost on this creature. As you
see, I am very clever; I even take unnecessary precautions.

His name is Michel Duhaut, but everyone calls him
Minime, in consideration of his small stature; in truth, he is
almost as short as a dwarf, though proportioned like a normal
man. He comes from a village near Bergerac in the Périgord;
he told me that when he was a child, his family walked to the
fields of Bordeaux every March to prune the vines, and again
in the summer to pick grapes, and walked back in the fall
gleaning chestnuts by the roadside and offering their services
along the way as menders of dry-stone walls. In bad years,
they begged along the way. He offered this observation of
his childhood, whose acridity I trust you will savor: you see
certain wild animals, he said, males and females, in the fields
and alongside hedges in the Périgord; they are black and
hairy, with curved backs, and they limp as they walk; they
possess a sort of voice that makes sounds, and when they
straighten up, their face is human, and at night they return
to their caves and dens, where they live on black bread and
roots, and sleep on straw, and there you discover them to be
your mother and father and brothers and sisters and cousins

and uncles; and you are one of them, bristles and all. You can see by this his amusing way of speaking, which is quite advanced for his type. He says things like this: "I don't know how old I am, my health is good, I never had a doctor. My nose has been broken sixteen times. If I don't have money, I tell someone to give me a coin and he can box my nose. As far as I know, God almighty made the world, and the poor masons built the houses afterwards." Well, my friend, here is some theology for you to ponder in the Holy City!

He speaks with a lisp, occasioned by the loss of his large front teeth, and he moves about nervously all the time, sometimes breaking into tremors as he speaks, either out of sheer excess of spirit, or because his feigning of fits has left a permanent mark upon him. His red hair is short, in appearance like the stump of a broom, and the hollows of his face are filled with dirt, giving the skin a brown hue. I would guess his age to be over thirty, but it is often difficult to judge with these poor people, whose ravaged lives and hunger age them quickly. When spoken to, he has a habit of approaching you directly and tipping his head to the side with an expression of deep distress and great want, which awaits the relief you might afford it with a coin or two. At other times, he breaks into a lascivious grin, as though privy to a secret you've told him, and his face collapses into a paroxysm of winks.

From his village, Minime was driven to Bordeaux at a young age by a famine occasioned by the severe winter of 1662, and by the death of his father, whose arm was broken with the kick of a horse, and who wouldn't have it cut off because he was stubborn, so it mortified and he died. No one in the countryside had food; they ate roots stolen from gardens, acorns, the grass in pastures, and the uncooked flesh of dogs, cats, donkeys, and horses they found and murdered. All the dogs in Bergerac were consumed. Those who could walk were forced to go to Bordeaux, to beg. In my lodgings, he had with him a folded, barely legible piece of paper he had once used in begging from door to door, in the manner of

dumb people who hand you a note explaining their condition. This paper he asked me to read to him, though he knew
it by heart. It described the amazing adventures and oppres-
sions of every kind he had suffered since leaving the Périgord, and was signed by a curé of his village, who testified
to its authenticity. There were famines, cattle pests, and
devils; his goods had been stolen, his children murdered, his
wife unfaithful, and so forth. His horse had dropped dead
with the mad staggers. At the climax of this story, he begs his
way across the Pyrenees into Spain, and all the way down to
Andalusia. He sweeps streets, empties latrines, carries water
and coal, and after a year of this accumulates four hundred
pesos to take back with him to France. But, begging his
return journey across the mountains, pretending to be a San-
tiago pilgrim—for he follows their route—he is robbed of all
his money in the Garonne Valley by the brigands there who
prey upon returning immigrants. They stab him and leave
him for dead, but he miraculously revives, and now must beg
all the time in order to survive.

Minime caused me to read him this story, though he knew
it to be false. His habit had been to approach the doors of
wealthy merchants and give them the paper, and hope for
alms, a practice he'd largely abandoned since coming to
Paris. As I read it, he greeted each new calamity with hearty
laughs, throwing his head back with all the oafish charm of
a peasant, showing the gaps in his mouth. He laughed so
much the tears came to his eyes.

In Paris, he lives in a quarter populated by people from the
Périgord, and he promises to take me there. If the King
receives our proposals with favor, we may have need of some
two hundred men for our expedition; and as the supply is
short for expeditions such as ours, this group of Périgourdins
might be as good a place as any to begin looking. Minime
guarantees me as many as I want, and some virtuous women,
too, to keep the men happy. He has made a living in Paris
by begging and by selling birds' nests, snakes, worms, ad-
ders, lizards, leeches, hedgehogs, frogs, and snails in the

summer, which he hawks on the street, or to apothecaries who give him orders. Once a week during the summer, he makes an excursion into the countryside to gather these wares. He has funny stories regarding this to tell: about the merchants who keep hedgehogs to eat their cockroaches, but find the hedgehogs have depleted their stores; or the lady whose apartment wall contains glass cases filled with birds' nests; or the gentleman who swallows whole the young frogs Minime provides in order to purge his insides.

But I see, Monsieur, that this letter has become overly long. Suffice it to say that we conversed all night, and now he is my valet for five sols a day, and sleeps in a sort of closet out in the hallway. He gives me good service—and unwanted advice—but has a nasty habit of drunkenness, which is very disagreeable to me, especially in public. He is, nonetheless, a most unusual experiment, and may even prove useful for our plans.

Moreover, he has a habit of mockery and imitation which is infectious. When my cartographer Goupil falls into a fit, Minime can't help but imitate his shaking and trembling, much to the delight of Chuka. Of course, there is something unhealthy in all this, and if it continues, I may be forced to ask Goupil to leave my service. His fits come once or twice a day, and Chuka must be vigilant to see to it that he doesn't harm himself. This falling sickness can lead to imbecility.

Yes, I have seen *Phèdre;* I am not entirely the Philistine you take me for, and the theater especially moves me, though I was vexed all the evening with two talking ladies, one of them masked.

de La Salle

G O U P I L
T O   F A T H E R   Z É N O B E   M E M B R É

Paris
17 March 1684

I hope you feel better my friend   the map is almost
finished, thank you for the letter   I am the instrument as
you say it is his map his deception   he has a new servant or
pet he'd better be careful this one could bite his hand   this
man has led a life of sin   but seems not to care for his
immortal soul   he is nothing more than a beggar and mis-
creant who insinuated himself into the Sieur de La Salle's
service while mocking him behind his back   strutting about
dressed in the master's clothes and wigs when he leaves
but he threatens me with a beating so severe my brains will
spill out of my ears if I tell about this,
   His name is Minime Duhaut   he imitates my fits to induce them in me,   pretends to be a famous savage hacks at
the air with Chuka's hatchet   often drunk he spits on the
floor   sometimes the Sieur de La Salle flogs him for his
insolence   I say he should be whipped & pickled both
his manners ugly false scurrilous   but the Sieur de La Salle
as you know for a man so particular has always given his
whims reign over his judgment   and seems to take pleasure
in observing this man's officious behavior
   When the master is gone he orders us about   he tells
us horrible stories about his life as a beggar and thief and
worse   dressed in the Sieur de La Salle's robes he acts out
the parts for Chuka's benefit   a beggar in Bordeaux   a
vagabond wandering from farm to farm across the countryside   he traveled with 20 or 30 of his kind   they begged
bread & asked to sleep in barns, if the farmer refused Minime
produced from a pocket in the rags he wore a little tinder-
wood showing it to the farmer   signifying they would
burn the barn down   or an ax signifying his hedges would
be cut and sold for firewood   Minime grinning as he told
this   they wandered from town to town, they wore fake

humps and clubfoots   blackened one eye to make it look
blind   acted out an epileptic's fit at this Minime commenced jerking & twitching but I turned away so as not to
be affected.   these vagabonds and beggars painted themselves with sores made from egg yolk and dried blood and
grabbed at the bourgeois for alms   who threw coins at
them and ran off   fearing contamination   they vomited
on the shoes of their victims   one without hands waving his
stumps in their faces, when they threw coins at him he picked
them up with his teeth.

their leader's name was Truquette he said   he married a
whore she broke a pot on the ground he waved a stick in the
air, that was their wedding ceremony.   the wedding feast
was stuffed fox crows frogs turnips,   she gave birth to a
creature with pointed ears and webbed fingers they threw it
in the river

they taught farmers' children to steal prayer books at
church, if the children told they ripped out their tongues

they broke into houses when all were at Mass   stole dogs
by coating their fingers with mashed liver thus taming the
dogs then stuffing them in bags & posting bills for their return
to earn a reward,   Minime brags he killed rats with his
teeth for a livre, if a rat was here now I'd bite off its head he
said   he demonstrated by falling to the floor & snarling
exactly like a dog, he feigned biting my foot   please rat
show me how he said   regarding my foot   I never had
my head bit off   show me how to do it he said

he was caught stealing from a poor box in Nantes with a
glued stick, he thought this showed more respect for religion
than pulling the whole box from the wall.   He was 5 years
in the galleys and branded on both shoulders, he showed us
the brands M for mendicant V for vagabond   he showed us
his back covered with marks from repeated floggings   he
claims these have no power to hurt him

All this he described and more,   with his sputter-
ing spitting manner of speech   I don't think Chuka
understood   but they have become fast friends he cheers

Chuka up   sometimes they wrestle on the floor
   I told him he should look to his salvation   but this he laughed at mocking me   saying as far as he knew only priests go to heaven having purchased their places there and other such blasphemous things
   I find I must keep my wits about me & always be alert with this mocking little devil around   because I fall into fits at his instigation then wake to find my clothes stripped off or my feet tied together or pockets picked   Minime no-where in sight   and my fits grow worse more each day I am seeking the physician you mentioned   as the cost is so great I have decided to sell my instruments   I can buy them back later   if I find other work   I am your friend,

Pierre Goupil

LA SALLE
TO THE ABBÉ CLAUDE BERNOU

Paris
17 April 1684

Here is success beyond our dreams; he gives us not one but four ships; not two hundred but three hundred men, includ-ing one hundred soldiers, and myself master and beneficiary of the entire enterprise; but you shall read it for yourself, once I have copied and enclosed his commission; though I suspect you know the details already, since it is your genius that I detect behind his words.
   The good effects of this have already begun to show. Yesterday, Plet extended his loan of thirty-five thousand until the end of 1685, and the Caveliers have set about to raise new funds, though I shall have to take half the family along with me, that they may keep their eyes upon me. My excursions into society are beginning to pay dividends, too, as Ninon (she is Tuesdays—remember?) offered me a loan of twenty thousand, and even Philippe de Vendôme,

drunk, offered me money which Philippe de Vendôme, sober, was unfortunately unable to account for. I suggest we write off Duduit, however; all he does is hang around the court and beg alms; that is to say, he litigates, he canvasses at court against this, that, and the other thing, and he attends to the revenues of the Bishop of Quebec. When he walks, his steps are so tiny he appears not to be walking at all. At Mme. de Lambert's (Wednesdays), his wife explained him to us. "Duduit labors for hours on a letter, then feels unwell. He looks pale, don't you think?" At this, Duduit smiled; evidently, the smile came from the fact that he was being discussed by everyone—and at the very moment he stood in their midst!

But you see from this letter that I am giddy, and unable to keep my mind upon one thing. Events move quickly; the good news has brought me out of my shell. Yesterday, Ninon insisted to me that she does not have a soul; such things, she says, are fairy tales. You may not have realized how scandalous these people have become. This is the price of victory: to tempt me with the doctrines of Epicurus.

In any case, write and tell me all this is real.

de La Salle

COMMISSION
FOR THE SIEUR DE LA SALLE
[ENCLOSED]

Versailles
14 April 1684

Louis, by the Grace of God King of France and of Navarre, greeting: Having resolved to cause some expeditions to be undertaken in North America, to subject to Our dominion many savage nations, and to convey to them the light of the Faith and of the Gospel, We have been of the opinion that We could not make a better choice than of the Sieur de La

Salle to command in Our name all the Frenchmen and Indians whom he will employ for the execution of the orders We have charged to him. For these and other reasons which have moved Us, and being moreover well informed of his affection and fidelity to Our service, We have by these presents, signed by Our hand, constituted and ordained, and do commission and ordain, the said Sieur de La Salle to command under Our authority, as well in the country which will be subject anew to Our dominion in North America, from Fort St. Louis, on the River of the Illinois, into New Biscay, as well among the French and Indians, whom he will employ in the expeditions We have entrusted to his care, cause them to live in union and concord, the one with the other, keep the soldiers in good order and police according to Our rules, appoint governors and special commanders in the places he shall think proper, until it shall by Us be otherwise ordered, maintain trade and traffic, and generally to do and exercise for Us in the said country all that shall appertain to the office of Commandant, and enjoy its powers, honors, authorities, prerogatives, preeminences, franchises, liberties, wages, rights, fruits, profits, revenues, and emoluments during Our pleasure. To execute which We have given, and do give unto you, power, by these presents, whereby We command all Our said subjects and soldiers to acknowledge, obey, and hear you in things relating to the present power; For such is Our pleasure.

In witness whereof, We have caused Our privy seal to be affixed to these presents. Given at Versailles, the fourteenth of April, 1684.

GOUPIL
TO FATHER ZÉNOBE MEMBRÉ

Paris
2 1 A p r i l   1 6 8 4

Thank you for the money the Sieur de La Salle assisted me
too and I shall not be forced to sell my instruments   now
I am indebted to him and must surely accompany him on this
next voyage about which he raves each day   but my epilepsy is gone & the manner of its cure & the horrible chirurgie which accompanied it,   I shall describe to you if your
stomach is strong

M. Chamfort the physician you recommended lives on the
Rue St. Denis near Les Innocents where many physicians
have their quarters   some people say it is because of the
cadavers in the cemetery upon which they perform their
experiments   these corpses being laid in open graves on lay-
ers of wood & sand in all stages of decay & putrefaction,
for Les Innocents is the most stinking indelicate & indecent
place I ever saw   and the smell arises to the rooms of all
these physicians along the Rue St. Denis,   whence you can
see men & women sticking out from the sides of those open
graves their bodies & ribs being still joined together and
partly hanging from the sides of such rough and unseemly
caves   : the refuge and last resort of French politeness and
delicacy.   but it seemed not to disconcert M. Chamfort
who must be accustomed to the smell   for he said nothing
about it   he is a dignified & sleepy man,   he hardly observed me but whilst I was there I felt a fit coming on   and
for this he prepared a couch and drew the curtains,   when
I awoke he was holding a candle to my eyes,   he gave me
some vinegar & honey I was wrapped in warm blankets,
the causes of my fits he says are the sufferings of the soul
brought about by anxious & terrible prefigurations   for the
soul then plays out its anxiety upon the limbs and organs of
the body like a musician playing his instrument,   and this
is the manner of the tune   : the body attempts to rid itself

with the assistance of the soul its master of some irritants and
other such foreign matter   a strong spasmodic copula dis-
tills itself from the blood into the brain   the copious evapo-
rations which ascend to the brain find no release, & the
animal spirits which lie in the brain being thus affected ex-
plode & a fit occurs accompanied by more explosions along
the rest of the limbs which jerk & twitch the body helplessly   the senses retire inward   if you were to open the brain
he said the smell would be poisonous & horrible,   these are
the vapors which affect the brain by the enmity of their
substance,   the solution he said is trephining   but when
he said this I was so frightened and began to tremble so I
thought another fit would ensue however he assured me the
procedure is simple many people have been trephined
one member of the court has been trephined eleven times to
cure his headaches and phlegmatic temperament,   and he
showed me some roundels of bone taken from the skulls of
trephined patients all of them survived   these were small
the size of coins   the hole allows the vapors to escape
and relieves the pressure upon the brain he said the wound
soon heals over & the trephined patient is normal again &
suffers no more fits,

I was going to write you my friend for your advice but after
this interview everything happened so quickly I was soon
indisposed to write   and for these three weeks now I have
been recovering from the operation but have had no fits
for this I thank the Lord who has seen fit to take this cup from
my lips & who must believe I have born the cross he formerly
presented to me long enough for his honor,   that afternoon
the physician met me at my quarters and together we walked
to the Hôtel Dieu across from Notre-Dame here he showed
me the instruments the surgeon would use   but gave no
indication this operation was to be performed upon the moment   & I handled and pondered these terrible machines
not realizing in so brief a time they were to pierce my skull
for this is his manner of dealing with his patients,   he
doesn't allow them the time to reflect.   there was a knife

a stop drill or non sinking drill so named because the drill has
a collar that prevents it from sinking in and going beyond the
thickness of the bone to what is beneath   the trephine
which makes the circular cut forceps for removing the bone
thus trephined,   his manner was so casual and soothing but
all around me were groans of the sick behind curtains & the
smell in this place was putrid due to the evacuations of bowels
bladders & blood on the floor   walls soiled with expectora-
tions,   when suddenly there enters a large man dressed in
the robes of a mendicant friar   carrying a stone in his hand
he has just cut from a patient   he resembles a butcher large
raw hands red face   and he looks upon me as though I am
thus to be sliced into morsels   this is the epileptic he asks,
M. Chamfort nods his head   has he had a fit today?   only
one says M. Chamfort,   then he shall have his last says this
surgeon whose name is Father John,   he has a manner of
inducing fits in such as us   in front of me he appears to swell
up in his robes   growing to twice his size & showing the
whites of his eyes & rolling his head back upon his thick neck
twitching and shaking all the while,   until I feel it swell up
in me also & my senses go dim   M. Chamfort must have
caught me.

but oh my friend this is the horrible part   I awake on a
board my ears stopped up   the smell is so putrid and
awful I think I shall vomit, something pinches the skin on
my skull in a horrible painful manner   I feel a hand on
my mouth and realize I am screaming,   & the enormous
pain somewhere in the room appears to be approaching
cold water pours across my head   a hot sharp stab comes
with the smell of singed flesh and hair & the pain then enters
my brain with the force of a hammer & I pass out again in
the blackness,

at last I wake up again with the pain as though of rocks or
shot being poured into my skull   but the wound has been
dressed with oil of roses and a poultice applied   I touch the
bandages,   & wondrous to say my friend I feel as though
the closed room of my brain has been aired for the feeling

of pressure is considerably lessened   & before I know it the
Sieur de La Salle is at my side   assuming his most solicitous
manner   Minime is there too the crude and vicious lack-
ey   twitching & convulsing his limbs in silence behind the
Sieur de La Salle's back in order to induce a fit in me   while
the Sieur de La Salle speaks mild words to me   but the
actions of Minime have no effect upon me whatsoever & then
I rejoice in my heart despite the great aching of my head for
I know I have been cured   for which I inwardly sing a *Te
Deum* & the tears come into my eyes   which the Sieur de
La Salle misunderstands continuing to soothe me with his
placid words.

   and since then my dear friend I have not had a fit, the
wound on my skull has healed & the hair begun to grow
I have returned to my quarters & being paid for the map I
made we are making plans for this new adventure since the
King has looked kindly upon it   & the Sieur de La Salle has
charged me to invite you to come upon it too   his kindness
after my operation has been such a comfort to me that I
couldn't refuse being in his debt   both as to money and to
the comfort of a friend   & it seems as though our past
enmity is finished   his family have given him money and he
talks of being favored in court so he may yet live to be the
hero he craves to be,   what think you of this?   he may
change again   but perhaps you will join us   he intends to
write your superior   I am your friend,

Pierre Goupil

LA SALLE
TO THE ABBÉ CLAUDE BERNOU

Paris
3 May 1684

The King has showed me his letter to La Barre, in which he
orders him to make reparation for seizing Fort Frontenac,

and places it into La Forest's hands. His words are icy; it will chill our old friend.

I leave for La Rochelle in a fortnight. The money continues to flow, now that I have been transformed by his privy seal from a ruined man into a burgher. I have sent my agents ahead to recruit in Rochelle and Rochefort, and the soldiers will arrive in a month.

My valet Minime, you may be interested to know, has left my service and returned in the space of a single day. To cure him of drunkenness, I withheld his few meager sols, which I had been paying him daily, and which immediately went into drink. So he quit my service in a huff, but returned the same evening, making a hundred apologies for quitting, and watching me carefully as he talked. He would serve me the rest of his life, he said, for only seven sols a day, payment for the first month in advance. I remained firm to our original agreement of five sols, and when he at last found that I was not to be imposed upon to waver from this resolve, he thanked me lavishly and in such an exaggerated manner, by bowing and genuflecting and kissing my hand, that I suspected he was mocking me; and I observed from his stumbling gait that he had been drinking. When he then hawked and spit on the floor, I had no choice but to flog him for his insolence, but he greeted my blows with laughter and, raising one finger, said words to this effect: Master, you can't hurt a Périgourdin; we are made of wood.

Quite frankly, I am torn by the desire to tame him and the pleasure I take in observing his antics. He may yet prove a good servant if I can cure him of his drinking. He is strong, despite his size, and I have discovered that his fellow Périgourdins are equally robust and vigorous (made of wood as they are) and thus especially suited for the founding of a new colony. Those whom I succeeded in recruiting in Paris for our voyage have already left for La Rochelle, more than one hundred of them. I supplied them with provisions in three carts pulled by donkeys, to lessen the temptation to beg and steal on their journey. Minime has enough money for their

needs, if he doesn't waste it on drink. Should they attempt
to return to Paris instead, they know that one hundred wild
savages from America will seek them out, each in his bed,
and scalp them alive.

These Périgourdins have been reduced by poverty to lives
of want and penury; their needs are few, they are not given
over to indolence, and they have grown accustomed to living
in hardship, so that we can expect them to work without
complaint under conditions more pampered men would find
intolerable. Many of them possess Minime's infectious spirit,
which, though unrestrained, is also resilient and adaptable.
Among them are several families, including women and
children, who may serve as the foundation of our colony.
Minime guided me to their quarters a week ago, and the
expedition was fraught with as many dangers as any I've
undertaken in America. Beyond the paving stones and lamps,
Monsieur, Paris is a wild and savage country, so that without
a guide one could wander for days among its hovels, risking
disease, senseless attack, theft, murder, and the troublesome
importunity of the natives, without ever discovering a way
out. I wish you had been with me; you could have baptized
a few dying infants. I am not being entirely facetious; many
of these people are beyond the reach of religion, so that if
missionaries are to be sent anywhere, we might as well begin
here.

Minime's former dwelling is not far from the Porte St.
Denis, in the shadow of the city's walls; I took Chuka with
me, to afford some protection. We threaded a maze of alleys
and passageways until the lanes turned to dirt, the houses
appeared tumbled into place at random, and debris and heaps
of ashes and offal lay piled in the streets. You have seen these
parts of Paris; the alleys are so narrow that the inhabitants of
the upper stories on either side could lean out and clasp
hands. Some of the buildings are propped up by huge but-
tresses and poles. Chuka and I were much stared at here, but
this was not the worst. In the midst of this place, we followed
a narrow alley, scarcely wider than a hallway, into a passage

which opened upon a lane of mud leading down between two crumbling walls into a valley of sorts. The people here were masses of rags and filth; chickens, dogs, pigs, rabbits, and other such animals as are forbidden in Paris wandered freely; but the police never come into this place. I remember having the distinct impression, from the appearance of the wretched shacks and buildings, the quantity of mud, the crumbling relics of stone walls and plaster, and the general oppression of the atmosphere, that the whole of Paris was dissolving and sinking into this spot, as though drawn down into a swamp or mudhole. Even Chuka seemed appalled. But Minime positively danced ahead of us, greeting everyone with a joke and laughter, and pointing us out as his great discovers and benefactors, until we were surrounded as though by the livestock of Périgord, with their bundles of rags and hair and barely visible faces, and I was apprehensive of my purse; but it may have been a mark of the respect in which my valet is held in this place that, after he had shouted to them in some argot which I could not understand, they parted and allowed us to pass unharmed, and my purse, though exposed, remained untouched.

The house where Minime formerly lived may be described as a sort of dome of mud. By the doorway were piles of dung and rotting vegetable stalks. Inside, all was darkness; this hovel had no windows. But the stench was overpowering, and in the darkness I perceived first one, then another, black bundle of rags taking shape and stirring, as each apparently observed my robes and wig outlined against the doorway. The ten or fifteen people here were some of them members of Minime's family, all from the Périgord. Through cracks in the walls I could see daylight; the floor was of dirt covered with straw. One woman whom Minime introduced as his sister carried a sickly child with a bulging forehead, half asleep in a stupor; she herself appeared to be drunk. As we herded them outside, I selected some to stand across the lane, in order to choose only those who were healthy and without disease for our voyage. Among the men were many former masons, carpenters, joiners, and such, some of whom were able to produce their tools, which nevertheless were rusted and broken from disuse. To those who appeared most eager for this adventure I gave each a token, in order to signify their admission to our company. Only those with tokens will be allowed aboard the ship. In this manner, we went from house to house, examining and questioning the most hearty among this wretched group of people, and passing out tokens to the number of 120; I noticed, however, that a few of the more officious ones inserted themselves into the ranks more than once, no doubt in order to accumulate tokens to sell to others; but these I caught and flogged. When I later discovered one of them whispering in a doorway with Minime, I had Chuka give them each a kick; for if my valet is king in this place, he must be made to acknowledge his allegiance to me. In this way, his people will become more docile to my rule.

The most healthy among these Périgourdins are clearly those able to master their poverty and, as it were, take advantage of it. They have managed to survive and become strong by being forced to hunt out the means of survival; the others have sunk into weakness and despondency. Among the leaders was one ragpicker whom Minime called the Minister of Finance; his hovel was termed Versailles. You can see by this how they ape our society. The street sellers are princes, the ratcatchers bishops, the acrobats dukes, and so forth. At the bottom of the heap are the dung gatherers and mud larks, called—you will be amused to learn—Jesuits.

Now they are making their way on foot to Rochefort, to join with our company in about three weeks. I have also recruited some gentlemen and burghers of condition, to act as leaders, and will find more in Rouen along the way. Tonty's friend Joutel will join us; he is a man of capacity and courage. I wish you could come too, to view firsthand your future domain; but all in good time.

I must say this, though I know you once adored the man: thank God Penalosa has lost favor at court. There is talk now of his being a spy. I could not have worked in consort with him, and it is his departure from grace that has won us considerably more than we asked for; in effect, we have become both expeditions combined into one. I have requested sole command upon departure, with a subaltern officer, and the necessary pilots to sail the vessels as I shall direct; can you see to it that this is done? Without seeking to bandy compliment for compliment, I will tell you that you have done so much for me already I can never sufficiently express my gratitude; your trust in me gives me strength, and I can assure you that it shall be rewarded.

de La Salle

GOUPIL
TO FATHER ZÉNOBE MEMBRÉ

Rochefort
20 May 1684

we have four ships the *Joly* the *Belle* the *St. François* and the *Aimable,*   the King gave the *Joly* to the Sieur de La Salle the *Aimable* is for cargo   Captain Beaujeu lives upon the *Joly* where we gather, there is some dispute about feeding the Sieur de La Salle's passengers out of his own pockets,   as to the command these two are at loggerheads   & the Sieur de La Salle raves that Captain Beaujeu is in the pay of his enemies while the Captain complains of the decks of his ships filled with packing cases & trunks so that one can hardly walk   luggage & cases of merchandise the Sieur de La Salle exchanged for the rations given him by the Minister which he hopes to trade in Santo Domingo but the Captain complains this leaves him no room in the hold for provisions and the provisions must do for nine months not six,   in truth the boxes & chests of prodigious size prevents the cannon and the capstan from being worked   boxes of beads good strong twisted thread fine broadcloth a whole crate of forks, which have lately become popular in Santo Domingo where a sailor told me buccaneers place morsels of food upon the tines with their fingers then thrust the forks into their mouths to emulate the French, the forks he can trade with the savages too who wear them around their necks.

we are all anxious to leave but much needs to be accomplished yet by way of preparation, the men recruited by the Sieur de La Salle have arrived & camped on the edge of town, their debauchery shocks everyone even sailors some have been caught stealing nearby setting fires begging thieving to colonize the savage world all France can offer is more savages their leader Minime wrestles each night with Chuka aboard the deck of the *Joly* for the entertainment of the Sieur de La Salle and some of the men who bet upon these wrestling matches Chuka always carries his basket with him containing the robes & other finery given to him at Versailles by the King.

the Sieur de La Salle and Captain Beaujeu sup each evening like gentlemen then insult each other over coffee they discovered both were Normans from the same province but that merely served to increase their enmity

a man here named Minet does question me often and the Sieur de La Salle too about our trip down the River Messipi to its mouth and all we saw along the way. the answers he writes in a book he wishes to speak with you about it too

please come soon we may leave in a month if all goes well we are not allowed to speak of our destination but say if we are asked that we go to Canada in order to prevent the Spanish from learning that we go to the Gulf of Mexico which they consider their own private lake

the Sieur de La Salle's lackey I mean his insolent valet Minime who gets into everything and toadies to everyone then ridicules them behind their backs, calls me Monsieur Hole-in-the-Head in consideration of my chirurgie but has stopped feigning fits before me as he knows this is of no

avail   in thanks for which I kneel and pray each morning
& evening that my illness is cured   but I need you here my
friend,   to pray with me,   please come soon.   I am
your friend,

Pierre Goupil

LA SALLE
TO THE ABBÉ CLAUDE BERNOU

Rochefort
30 May 1684

Your suggestions perplex me, Monsieur, after all we have
accomplished; in another's man's name they would be accusations, but I accept them from you in the spirit of friendship.
It will not be found in any case that I have treated any men
harshly, except for blasphemies and other such crimes,
openly committed. As for my servants, what is said about
them has not even a show of truth; for though I have a valet
and a savage who follow me, all my men are on the same
footing. Because those who have lived with me are steadier
and give me no reason to complain of their behavior, I treat
them as gently as I should treat the others, if they resembled
them; and, because those who are my so-called servants are
the only ones I can trust, I speak more openly to them than
to the rest, who are generally spies of my enemies. So you
can see I do not know what you mean by having popular
manners. There is hardly anything special in my food, clothing, or lodging, which are not the same for me as for my men.
How could it be that I do not talk with them? Except for the
sailors and their offensive captain, I have no other company.
You fail to understand these men when you exhort me to
make merry with them. These Périgourdins and the other
men we have recruited are a vigorous lot, but their drunkenness and other vices should not be given free rein. If that is
what you call popular manners, neither honor nor inclination

would allow me to stoop to gain their favor in a way so disreputable; and, besides, the consequences would be dangerous, as they would have the same contempt for me that they have for all who treat them in this fashion.

You write that even my friends say that I am not a man of popular manners. I do not know what friends they are. I know of none in this town. To all appearance, they are enemies, more subtle and secret than the rest. I make no exceptions; for I know that those who seem to give me support do not do it out of love for me, but because they are in some sort bound in honor, and that in their hearts they think I have dealt ill with them. Renaudot will tell you what he has heard about it himself, and the reasons they have to give. I have seen it for a long time; and these secret stabs they give me show it very plainly. After that, it is not surprising that I open my mind to nobody, and distrust everybody. I have reasons that I cannot write.

Of more pressing concern is this sailor Beaujeu; I hope you are not in correspondence with him, or that it is he who has said these things against me. His wife is devoted to the Jesuits; that should tell you enough about him. Captain Beaujeu appears to be astonished that I should have command of everything concerning this voyage, and seems to forget that it is I who has made the discovery and who possesses the commission from the King. He may have been charged with the safety of the *Joly* and the other ships, but that gives him no precedence of command over me. I suggest that you try to find out who appointed this man, for whoever it was must have taken money from my enemies to wreck our enterprise. He begrudges the presence of me and my men at his table, as well as the space in the hold of his ships for those goods and materials necessary for this enterprise, and the room and provisions for the additional one hundred men given to me by the King; and he never tires of the attempt to pry from me the secret of our destination, so that he may publish it to the world. He seems to think that while the soldiers are on board he has command over them; but how can I make

Captain Beaujeu or anyone else do their duty if I do not have complete control of the soldiers on board? The man isn't a fool, and he knows what there is to know about outfitting a ship, though he is overly nice about it. But he is not one of those content to do well; doing badly, he calls it perseverance; his attention to detail is selective and capricious, like an insect's; and this he terms duty, and I am expected to admire it. His assumed dignity is really quite bloated, and reminds me—if you will excuse me, my friend—of certain clerics we both have the misfortune to know. In short, this Captain Beaujeu is a menace, and I shall labor eternally to prevent him from gaining the upper hand. He will know this war is one he cannot win without unacceptable losses; my strategy shall be to make him bluster and protest, to mimic all the distress of combat, in hopes that this will either satisfy or exhaust him. As for me, as you know, I am inexhaustible.

For the rest, Monsieur, pray be well assured that the information you are so good as to give me is received with a gratitude equal to the genuine friendship from which it proceeds; and, however unjust are the charges made against me, I should be much more unjust myself, if I did not feel that I have as much reason to thank you for telling me of them as I have to complain of others for inventing them.

de La Salle

M .   D E   B E A U J E U
T O   T H E   M A R Q U I S   D E   S E I G N E L A Y

R o c h e f o r t
1 7 J u n e   1 6 8 4

Monseigneur,

You have ordered me to give all possible aid to the undertaking of the Sieur de La Salle, and I shall do so to the best of my power; but permit me to take great credit to myself, for

I find it very hard to submit to the orders of the Sieur de La Salle, whom I believe to be a man of merit, but who has no experience of war except with savages, who possesses no rank, and who never commanded anybody but schoolboys, while I have been captain of a ship thirteen years, and have served thirty by sea and land. I beg, Monseigneur, that I may at least share the command with him; and that, as regards war, nothing may be done without my knowledge and concurrence; for, as to his commerce, I neither intend nor desire to know anything about it.

Thus far, he has not told me his plan; and he changes his mind every moment. He is a man so suspicious, and so afraid that someone will penetrate his secrets, that I dare not ask him anything. He says that M. de Parassy, commissary's clerk, with whom he has often quarreled, is paid by his enemies to defeat his undertaking; and many other things with which I will not trouble you.

He pretends that I am only to command the sailors, and have no authority over the volunteer officers and the hundred soldiers who are to take passage in the *Joly;* and that they are not to recognize or obey me in any way during the voyage. Yesterday he said rather haughtily and in a tone of command that I must put provisions for three months more on board my vessel. I told him this was impossible, as she had more lading already than anybody ever dared to put in her before. He would not hear reason, but got angry and abused me in good French, and found fault with me because the vessel would not hold his three months' provisions. He said I ought to have told him of it before. "And how would you have me tell you," said I, "when you never tell me what you mean to do?" Monseigneur, I have measured the hold of the *Joly;* it cannot contain more than 140 tons; if, when we had met in Paris, the Sieur de La Salle had confided the truth to me concerning his destination, I would have suggested the ship *Fendant,* which has a large hold and is able to carry at least three hundred men with supplies for a year, as well as all the Sieur de La Salle's baggage.

Last week, he told me that he meant to go to the Gulf of Mexico. A little while ago he talked about going to Canada. I beg, Monseigneur, that you order him to tell me his secret once and for all, for it is necessary to know the route in order to know how many months we will be gone, and to select a pilot who has been in those parts. I think him an honest Norman, but Normans are out of fashion. It is one thing today, another tomorrow. It seems to me that he is not so sure about his undertaking as he was at Paris. I think, by what he says, that he wants to find a scapegoat to bear the blame, in case his plan does not succeed as he hopes. If you can settle this matter of the command, Monseigneur, I shall do my best to help him; and were it not for the matter of provisions and the selection of a pilot, I would be delighted to have him keep his secret, so that I should not have to answer for the result. Awaiting the receipt of your reply, I remain,
Monseigneur,
your most humble, most obedient,
and most faithful servant.

de Beaujeu

M .   D E   B E A U J E U
T O   T H E   M A R Q U I S   D E   S E I G N E L A Y

R o c h e f o r t
2 9 J u n e   1 6 8 4

Monseigneur,

I take the liberty to reply to you that I will obey without repugnance, if you order me to do so, having reflected that there can be no competition between the Sieur de La Salle and me. But it vexes me, Monseigneur, that you should have been involved in a business the success of which is very uncertain. The Sieur de La Salle can leave any time he wishes; nothing remains but to take aboard the extra months' rations for the *Joly*. He still appears to change his plans every moment, and when I ask him to tell me, he can hardly keep his temper, and uses expressions which oblige me to remind him that he was brought up in the provinces, and that the King himself would not speak as he does. When I am courteous, he replies with insults; I have always thought him a gentleman, but at present I can see clearly that he is much less than that. Perhaps I should excuse him not knowing how to behave himself, having spent his life among schoolboy brats, wild savages, and the beggars and vagabonds he has engaged for this voyage. He is a man so defiant and so afraid that someone may penetrate his secrets that I do not dare to ask him anything further on this topic. His fastidiousness has gone so far as to tell me that he will prevent people on board from taking bearings. I beseech you, Monseigneur, to at least modify my orders to allow me to live in such a way that he will be able to impute nothing to me, in case he fails to carry out all that he has promised. I beg you to let me know what my authority is over the soldiers on board after we land; for the Sieur de La Salle claims that when we arrive and he disembarks, I must place them all in his hands. My instructions say nothing about this point. It is evident to me that, left with only seventy men, I would be unable to either defend or sail the *Joly* alone on my return voyage.

I am bound to an unknown country, to seek what is about as hard to find as the philosopher's stone. Let Abbé Renaudot glorify the Sieur de La Salle as much as he likes, and make him a Cortez, a Pizarro, or an Almagro; that is nothing to me. But do not allow him, Monseigneur, to speak of me as an obstacle in his hero's way. Let him understand that I know how to execute the orders of the court as well as he does. The distrust of this man is incredible; if he sees one of his people speak to the rest, he suspects something, and is gruff with them. There are very few people here who do not think that his brain is touched. I have spoken to some who have known him twenty years. They all say that he has always been a bit of a visionary. He cannot keep his mind upon practical matters, and not being of the profession, and not liking to betray his ignorance, he is puzzled what to do.

We must sail within two weeks, if he plans to go to the Gulf of Mexico, since one never sails in the Gulf between the months of September and February, unless one wishes to perish from the northerly winds which prevail at that time. I shall go straight forward as you suggest, Monseigneur, without regarding all his whims and bagatelles. His continual suspicion would drive anybody mad except another Norman like me; but I shall humor him, as I have always done, even to sailing my ship on dry land, if he likes.

I beg of you to protect my family during my absence, and to guard these letters and publish them in case my honor should be impugned by anything that happens on this voyage, for you know that I am, with respect,

Monseigneur,
your most humble, most obedient, and most faithful
servant.

de Beaujeu

III

TEXAS

1686–87

GOUPIL

sunshine all day we aired some of the sick outside,   a controversy today put us all out of patience   concerning the
privileges the King grants to the first-born in a new colony
whether it shall be the Sieur Thibault's child his wife is with
child he claims the privilege granted for that child   or the
widow Jupien whose child was born in passage here from
France   whether her child ought to be preferred but the
boy is so ill he will probably die so the dispute be decided
     I found Mathieu Durand eating rats again today he will
surely die from it   cornmeal for the sick.

today out hunting near the river our party spotted a man in
a pirogue he was cr ing Pierre Pierre then Sieur Hole-in-the-
Head   we drew near & saw it was Minime Duhaut who we
thought was with the Sieur de La Salle   the sight of which
made me apprehensive lest some disaster was befallen the
master's party   Minime grinning all the while he landed
dancing feverishly upon the shore   we asked him whether
he had any letters from the Sieur de La Salle he had not
but M. Joutel was forbid admitting any man without an order
in writing & we were almost resolved to arrest him   but the

account he gave M. Joutel wholly cleared him in that man's
eyes   I have my doubts as he rendered himself privately
odious   M. Moranget was for knocking out his brains,
here is his story

he said the Sieur de La Salle when he left in May having
stayed some time on the seashore & exploring the bay in the
bark *La Belle*   caused some men to go ashore to hunt &
provision the ship   they made a fire but neglecting to stand
upon guard were surprised & all 6 of them murdered by
savages   who thus avenged themselves for the irruption
the Sieur de La Salle had lately made among them.

more time being elapsed than the Sieur de La Salle had
allotted those men to return   growing uneasy he went
ashore himself to see if any news could be had of them
there he found the sad remains of those unfortunate wretches
their carcasses strewn about torn half devoured by wolves
wild dogs   a spectacle which went to his heart.

However this loss which affected him did not quite cast
him down exerting himself against his misfortunes   he victualed the bark *La Belle* put a good number of men on board
to secure it   charging them not to stir from that place till
they heard from him, next he chose out thirty men and
embarking on shore set out across the land every man with
his bundle   consisting of arms tools utensils for the kitchen
goods to trade should they find any sociable savages   & so
advancing into the country to try to find if any notice could
be had of his fatal river Messipi

after a march of several weeks crossing rivers   Minime
stopping to mend his knapsack & shoes the Sieur du Hamel
coming up commanded him to march he desired him to stay
a little   but Minime says the Sieur du Hamel would not stay
but held on his way, Minime followed some time after but
having stayed too long could not overtake the company
& found himself about nightfall in a plain full of weeds where
there was several tracks the way buffalo had gone but knew
not which of them to take.   fired his piece several times

without hearing a reply and so was obliged to pass the night in that same place,

in the morning he shot again spent the day & night in that same place so that not knowing what to do he attempted to return the same way he had gone   losing his way several times   and marched for a month traveling only at night for fear of meeting with savages   living upon what he killed with much difficulty & danger   at last he arrived at the place where they had left some canoes & took one of them with incredible labor & too long to relate came to our fort of St. Louis   thus it pleases God to preserve scoundrels when the best men fall sick & perish.

this account carries only the face of probability   but we shall know when the Sieur de La Salle returns   6 months since he left   I hope he throws this vicious lackey in the stocks

27 September 1686

Henri Cossant died in his sleep   buried him this morning

Paget's party out gathering salt by the bay spotted a new village of 50 or 100 savages rushed back

later our hunters harassed by savages.

we boiled and eat an alligator Jacques Ory killed the flesh white I could not eat it   though it was our first meat in weeks   a taste of musk

now the alligators have returned to our creek as they did last year I won't sleep at night   for fear they are crawling up the steep eminence on which our fort is built   even though they never exert themselves in such a manner Membré says such monsters are part of the divine intention too as He tells us when He sets Behemoth & Leviathan before Job they reveal His glory too   but I would rather be in Paris where they never saw alligators

2 9   S e p t e m b e r   1 6 8 6

because all the land shall be briars & thorns where once there
was a thousand vines   and with arrows & bows shall men
come thither   the savages came in the night to range about
our fort howling like wolves or dogs, 2 or 3 muskets shots
put them to flight

3 0   S e p t e m b e r   1 6 8 6

the groans of the sick & dying begin each morning before
dawn   after their small pittance of sleep   Michel Fouillou
crawled out in the night no one knew it   to see if a miracle
could be performed on Father Désmanville's grave as it was
for the Sieur Moranget after he was bit by the snake   we
found him in a ditch dead of fever   buried him in his foul
rags   this makes 48 dead by my count   50 went with the
Sieur de La Salle but some of them are dead now too.   of
the 180 who landed on this shore 17 died who were de-
bauched & given diseases by the whores of Santo Domingo
on our passage   9 deserted no one knows where they
went   16 died of the fever & plague more every day   5
killed by savages the Sieur Planteroze bitten by a snake Bissy
drowned Pucelle found dead Lefranc shot himself,   I have
seen men reduced to slamming their heads against a stone in
order to induce unconsciousness or even death   merciful
God what tribulations   what hunger for persons so weak &
sick   it is one thing to die in battle or be drowned on a
voyage in which many others perish too,   because the ship
is lost due to weather or some calamity the men who dies in
this manner do so serving their prince having made their will
put their soul in order by confession, they die on the road to
salvation.   but to be struck by pestilence hunger disease
delirium to gradually weaken in body & mind to suffer your
death over & over again   who can be equal to having their
bad fortune & their sins so constantly opposing them while
they waste to skeletons you can count the bones,   these

poor men and women should have stayed at home.   the
artisan should not leave his trade nor the farmer his plow
these men left their digging & other labor begging too in
order to come to America lured by dreams of gold & silver
in abundance   but there was more security & peace in
France more wealth too   than there was in following the
Sieur de La Salle   who cannot prevent death from overtak-
ing them all   for death is come into our windows & entered
into all our hovels to cut our people off from within.

oh damned gold!   oh such dangerous schemes!   oh
cursed river!   oh wretched country where Frenchmen die
without seeing a paving stone a church a carriage their
mother's face & not one familiar thing   but everything is
strange new ugly & the people who inhabit it are brutes

when a gentleman becomes deluded by dreams he knows
how to wag his tongue in order to recruit foolish people to
follow him & serve his ends.   the poor Frenchmen who
listened to the Sieur de La Salle thought that everything in
America was well known and understood   every corner of
this country explored   but nobody knows where we are,
these ignorant peasants believed the place would be similar
to Brittany or the Périgord, you can simply walk from village
to village with ease as from Tours to Rouen to Paris,   even
in Canada foolish people address their letters to My Dear
Son Jean in Canada just as though they might write to Mo-
hammed in Africa   it is the same thing as addressing the
letter to the moon   they have no idea of the size of America   which may be as large as the two parts of the rest of
the world Asia Africa Europe, their minds are beclouded
they measure their ignorance by what they know   and what
do these foolish peasants do they grumble about being paid
as though they would ever see France again   they should
know that the paper the Sieur de La Salle gave them is worth-
less   what good is paper to a corpse   who needs money
when he shall never see a store again a fair carnival merchants goods, the King never puts money into enterprises such
as this one   only privileges & nice words license & power

to conduct trade to plunder   and the poor volunteer is obliged to give up what little money he has for the freighting of his belongings, he sells his coat & cloak to do this believing he will arrive well dressed & the gold will pour into his pockets   but the voyage is long money is scarce life is short & the occasions for losing it numberless.   here they are obliged to stay under contract to the Sieur de La Salle who would not let them return to France even if they had the means to   or knew where they were

we cannot be near the Messipi if what Minime says is true,   when we landed the Sieur de La Salle said the river was here but nobody recognized this place who was with him before   the savages about this place know nothing of the Messipi   the landscape being different too little that you plant springs up,   no trees   having come to believe in his own deception the Sieur de La Salle raved about sailing up this creek to meet Tonty and recover his furs   saying this was a branch of his river the latitude is the same, the mouth of a great river is like a rope unbraiding   but I say his brain was touched during his fever on Santo Domingo   now he'll come back and announce some grand discovery   such as his cursed river is just around the bend or in the adjacent bay or we are on the moon maybe we are

1 October 1686

the Sieur Thibault's older child died today   49 dead
   Fleury contracted the fever Joubert too
   the hunters harassed by savages north of here

4 October 1686

Chételat and Le Jeune both died during the night buried them at noon   51   during the ceremony Fleury fell on Father Désmanville's grave to cure himself by miracle and strange to say he rose up without his fever   this caused a great commotion now others fall on the grave or rub their

bodies with dirt from this grave   for it is said that Father
Désmanville died in the odor of sanctity   everyone remem-
bers the good he did caring for the sick & the mortifications
he underwent   Zayère claims to have a tooth he removed
from Father Désmanville's mouth before he died & touches
it to the bodies of the sick to cure them   saying he cured
Mme. Thibault of a painful fistula in her eye with this tooth

6 October 1686

Minime has a way of strutting about like a cock as short
people do   indifferent to the groans of the sick   a manner
of pursing his lips with mocking fastidiousness that drives me
into a rage it is so false,   He bounces about like a mechanical doll & spits wherever he pleases as though he was God
& creation at his disposal   he can talk of any worldly thing
but he has no knowledge of religion   shows no respect to
Father Membré & the other priests but mocks them when
they pray   don't scream I tell him   I won't he screams
he always does the opposite of what he says   I'll drive off
the Spaniards with civility he says   he meant the ship which
our fishermen saw yesterday out at sea   they hid in the
reeds   we supposed this might be the Spaniards who had
heard of our coming & were ranging the coast to find us
out   that made us stand upon our guard but today the ship
was gone
     the fishermen took a prodigious quantity of fish at the
fishing grounds M. Joutel discovered   dorados or gilt-
heads mullets & others about as big as a herring   but those
with the smallpox and fevers have no use for this fare   their
stomachs unable to hold it

7 October 1686

as expected Chauvelin died   52   we drew lots Languet
got his clothes

8 October 1686

Daguesseau died peacefully in his sleep   Maurepas & Marais   55

9 October 1686

Barbier who was with us on the Messipi   56

10 October 1686

Belsunce & Lallemand   58

13 October 1686

a third part shall fall sick of disease & a third part of the pestilence and blood & a third part will be scattered to the winds   for you are a stiffnecked people & rebellious stubborn in your iniquity
    one of Daguesseau's children died followed 5 hours later by his mother   60   after the service a large gathering of the sick & healthy prayed at Father Désmanville's grave sending up wails & prayers   Claude Péret lay on the stone & shook   being a slab of stone on four pillars of wood on each corner with just enough room for someone to crawl underneath which a few did.

14 October 1686

Vintimille has followed the others Turpin will soon   61
Joubert's fever has broken into swelling & pox   Membré holds the water to his lips   his features unrecognizable in his delirium he shouts execrations against the Sieur de La Salle

Turpin dead   62   Joubert burning up   19 in bed with
fever or pustules   Membré washes them brings them
water   he makes such a saint as even Father Désmanville
might admire, he washes their feet comforts them holds their
hands hears confession,   for this holy man even the tribulations God sends are not enough   but he must make his
suffering equal to those who are dying he sharpens the iron
points of a girdle all covered with spur-rowels & wears it
about his waist   in order to be worthy of praying that God
will forgive his pride, even this is hardly sufficiency of attri-
tion   his blessed face perfectly serene   happy to do the
Lord's work   he always wears a hairshirt   for a week he
eat just water & meal.

now Languet Stapart Brongiart   65   the savages come
again last night howling in the darkness, we laid wet blankets
on the fort & huts to prevent them being burnt by the fire
these savages sometimes shoot with their arrows

mutterings & imprecations against the Sieur de La Salle if he
should return   Father Maximus has written some memoirs
concerning the Sieur de La Salle's conduct condemning him
upon several occasions but M. Joutel found these out & threw
them in the fire.   others of the disgusted party are for leaving this place, M. Joutel uses all possible means to keep them
employed as much as he can the healthy ones some to cut
down the bushes about the fort & dwellings others to mow
the grass that fresh might grow up for our cattle   he diverts
them with dancing and singing at night it cloaks the moaning
of the sick
    Joubert   66

1 9   O c t o b e r   1 6 8 6

some men deserted last night Comine de Tesse & some others   the Sieur Moranget was for pursuing them but M. Joutel dissuaded him
    the Sieur de Villeperdy who had the fever once but survived goes about casting meaningful glances at everyone the healthy and the sick   he wrings his hands clicks his tongue   sometimes he mimics the walk & gestures of others as if in a dream but can find absolutely nothing to say except an occasional Mon Dieu or a thing like that.

2 0   O c t o b e r   1 6 8 6

Regnier & Le Grand   68

2 1   O c t o b e r   1 6 8 6

after much suffering Etienne welcomed death   69

2 3   O c t o b e r   1 6 8 6

Marcel Ory   70   our chief work now consists of digging graves   rain today the first rain in weeks   I think of plowing in the spring whether I shall turn up any corpses   for it is difficult to conceive of any part of the soil without its carrion beneath the surface
    the *convulsionaries* who gather each evening to pray & tremble at Father Désmanville's grave say this place is the New Jerusalem   they say the prophet Elijah will come they will be restored to their homeland they announce by these signs the imminence of the Last Days   Louis Sabinet who is 3 years old they say was cured of the blindness induced by his smallpox by Father Désmanville's tooth   but I never knew he was blind,
    they perform endless novenas & rosaries at Father Désmanville's grave   the sick who cannot leave their beds hire

others to say the rosaries for them   pass around portraits of
Father Désmanville scratched on bark by M. Talon   pieces
of his clothing bits of wool from his blankets hair they say is
his.

Minime mocks their trembling with his officious behavior
jerking & twitching   rolling his head back

2 5   O c t o b e r   1 6 8 6

at our fishing grounds one of the fishermen swimming about
the net to gather the fish was seized by the current carried
away & could not be helped   7 1   it was Claude Chambon

2 8   O c t o b e r   1 6 8 6

yesterday our sentry at the top of the fort spotted 10 or 11
persons on horses coming toward us & gave the alarm
some thought it was Elijah & his angels others that it was the
Spaniards come at last to murder or arrest us   M. Joutel
sent out some armed persons to go & meet them I was with
this company, as soon as we drew near we saw it was the Sieur
de La Salle M. Cavelier his brother the Sieur du Hamel the
Chicaza brave Chuka and 8 or 9 others   the rest being gone
another way to find the bark *La Belle* & give notice of the
Sieur de La Salle's return.

They were in bad condition their clothes ragged,   M.
Cavelier's short cassock hung in tatters   most of them did
not have hats their linen was no better.   the Sieur de La
Salle had not found his river nor been towards the Seignelay as we had hoped.   only 19 men returned of the 50 he
had with him   7 went to the bark *La Belle* where 12 more
were   3 deserted 11 died because of disease 2 of attacks
by savages   he asked M. Joutel whether the Sieurs Clerc
Hurie Theriault & 2 others were come because not being
able to endure the fatigue of the journey he had given them
leave to return,   hearing they were not he concluded they
had deserted or been murdered by savages.   we were also

told that the Sieur Valentine had strayed & was lost that one
of the Sieur de La Salle's servants had been dragged down
to the bottom of a river & devoured by an alligator & 4 others
had deserted & abandoned the Sieur de La Salle when he was
in the country of the Ceni savages,

   this was a very dismal & deplorable account and the Sieur
de La Salle distracted to boot   as though ravished with
astonishment by his arrival at this place   but he curled up
like a babe & slept the rest of that day to the tune of the
groaning sick,   while the rest of us unloaded from his
horses the only visible advantage of that journey consisting
of skins filled with beans wheat & some other grains which
was put into the store

   then this morning the Sieur de La Salle rose up refreshed &
proposed to take another journey with the bark *La Belle* toward the mouth of the River Messipi   an account of which
he had heard from the Cenis   convinced now that we had
sailed past the river's mouth in a fog   how can we sail the
ship without a pilot, he was murdered by savages   the Sieur
de La Salle hasn't taken this into account   but raves & paces
to enspirit the men & revive the lowest ebb of hope   raving
about the weight of a mighty enterprise on their shoulders it
bows them down they are so morose   one died in the night
while he slept Pierre Vaillant   we discovered it this morning, with the Sieur Rochebouet 2 days ago this makes 73 by
my count   12 more counting the dead among the Sieur de
La Salle's men more if the lost & deserters died   the 6 from
the bark *La Belle* murdered   91 half our colony

   today the Sieur de La Salle paid no attention to the sick
who have been in need of his assistance ever since the surgeon M. Taveneaux died to bleed them or administer medicines   but fell into a rage when he spotted his valet Minime
among the men at noon,   not having seen him yesterday or
perhaps Minime was hiding   & began beating the officious
lackey inquiring of M. Joutel in an angry voice why he received deserters against his orders but Joutel gave Minime's
reasons that he was lost & could not find the company.

whereupon the Sieur de La Salle seemed not to be satisfied
with this and ordered the entire company to work with so
many contradictions & extravagances, in such a confused
manner   to make a new magazine or storehouse he said
the design of which he sketched in the dirt before going off
in a rage without giving orders as to the execution of it
or who should be in charge,   and he was gone all day no
one knows where until evening   accompanied by the savage Chuka, whence he returned before dark to witness the
convulsionaries and their antics   but it seemed not to entertain him at all as he moped in a corner of the fort sunk in
melancholy

L A   S A L L E

1 N o v e m b e r   1 6 8 6

Of those who return, only Jason has grown old. Medea possesses the secret of youth and the sorcery with which to
conquer death. *Jason's Return* tokens both his return to Ioclos to assume the crown and his subsequent desire to return to Colchis and renew the fleece, which has become a
rag on his shoulders. Jason to be shaggy and bestial, having
undergone debilitating adventures, and having in his youth
been tutored by a centaur, who may have been wise, but
who himself was required to be shod by a blacksmith, and
who emptied his bowels wherever he pleased. Jason should
smell of the stables.

In a dream, he perceives the ghost of the minstrel Eliym
singing of Colchis and the golden fleece, just as it happened
upon his first entrance into Ioclos years before.

G H O S T: Finding is the first act; the second, loss. Third, to
    search
For the fleece made of gold, which rises in the east
With the light of the sun. Have you heard of the fleece?
Its light outshines all light. It was taken from the place

Where the sun dies in the west, and he who brings it home
Allows the sun to rise again, Apollo's throne,
Restores our loss, conquers night, and paves our streets with
    gold.
East in Colchis lies a great river, swift and bold,
Where men catch golden nuggets washed from distant moun-
    tainsides
With fleeces used as nets, and some say this will be his prize,
Gold for the hero who finds the golden fleece.

Goupil would make a convincing ghost, he appears so debili-
tated and thin. The solidest of peasants becomes transparent
in this place, I've observed, either from lack of food or excess
of evacuation. Barbier's widow could play Medea, or Minime
in woman's dress, if he mends his ways. Assign roles in consideration of character: Minime as Medea, in view of the fact
that he has much of the devil about him.

5 *November* 1686

Work on the new storehouse goes well, under Joutel's direction. I have discovered that those who claim to be ill quickly
cure themselves with the medicine of labor; some have secretly admitted to me that they wasted away in idleness during my absence.

    And now, having hitherto said nothing of the situation of
our dwelling, nor of the nature of the country we possess, I
will here venture upon a plain but true description. Our fort
of St. Louis, built with timbers and standing palisades, sits
upon a rise of ground surrounded by pens for the livestock,
cultivated fields and gardens, and six smaller buildings constructed in the manner of the savages with poles, mud, and
buffalo hides, the largest of which serves as a house for fatten-
ing pigs. From our little hill above the River of Bullocks, vast
and beautiful plains extend far to the west, all level and full
of green, affording pasturage to many wild goats and buffalo.
To the south, other plains may be seen adorned with little

tufts of woods of oak and other trees. North lies the River of Bullocks, beyond which the plains terminate in a border of wood, and east and southeast one or two leagues is the bay and the shoals which hem it in and protect it from the Gulf of Mexico.

Here, we have an abundance of wild fowl, such as curlews, water hens, and other sorts, in a marsh near the river. We have as well an infinite number of buffalo, wild goats, rabbits, turkeys, bustards, geese, swans, plovers, teal, partridges, and many other sorts of fowl fit to eat, and among them one we call the "great gullet," because he has a very large one; and another as big and fleshy as a pullet, which we call the "spatula" after the shape of its beak. The pale red feathers of this bird are very beautiful.

As for fish, we have several sorts in the river and bay and lakes around the bay. The river affords a sort of barbel, differing from ours in roundness in their having three bones protruding, one on the back, the others on either side of the head. Their flesh is like cod. The bay affords us oysters, eel, trout, a kind of red fish, and others whose long and sharp beaks tear our nets. We also have tortoises, whose eggs serve to season our sauces. The land tortoises differ from those of the sea, being smaller and more round, with gaily decorated shells. It was in looking for one of these tortoises, who hide themselves in holes in the earth, that our surgeon was bit by some venomous creature in a hole, which resembled a toad but had four equal legs, a sharp back, and was very hard, with a little tail. His arm swelled up and it cost him a finger, which was cut off.

Among the venomous snakes, such as vipers, asps, and others, those called "rattlesnakes" are the most common. They make a noise by the motion of two scales at the end of their tail which can be heard at a considerable distance. Some of our men have cooked and eaten these rattlesnakes and found their flesh was not amiss; but usually we feed them to the swine.

Of the trees, there are oaks like ours in France, bearing a

fruit much like our galls, as well as nut trees and berry trees and others the fruit of which are full of prickles, which must be carefully rubbed and taken off before being consumed. One kind of tree resembles the palm, whose lofty and long branches spread out majestically; another possesses leaves like gutters, harsh and sharp, capable of piercing the thickest skins. This tree has a sprout on top which shoots out yellow flowers in the shape of a nosegay; and some of these have sixty or eighty flowers hanging down like our flower-de-luce, while beneath the flowers follows a fruit as long as a man's finger and thicker than the thumb, full of little seeds, the rind of which is sweet and delicate to taste. Mulberry trees are also common here along the rivers; their leaves are beautiful and large, and would be of good use for the feeding of silkworms.

The climate is mild and temperate, even though the seeds we caused to be sowed did not thrive well. The plains are strewn with a sort of small sorrel, the leaf of which resembles our trefoil, with a sharp taste like ours. Wild onions no bigger than a man's finger grow in abundance, even in scorching heat. Indeed, nothing is more beautiful than to behold these vast plains when the blossoms of onions and other wild plants appear. A thousand different colors, a thousand agreeable scents, adorn the fields and afford a most charming object to the eye and the nose. I have observed some flowers that smelled like a tuberose, although the leaf resembles our borage, and primroses having a scent like ours, as well as African gillyflowers, and a sort of purple windflower. The autumn flowers about here now are almost all of them yellow, so that the plains take on a golden hue, the richness of which is enhanced by sunset.

6 November [*?*]   *1 6 8 6*
[*Date uncertain; two pages missing here.*]

tipped on
This beach and broken apart like a cask of wine
Dropped by some clumsy god, who allowed all that fine

Romance to trickle out. Welcome to my home,
Pelias. The *Argo.* Corpse of my ship. My throne.

PELIAS: You are King now, Jason. You could live in the
city.

JASON: This is my city, I sleep beneath the third vertebra.
See back there where the spine cracked and a rib jammed the
sand?
That's the room I share with crabs, water rats, lice, ants,
Beetles, snakes, spiders, and the dung of all those sheep
We brought with us from Colchis, in hopes some would mate
And make a new golden ram. This fleece has lost its shine,
Don't you think? See where it sheds? The stains and grime
Are due to adventures, the mildew to the air of the sea,
The holes to moths, the bare patches to worms and fleas
Who live in it now—hence, live with me. For I sleep
On the fleece, wear the fleece, gnaw and chew upon the
fleece,
And dream about the fleece, about a prize so rare,
And think about its gold that turned to filthy hair.

PELIAS: Jason, don't be a fool. How can a hero and a King
Live in such a rotting hulk in filth and decay?

JASON: I love decay! I love to touch it, though it can't
Affect me. Nothing clings to my hands. I have no wants.
I eat little, sleep less, and dream awake. I walk
Around in my aging flesh as though in a sack
Carried by the gods, accomplices in my freedom
From touch. Therefore, putrefaction is my kingdom,
Disgust my realm, death my castle. And my soul
Of ice never melts in this warmth. Free and whole,
I can do anything—sleep with apes, smelling their glands,
Befoul myself and my nest, and plunge my hands
Deep into the belly of a freshly killed deer.
I could scrape out the entrails and curl up in there.

Pelias too passive in this scene. Develop his clever scheming.
He plots to tempt Jason with the prospects of a new expedi-

1 5 5

tion whose goal will be to repair the *Argo,* sail to Colchis, and dip the ragged fleece into the River Phasis, thus renewing its vigor; all this, in order that he, Pelias, may once again assume the crown while Jason is gone. Exactly as it was done before. Pelias assumes that this expedition will be the decrepit hero's death, but Jason, tempted, outwits his adversary with the help of Medea, who gathers herbs to restore his lost youth just as she had for Jason's father, Aeson.

The female parts should go to men, as the English do, so as not to excite the infirm unduly. Joutel thinks it a good distraction to perform a play, but he concurs with all I suggest regardless. Joutel as Pelias: he has that tarnished nobility, which clings in a sticky way to what it reflects.

GOUPIL

9 *November* 1686

Boursier wailed for a steady hour in the night before dying, needing sleep we waited until morning to remove the body   97

12 *November* 1686

Jourdain & Cognet   99

13 *November* 1686

I will lay the dead carcasses of the children of Israel before their idols   scatter your bones round about your altars the vintage shall fail the gathering will not come the teats shall dry up the oxen starve the eggs become dust worms eat the fruit figs rot corn be blasted grass turn brown weeds & thorns come up   you shall conceive chaff & bring forth stubble & your own breath shall burn you up,   frogs plague the land and lay in huge stinking piles   flies deposit their eggs in your food   boils break out on your skin.   locusts cover the land   Membré says death has a face like a locust his eyes bulge his hiss is unbearable his serrated jaws working back & forth fill with froth, his wings carry him in all our windows

14 November 1686

Chuka sleeps on the robes given him by the King which have become ragged & filthy with lice, they never part from his company   keeps them in a basket,

Now the Sieur de La Salle raves about building a play-house not a storehouse he wants to perform a play for the entertainment of the men

Nicolas Blet who was with the Sieur de La Salle on his trip told of some Frenchmen becoming savages   at one village they found Valentin Durand who deserted when first we landed   his face was painted, he could not converse in the French tongue   having forgotten it,   he pretended to recognize no one

5 other deserters who the savages would not take in were so driven to desperate ends by hunger that they ate each other up,   these were 5 men they ate each other until one remained who was left alone   there being no one left to eat him.   Blet heard this story from this man himself who was Joly Petitpied, they found him outside the village of the Cenis   he later expired

Father Membré wrings his hands in despair about the Frenchmen who become savages   they succumb to the lures of promiscuity   let us go and withdraw & serve other gods   they go whoring after the gods of strangers but the Sieur de La Salle too lightly opposes them   it frightens me to think of putting on feathers rubbing my skin with the grease of bears painting my face speaking gibberish   and forgetting all I have ever known   trading in my immortal soul for the gratification of such lusts as we know to be unspeakable   unclean defiled

there is less people with fever now 10   2 of the men who
returned with the Sieur de La Salle have become sick
having survived his expedition.

we were forced to kill one of the horses today cooked him
after I wrote this the sentry gave the alarm this evening
having spotted some men,   they were the Sieur Chedeville
the Sieur de La Sablonniere & some others who had gone to
the bark *La Belle,* they carried bad news which sent us all to
bewailing our misfortunes in this place   that the ship had
run aground on the other side of the bay its side was stove
in it could not be saved   and so runs aground our means
of returning to France   the *St. François* was taken by pirates
the *Aimable* sunk in the bay   whose timbers we salvaged to
build our fort,   M. Beaujeu returned to France with the
Joly   now the *Belle* is lost,

of the men the Sieur de La Salle left with the *Belle* only 3
were still living when the party reached them   & these gave
our company an account of their misfortunes, they waited
some time with the bark in the place where the Sieur de La
Salle had appointed them to wait when first he left our fort
on his trip, their water fell short they sent the boat ashore
with some casks to fill with water   the Sieur St. Germain
went with 5 of his best men, toward evening they saw the
boat returning but the wind blew contrary night coming
on   they put out a light but the wind blew it out, in all
likelihood the boat could not see the bark & they never heard
of it after   nor of the 6 men who must have perished.

after that they continued on the ship   2 men died,   at
last having no water they resolved to weigh anchor and draw
near the shore but having few hands & no pilot   to add to
their misfortunes the wind was contrary   driving them to
the other side of the bay where they run aground on a sand-
bar & the ship split open.

still they could not go ashore as the waters of the bay at this
place was over their heads,   having no boat   they con-

structed a raft with planks but it sank losing 2 men, 3 men were left they made another raft better fastened than the first & taking with them from the ship some sails & rigging linen clothes & papers belonging to the Sieur de La Salle   they went to the shore where the other party found them

the Sieur de La Salle needed all his resolution to bear up against this   he began to talk this evening of taking another journey overland after Christmas   toward the northeast & making it his main business along the way to find the Messipi   because by accounts the Cenis gave he avers it is the journey of a month from their country   itself a month's journey from here, then once having found his river to go by way of Canada to France & obtain succors for the colony here

19 November 1686

the child of M. Boyer died making 109 with those from the bark *La Belle* who perished,   the Sieur de La Salle today assisted Father Membré in washing the sick, he washed their feet   bled them gave them water but by evening he was in a rage again beating his valet Minime for some insulting thing he had done   then sunk in melancholy

21 November 1686

Last night an extraordinary event occurred while the convulsionaries were praying at the grave of Father Désmanville their numbers having swelled by some of the sick who became well   they say they were cured by miracle

these convulsionaries pray feverishly out loud   some fall down shaking to the earth   this reminds me of the fits I had when I see this happening I break into a sweat   but I think their fits are induced or occur by miracle because they rise up refreshed   cured of their ailments,

for some few days now Minime has enjoyed mocking these convulsionaries by imitating their twitching & jerking, thus

affording sad amusement to those in our colony who aren't
of their number and gather about the cemetery to observe.

he pushed through their ranks last night shaking in every
limb mocking their prayers   blessed Father have mercy on
us all cure me of my fits he shouted,   and at the grave of
Father Désmanville threw his head back violently & making
a sound through his teeth unnnhhh   fell to the ground
writhing thrashing foaming at the mouth   his entire body
forcibly lifted in the air like a bow, some began screaming
uttering ejaculations   more fell down Minime continued
his violent spasms,   whereupon all dropped to their knees
to pray   this was no mockery but a genuine seizure
involuntary writhings of his limbs and amazing contortions.
2 or 3 had to hold him down.   While the muscles of his face
contorted into the most misshapen grimaces.

   this lasted nearly an hour,   when at last he recovered
from his fit all who were present saw it as the manifestation
of God   for this offensive mocker had been striken with
exactly the same kind of fit he had feigned   but when told
of this he grew angry & violent striking out at leaders of the
group   At last Father Maximus who is one of their leaders
induced him to leave he went off sulking   chastised by this
species of miracle which convinced more of our colony to
join the convulsionaries,   but I feel obliged to hold myself
apart, their demonstrations frighten me by reason of their
violence   for having been cured of the falling sickness I
have no desire to excite it again

22 November 1686

some of our hunters harassed by savages one shot put them
all to flight.

   M. Gayen died   110

   the Sieur de La Salle has set the women & the sedentary
to sewing clothes from the sails salvaged from the bark *La
Belle.*

2 3 N o v e m b e r   1 6 8 6

Minime seized by a fit again tonight praying with the convulsionaries,   now he is one of their number urging them on
to greater frenzies   he argued with the Sieur Moranget
about miracles   they had a fight the Sieur Moranget's ear
all bloodied

LA SALLE

2 1 N o v e m b e r   1 6 8 6

I have discovered that the convulsionaries in our colony are
every one of them secret devotees of Father Jansenius, Father
Quesnel, and other such heretics as have been condemned by
the Pope and King. From the Jesuits I expect censure, disallowance, and plotting, but not heresy; and, though I love not
the Jesuits, everything in my temperament leads me to abhor
the heresies of their enemies even more, leading as they do
to seditious behavior insulting to all secular authority as well
as to the church. Some of these men have Quesnel's *Réflexions
morales,* which they brought with them from France. Under
my orders, Joutel will seek out all copies of this book, which
we shall burn. Taken in the sense in which they have been
condemned, the famous propositions of Jansenius raise a
spirit of audacity and insubordination disrupting to the tran-
quility of the colony, and causing confusion and division
among the simpleminded. Besides, these people claim that
miracles have been performed and cures effected; but a cure
may be regarded as miraculous only when the malady was
incurable or when the recovery is too sudden to be attributed
to natural causes. All such cures as they claim for Father
Désmanville are either frauds or the effects of those princi-
ples which nature keeps hidden within her bosom.

It is to be observed that under great strain, weak men
break down. The losses we have suffered, the great misfortune of the *Belle,* are judgments of God which we cannot

investigate, pull our hair though we may. If it pleases our Lord in heaven to torture this enterprise, strong men must bear up without forsaking their resolution, and without allowing themselves to be reduced to twitching puppets.

2 3   N o v e m b e r   1 6 8 6

Jason must smell of the stables. How to hint of this? Even his inferiors dare not approach too closely. The bulk of the play to take place beneath the wreck of the *Argo,* whence various people from Ioclos come to persuade him of the necessity of this or that: another expedition; a triumphal march through the city; revenge upon Pelias.

Ophraedes a clubfoot. The servant forced to arrest his true leader precisely in order to prove his allegiance.

Jason's farewell to the fleece. His oration upon the prospects of a return to Colchis, where dragon bones bleach in the sun. His address to the rotting hulk of the *Argo.*

2 6   N o v e m b e r   1 6 8 6

It is a painful spectacle that has dawned on me; I have drawn back the curtain from the corruption of men, which is nothing more than their overbearing pity, which leads to whining. Their pity for the ill and dying makes such suffering contagious, and this becomes especially annoying to me when I try to write my play. I could walk away from this place without a word and leave those who are left to seize each other's throats, but the joyous act of accomplishing our weighty enterprise would then fall to other shoulders, weaker and less worthy than mine. I suspect that God must have decided that our existence here was too large, and wanted to reduce it in the only way he knew how. This extreme hatred of reality is a consequence of an extreme capacity for suffering, which God has manifested in the various monsters of his creation, not the least of which [Entry breaks off.]

The scarcity of wood about this place encourages the laziness of the men, who grumble for horses to drag the logs here; but we must spare our horses for the expedition. Of the carpenters left in our colony, all are so ignorant that I've been forced to act the master builder, to direct them in squaring the trees and to mark out pieces for the playhouse. Death weeds out the weak, but not the stupid.

The savages about this place, called the Clamcoëts, with whom we are at perpetual war, continue to harass us. Edmond Richer disappeared, having stepped aside to shoot some wild fowl on a hunting party; in all probability, he was abducted by these savages. They know better than to attack us in our fort in consideration of the cannon and muskets, and instead prefer to lurk about unseen and murder or kidnap those who venture out unprotected. The men of this tribe go about naked, and have one nipple perforated from side to side with a thick reed as long as a forearm; their lip is perforated with a thin piece of cane.

Jean Portefaix came to me in private last week, desiring leave to marry a young woman who sometimes accompanies the hunting parties to dress and dry the flesh, and with whom he was said to slip aside from the company; a dangerous practice due to the savages. I made him some difficulty at first, but at last, considering that they had undoubtedly anticipated matrimony regardless, gave leave to M. Cavelier[1] to perform the service, which was done this evening, in honor of which I allowed a ration of brandy to be distributed to the healthy and the sick alike; which afforded some distraction to the men. M. le Marquis de La Sablonniere, following this example, asked the same liberty after the service, being in love with a young maid; but this I absolutely refused, and forbade them seeing each other.

Joutel has found seventeen copies of *Réflexions morales* and

---

[1] La Salle's brother, a Sulpician priest.

three of Pascal's *Lettres provinciales;* these shall afford a fine hand-warming of a cold evening.

GOUPIL

25 November 1686

now Chuka has fallen ill of the fever Minime touched him with Father Désmanville's tooth some hairs but it does no good   as with most savages the disease proceeds more rapidly than with us already pustules have appeared on his skin   he lies upon the robes given him by the King makes no complaint while all around him moan   the sick are lucky they don't have to work   for the Sieur de La Salle drives the rest of us day & night with excessive toil   to build his cursed playhouse which now he says will serve also as a chapel to enlist the priests on this foolish enterprise.   he whips the men denies them food speaks of executions to suppress their insubordination   but with all this they mutter imprecations against him saying we shall all die in this place

he drives the men until they visibly decline then for an entire day mopes about not attending to the construction which in consequence of his neglect slacks off,   then flies into a rage the very next day against the laziness of the colony   for nothing he does or says will he press upon us with firm or even patience   always waxing hot & cold

26 November 1686

Jean Portefaix married today to the woman he whored   we drank & sang ate a pig

now the Sieur de La Salle who always changes his mind says his playhouse will serve as a hospital for the sick   to isolate them from the colony good.

———

Merciful heavens he has beat me until I can scarcely walk
for my insubordination he says   as I had an abscess in the
mouth which suppurated continually I manifested to him my
repugnance at doing this filthy work   dragging trees cutting them down   telling him it needed to be treated   but
he replied with biting words asking where did I think I was
in Paris?   and he would consider me the cause of the want
of success of our colony & accused me of Jansenism having discovered Quesnel's book in my belongings,   I
searched for the book & found it gone   whereupon he
followed kicking & abusing me & accused me of leading
these convulsionaries whose actions frighten me as much as
they do him   and shouted at me with great violence but
what have I done   I have done nothing but his bidding
since we arrived at this place   executing his orders with
diligence & smothering all my repugnance   I defended
him before Nicolas Blet & the others who wanted to seize the
colony   the ones who muttered against him Father Maximus & the others   having followed him all this way here
and there when I could have been in France instead of this
waste of earth filled with slimepits where the boils and lice
plague us & we listen to the sick moan all day   who out of
their misery take death as their Messiah   because there
weren't enough graves in France he took us here to die in the
wilderness   & now he lords it over our feeble remnant too
weak to oppose him   he himself planted this enmity in our
hearts for which he blames us now   but tomorrow he'll
probably mope & pare his nails & wander off melancholy
gnawing on his own forearm without anyone to whip
leaving us to our own ends neglecting the proper supervision
of this place   then return to beat those he imagines are his
enemies   and so on until none are left to beat.

    he spoke softly to me afterwards,   requesting that I assist
him in suppressing these convulsionaries by serving as his
spy   I had to say yes what could I do but my heart is against

him   he stinks of vanity his head is touched   he speaks of
excommunicating the convulsionaries as though he were the
King or Pope,   between him & his brother there is no
affection   Minime is now of the convulsionary camp,
only Chuka continues with unabated loyalty but he is ill with
disease   lies on his robes eyes ajar not a sound

1 D e c e m b e r   1 6 8 6

Péronnet   114   more become sick driven so hard
     inventory 8 pieces of cannon 200 muskets as many cut-
lasses 100 barrels of powder 1000 weight of balls 300 weight
of other lead some bars of iron 20 packs of iron for nails some
iron work & tools such as hatchets & the like
     20 casks of meal 16 skins of beans & grain 2 hogskins of
wine 1 of brandy 23 swine 34 hens 9 cocks a goat

4 D e c e m b e r   1 6 8 6

Chuka's fever has broke, all at once this morning he rose up
& joined those working without a word   some said it was
a miracle,
     each evening Minime enacts Paul struck down on his way
to Damascus & induces the others to greater follies & inde-
cencies   in their fearsome attempts to be noticed by God
like little twitching insects some of them beat each other
shouting *secours secours*   they shake & tremble barking on
all fours like dogs or howling at the air   twisted in strange
freakish postures
     in a corner of the cemetery a man stood swearing a solemn
oath with his hands on his private parts   Jacques Gayen
displayed the stigmata on his palms   anyone could see these
were self inflicted fresh
     everywhere Minime urges them on when he is not sunk in
a paroxysm of trembling praying wailing   he shouts *secours*
& Portefaix beats him with a stick   the *secouristes* come up
with swords bats pins knives ropes & whip & flail those who

scream & sigh with relief & call for more   they press the knives against their bodies but nevertheless fail to do damage   Minime drags Paul Grégoire across the ground by his arm   then André Darricau places a board on his stomach and invites the others to dance on it all the while howling good! more!   one *secouriste* surveys the scene & deals André a kick which should knock all his teeth out but he sighs with relief

the convulsionaries rise up calm and refreshed the *secouristes* who beat them appear exhausted   Marguerite Charcot declared to me she would gladly endure the *secours* all her life in exchange for the small moment of joy the Lord pours into her heart after each torture   Father Maximus says they do this because they will triumph with Jesus Christ only through suffering & that God's wrath is appeased through their sacrifice but Membré who only looks on says it is a perverse ceremony   *secours* are the evils and corruption of the church, they use heresies & other such rubbish to justify their madness & indecency   Duval was completely stiff for 4 hours   sunk in a trance   they sing & chant hymns & speak strange languages some expect Father Désmanville to rise again,   what will he do lead us all to heaven   France would be enough.

LA   SALLE

6 December 1686

As Goupil's inventory revealed one hogskin of wine to be missing, I have ordered a search. The necessity of rationing the cornmeal has been reduced by our losses, but I am sensible of our inability once more to cultivate this land, now that the winter, such as it is, has come. Should we be forced to trade with the savages in these parts our iron will prove invaluable. One thousand weight of balls, but no large balls for the cannon. Three hundred weight of other lead, sixteen bars of iron, twenty packs of iron for nails; our store of tools has diminished suspiciously. Sails for clothing, blankets, skins, needles, thread, candles, surgical instruments. We have no more medicine except miracles and convulsionaries.

Now that our playhouse is completed, I will set the men to erecting a palisade around the cemetery, then set up a guard and order it closed. If worst comes to worst, we could exhume the good Father Désmanville's corpse and suspend it from a tree.

11 December 1686

Today I ordered the sick removed from the fort and with their bedding and clothes carried to the playhouse, where they may be distracted by our rehearsals. Membré carried some of them himself on his back. He is weak, but they are paper. For some, this was their first view of daylight in weeks, as well as their first fresh air. Some were dead, but this emetic revived them. Minime assisted, aping the priest, aping the bustle of Joutel, aping my dignity. My Périgourdin servant survives in this unmerciful land by adopting the ways of whatever comes near him; without liquor, he drinks manners, and would equally make a French King or an American savage, a Cortez or a beggar, a Pope or a convulsionary. But my suspicion is that, just as he can mimic any of these roles equally, so in secret he laughs at all of them equally, since, whatever the pose, his eyes invite unspoken conspiracy; as if they should say, "What have we here, Monsieur? You and I both know it. A farce."

14 December 1686

OPHRAEDES: I watched her gather herbs for nine straight
    nights by moonlight
With both feet unshod and black hair unraveled. The sight
Of this sorceress creeping half naked through the bare trees,
Wheeling about, lifting her arms and pale face three times
    three

168

To the stars and moon, then bending down and dipping
Her hair in a stream, and rising up with bare breasts
   dripping—
My lord, this sight made me dizzy with—with impatience.

PELIAS: You followed her each night? I admire your—your
   diligence.
And where was Jason all this time? Moping by his ship?

OPHRAEDES: He charged me to follow her while he lay
   asleep
In his foul nest beneath the *Argo.* Each morning
I reported back to him, but he seemed strangely
Unconcerned. His mind wandered. My lord, he seemed old.
Older than his years. Reluctant to act, less bold.

PELIAS: Medea's potions can bring a corpse back to life.
You followed her for nine days. Did she have the knife?

OPHRAEDES: Yes, in her belt, though I missed it till last
   night.
Last night she made two altars of turf, to Hebe and Hecate.
To Hebe she bowed down, exposing her private parts.
To Hecate she sacrificed three rams, then ate the hearts.
She hung the altars with green branches and sprays of ver-
   vain,
Then, mumbling, poured forth libations of milk and wine.
In a caldron she brewed her magic liquor, stirring
It with a dead ram's leg. To the blood, milk, and wine
She added roots and seeds from distant mountains, mosses
From Anthedon, leaves and plants of Enipeus, grasses
Plucked from the sides of Apidanus, and the scaled skin
Of a water snake, bowels of a werewolf, the torn
Breasts of two screech owls, and their worm-eaten wings,
A crow's head, glands of a deer, unspeakable things.
I watched her from behind a bush, crouching in the dark.
When she turned toward me, I held my breath, my heart
Fluttered like a helpless bird. I don't think she saw me there.
Her eyes were burning. Her face, breasts, arms, even hair

Seemed to flare up from within, like pale embers blown
By the wind, swelling and snapping, whipped into flame
Until her very blood appeared on fire, outlined by the dark
Like a burning tree at night, and from her hair flew sparks.
Like a she-wolf she uttered a cry, then with her knife
Cut a dead stick, dipped it in the brew—and it sprang to life!
It pushed leaves out along its length, then white flowers,
And at last huge golden fruit, in tribute to her powers.
In one hand she held the knife, whose blade trapped the
    moon.
With the other she dipped a shell into her brew
And walked back toward Jason's ship. I followed her trail
By finding places where the magic broth had spilled
And brought forth flowers and grass, turning the earth green.
I could see the knife too. I followed its gleam.
By the time I came to the *Argo,* she'd already raised
The knife and brought it down across his sleeping face.
With one stroke she cut his throat. I screamed where I stood.
He gurgled once, jerked, and the earth ran with his blood.
Then, with the shell in her hand, she poured her magic broth
Into the gaping hole in his throat, which had released his
    breath.
The liquor filled his veins, he glowed, stirred, came back to
    life,
His wrinkles disappeared, his throat closed where the knife
Had opened it, and his gray hair turned black and grew,
His arms and chest swelled up, and while Medea howled—
I think I did too—he rose and staggered toward the beach
And raised his arms in triumph, as far as they could reach.

This scene could be played out in silhouette or mime in the
background while Ophraedes speaks. Pelias and Ophraedes
off to one side; the slitting of Jason's throat, the pouring in
of the magic liquor, and the subsequent resurrection of Jason,
to howls and screams, all center stage, but recessed in the
shadows. When Ophraedes finishes speaking, Jason steps forward into the light, young again, and this may serve as the

transition into the next scene, in which Jason speaks with vigor and hope of his newly awakened desire to return to Colchis.

GOUPIL

19 December 1686

The convulsionaries meet in secret now that the cemetery is closed locked up   which seems not to affect them at all, they gather in twos or threes to incite each other to virtue

making agreements to cause each other suffering, Jeanne Egret & Madeleine Dillay meet in the smokehouse & chastise each other with blows from a whip   willow shoots branches of thorn

sometimes they all gather in the playhouse which is our chapel   some fall down during prayer but they drag them off.

Paul Broutin jumps in the river to punish himself with the cold water,

the Sieur de La Salle has set up a guard at the cemetery Moranget & du Hamel with their muskets

Denis St. Martin's hair has fallen out

I never thought I would spend another Christmas in this wretched land but here it comes again in six days   no one cares

21 December 1686

at rehearsal today in the playhouse the Sieur de La Salle commenced once more to enjoy his sport of thrashing Minime to within an inch of his life   but the scoundrel only infuriated the master all the more by shouting *harder! good!*   dressed in woman's clothes

he has give me the role of a ghost with one speech   this play is all his vanity he raves & struts about in a huff

I forgot 13 kettles   there is no end to his inventories.

of the 30 hogsheads of wine & brandy saved from *L'Aimable*
3 are left   powder 100 barrels   no large balls for the
cannon 8 pieces   more than 200 muskets cutlasses pikes
halberds   3000 weight of balls & other lead 600 weight of
iron 73 hatchets 189 knives 57 blankets 819 candles
thread & needles in abundance a gentleman's library of
books 18 casks of meal   the swine hens cocks goats he can
count himself they are of no consequence

  Joseph Augustin was bit by a rattlesnake   he was shooting snipes about the fort, he shot one which fell into a marsh
& took off his shoes to fetch it out   & returning through
carelessness trod upon a rattlesnake which bit him a little
above the ankle,   Membré dressed it & put him to bed in
the playhouse   his leg swelled up enormous, apprehensive
of a mortification the Sieur de La Salle resolved to cut it
off   Augustin agreeing with regret   the Sieur de La Salle
cut it off with a saw but now he has gone into a fever.

2 4 D e c e m b e r   1 6 8 6

I am sent to speak unto thee & show thee these glad things
thou shalt be dumb & not able to speak   thy soul shall
magnify the Lord

  Augustin died never having regained consciousness   119

2 5 D e c e m b e r   1 6 8 6

the midnight Mass was solemnly sung Membré led us
afterward we cried *the King drinks* though we had only
water   the Sieur de La Salle preserving the brandy & wine
for the ill.

  every day there is some discourse of his journey toward the
Messipi,

  toward evening today we saw a herd of buffaloes rushing
past our fort, we guessed they were pursued by savages,
afterwards this appeared to be true   some of them had
muskets they had taken from our men they made some shots

but very weak   the Sieur Joutel was on the river in a canoe
& designed to have gone upwards but the savages perceiving
it 8 of them swam over the river hastening to get before the
canoe   hid themselves in the weeds & let fly their arrows
wounding several men   one shot from the Sieur Joutel's
musket put them all to flight, he held on his way and returned
to our habitation,   but 2 of our men were killed   unable
to recover their bodies in the darkness   121

2 7 D e c e m b e r   1 6 8 6

Raymond Lecler who we thought broke his fever was found
dead in his bedding this morning   122   the Sieur de La
Salle has begun a new cemetery   the one under guard
being full.
   rain again last night it prevented me from sleeping   part
of the top of our building being uncovered because the sun
has dried & shrunk our hides   the rain came in dripping all
night,   Joutel resolves to provide bark for the roof instead.

2 8 D e c e m b e r   1 6 8 6

Rehearsal much of the day as it rained   the Sieur de La
Sablonniere infuriates the Sieur de La Salle for the forgetting
of his lines   he is the only one who has acted before, because of his noble profile he has the role of Jason   he de-
claims the speeches in a dainty fashion swells up when he
forgets some words & thrashes about with his arms like a man
tongue-tied   or drowning,

2 9 D e c e m b e r   1 6 8 6

Louis Theriault spilled powder on his cloak while out hunting today, it caught a spark from a fire & burned his whole
side from head to foot
   Cloudy disagreeable day,   we purchased 1 2 dogs 4 sacks
of fish from some savages who came by today we never saw

before   watching them carefully   this is the first instance
of this I ever knew   one had his eye blind & white.

30 December 1686

drying meat all day   sufficient stock for our journey
  I have made a map of this place the bay rivers fort &
vicinity
  one of our canoes broke its rope and was going off with
the tide this morning   Joutel and some men recovered it

2 January 1687

yesterday we performed the Sieur de La Salle's play *Jason's
Return* but a horrible catastrophe halted the performance and
now all is laid to waste about here,   the fences have been
broke down around the cemetery & Father Désmanville's
grave dug up & carried off no one knows where   the Sieur
de La Salle after the day's events too sunk in his wretchedness
to do anything about it,   such as punish the brutes   but
surely this is God's judgment upon us for painting our faces
  I wore a mask I was the ghost   when my part was said I
stole into the audience to watch the rest,   there was all manner of the sick lying about on the floor or raised onto platforms in the back of the place tended by Membré   some
of them was moaning,   the German Hien unconscious
everyone else from the colony filed in at sunset almost
filling the hall   illuminated by candles and torches
Moranget & Talon stayed behind as sentries at the fort.
  the Sieur de La Salle sat in front with his play prompting
the actors   dressed in his wig finest robes knickerbockers
linen   which are ragged because he was forced to wear
them on his last journey   not having any other clothes.
  he made a little speech before the performance,   the
entire play he said takes place beneath the wreck of the
Argo,   it is a study in degradation & personal honor   how
the gods plant eternity in our hearts,   and he explained that

Aristotle did not want tragic characters to be entirely good
or bad, therefore in this play we will see virtue liable to
weakness & misfortunes,   but vice is painted in such colors
that its hideous face may be recognized & despised and virtue
in the end is shown to advantage,   and other words to the
same effect I wrote them down   his eloquence wonderful   polite applause

Then the play begun with Jason talking   I said my part
without an error for which I received no acknowledg-
ment   when the guards seized Jason there was some horse-
play & this woke up the colony many of them laughed or
shouted,   until the Sieur de La Salle was forced to rise &
call for silence   Groethuysen beat the drum, there was a
drum and a flute   a chorus of the children of the Argonauts

the Sieur de La Sablonniere playing Jason staggered about
the stage   having contracted the fever the previous day,
he forgot his lines the Sieur de La Salle had to whisper them
to him   but everyone heard the whispers some laughed he
coughed a great deal   finally driven to slump against the
back wall & deliver his lines about the injustices of heaven
in a voice so weak & dispirited many in the audience grew
restless   only M. Talon's oldest boy Lucien woke them
up   & Minime dressed as Medea he looked like a witch
his appearance greeted with cries of horror & delight

Lucien played Ophraedes in a loud voice, his talent for
speaking bewitched the audience   as he was one of the
convulsionaries who used to preach & speak in strange languages.   when it came time to describe the rejuvenation of
Jason the audience was perfectly silent, the Sieur de La Sablonniere lay beneath a shroud in back of the stage & Minime
crept about like a shadow upon the darkened stage   the
Sieur de La Salle having removed some torches, Lucien stood
to the side & spoke beneath a torch which illuminated only
his face   we couldn't see Joutel he was playing Pelias, some
people stood up   then Minime pretended to slit the Sieur
de La Sablonniere's throat there was screams from the audience, some thought it was real   then Lucien describes

Medea making her potion, Minime is in front of everyone
with a kettle   then he pours it onto the Sieur de La Sablonniere's neck & strange to say he rises up with great effort like
Lazarus   & staggers toward the front of the stage mumbling
his lines while Minime screams someone shouts   another
commences to pray   and no one can hear the Sieur de La
Sablonniere as people in the audience begin shouting & praying   then O lamentable someone falls down with the convulsions   while the Sieur de La Sablonniere staggers about
in a trance Minime's body stiffens he throws his head back &
drops to the floor   Lucien does too with a shout trembling
& twitching like a puppet   & heavenly Father the cataclysm
begins   I saw someone strike the Sieur de La Salle from
behind, some colonists run for the doors screaming some fell
down climbing across each other   while the Sieur de La
Sablonniere wanders about still mumbling   M. La Barre
rushes up to me sobbing & kneels down before me seizing
my legs & sobbing & crying   some people are leaping into
the air   tears groans & frightful screams   it is a terrible
sight to see so many Christians shaking and trembling upon
the ground   crawling up & down   Mme. Lefebvre down
on all fours like a dog exposing herself,   this was the worse
convulsions I ever saw, I had to kick M. La Barre to release
his grip but he called for more   trying to attain the door
while all about me are writhing contorted   twisting themselves into strange violent postures

   I heard Father Maximus uttering horrible profanations &
blasphemies, he struck himself with his fists   shouts of *secours,* Lepaysant ran about with a sledgehammer   some of
the women demanded their breasts & nipples be pinched &
bitten by *secouristes*   and the faces!   ugly twisted mouths
jaws jutting out like an idiot's eyes crossed tongues swollen
up   Minime was twisted up twitching every joint arthritic
& bent   he rolled around on the floor sobbing & laughing
immoderately at turns   he rises up his shoulders distended
arms aflap he appears to be arching back & rising into the air
as though 2 enormous fingers are hooked beneath his

arms   while the Sieur de La Sablonniere picks at the walls
as though picking hairs off them   amidst exclamations &
incoherent babblings   choking on smoke   someone at
my feet a lump of head & chest with bunches of limbs splayed
out and twitching,   Georges Avenel was attempting to cru-
cify himself upon a board,   my thumb stiffened folding up
inward   it flowed up my arm I shuddered once a woman in
black approached me,   then my eyes closed & I was taken
up   a rushing sound and the noise of wheels   the name
of the Lord burning with anger his tongue on fire hanging
out dragging,   everything aflame then dark

   later we discovered the fence around the cemetery was
torn down   not being guarded   and the Sieur de La Sablonniere was stabbed he may not live   Mme. Lefebvre's
arm was broken   the Sieur de La Salle has a contusion on
the back of his neck   others have injuries too Membré
struck by a club   while tending to me he said when the fit
came upon me   to prevent me from the swallowing of my
tongue.

                                   4 January   1 6 8 7

2 days spent in bed for fear my falling sickness would recur
again it hasn't   repairs to the fort & cemetery   6 deserted
where could they go?

   the Sieur de La Sablonniere's death as a consequence of
wounds suffered during the performance of the play   has
laid the convulsionaries to rest   but the Sieur de La Salle
does not seek out the malefactors to punish them   nor pursue the deserters he throws up his hands in despair at all our
misfortunes   and plots our way home on the crude maps he
drew amongst the Cenis

                                   7 January   1 6 8 7

Gabriel Lovaquery   1 2 7   Hien has recovered from his
fever another scoundrel   a buffalo knocked down Father

Membré took some skin off his face, he thought it was dead   it sprang up after Joutel shot it with an effort of expiring fury   my friend was not hurt too badly & repents his rashness

LA SALLE

12 January 1687

Preparations for our departure proceed according to my designs. Of the fifty or so left in our colony, half will come with me, and half remain here, the latter to include the women, children, and infirm. Talon, who manages his family well enough, with the exception of the older son, will be in command during my absence. The son Lucien will travel with me, as will the other troublemakers such as Blet, Hien, and Paget —not to mention my valet Minime—so that I may better keep my eye upon them. Goupil shall come and draw a map. Fathers Douay and Cavelier will come, but Membré will stay behind to tend to the sick, saint that he is. I will take with me the strongest and most healthy, as the journey will be long and there shall be no occasion for turning back. Those who stay have manifested to me their fear of attack by the savages hereabouts; but they will have ammunition sufficient to kill all the savages of America, as we can only carry a small portion of it with us, in each man's bundle. As the Lord says, I will not leave them orphans; but, once having recovered my furs and dissolved my debts, will return with provisions and supplies for their relief, and for the expansion of our colony.

15 January 1687

In placing our expedition under the protection of the Lord, I do not imagine that he holds our interest foremost in his heart; nor do I underestimate the uncertainties and dangers of this attempt; for, first we must find the Colbert, or Messipi; then follow its perilous course more than three hundred leagues to the Seignelay [Illinois], which will then be the starting point of a new and not less arduous journey, from the Seignelay to the Lake of the Hurons, thence through the other lakes to the River St. Lawrence and finally to Quebec. But even here our voyage will not be completed, until we cross the ocean to France, and return to the Gulf of Mexico, where in all likelihood we will find everything we part with now reduced to ashes.

Nor am I insensible of the misfortunes I have already suffered, the blows of fate, death by starvation and disease, mutiny, insubordination, the weaknesses of untutored minds, religious heresy and fanaticism, murderous savages, monstrous alligators, the breakdown of order, the difficulties of arduous labor, the ungrateful behavior of spiteful men. On our voyage, we shall be forced to suffer further the ravages of hunger, to sleep on the open ground, watch by night and march by day, loaded with baggage, such as blankets, clothing, kettles, hatchets, guns, powder, and lead; sometimes pushing through thickets and cane, sometimes climbing steep ravines, sometimes wading whole days through marshes where the water is waist-deep or more; and cutting our feet on shells; to say nothing of the danger of meeting savages from a hundred different nations.

Nevertheless, despite all this, hope floods my heart with exultation.

GOUPIL

9 *January* 1687

a great belt of M. Joutel served to make shoes for the Sieur de La Salle and M. Cavelier   the clothes belonging to Thibault Le Gros & Carpentier who are dead,   have been distributed to those making the journey   as well as several

effects of the Sieur de La Sablonniere after he died such as
linen hatchets & other tools   which he saved from the bark
La Belle,

I supplied the Sieur de La Salle with some linen I had at
his insistence   as well as 1 2 pounds of string & beads some
knives & nails to make gifts to the savages,

We must dry more meat as some we had provisioned for
this journey has turned up wormy.

1 1 J a n u a r y   1 6 8 7

nothing remarkable happened during today.   everyone
anxious to be off   to find what we have come here for that
was hid from our eyes.

thank God no more fits

1 2 J a n u a r y   1 6 8 7

prepare the table anoint the shield   thy dead men shall
live   wolf dwell at peace with the lamb the leopard lie
down with the kid,   lion eat straw like the ox

Membré says this land devours its inhabitants   at the
same time there came into his mind the speech of Joshua and
Caleb, the land is very good   if the Lord be favorable he
will bring us into it,   but at this I wept on his shoulder at
the thought of departing from my dear friend and he said he
has never been so sensibly touched at parting with anyone,

he cautions me not to place too much confidence in the
Sieur de La Salle but in this I feel he is wrong.   the immen-
sity of our journey the unknown country we enter,   I say
send up a cheer that we shall come to the Messipi Quebec &
afterwards France,   since the way is closed we came
anxious to be rid of this place an abode of weariness &
perpetual prison,   forgive this sentiment it blasphemes the
suffering here   I cannot help it

15 January 1687

Birobel taken last night with a violent pain in his side.   M.
Cavelier & M. Chedeville also complain of pains, it is unfortunate that they should be sick at this moment

we made some repairs on M. Moranget's musket

parceled out the powder 4 pounds each & 6 pounds of lead
2 axes 2 dozen knives as many awls some beads   several
kettles hogskins of grain meal dried meat on the 3 horses

the Sieur de La Salle made a lasting speech tonight to those
who will stay behind,   everyone persuaded of the necessity
of this voyage & his great audacity of hope.

then Membré said Mass & elevated the host with trembling
hands   some almost moved to tears but I secretly rejoiced
in my breast at our departure & the great path before
us   for the ransomed of the Lord shall return to Zion with
joy upon their heads,

LA   SALLE

16 January 1687

Taking our leave with as much tenderness and sorrow as
possible, we set out today in the direction of the place we call
Le Boucon, where we have often dried the flesh of deer and
buffalo, there being seventeen of us, including my brother,
M. Cavelier, my nephews MM. Moranget and Cavelier, Father Anastasius, the Recollect, Blet, Hien, Paget, the young
Talon, Liotot, L'Archeveque, Saget, Joutel, Goupil, Minime,
Chuka, and some others, along with three horses to carry
some of our equipment. A few of the men were lax and heavy
at the stomach, complaining of their bowels, and we were
obliged twice to halt while they lay on the side of the trail.
Twenty-eight stayed behind, with the elder Talon in charge
and Membré to tend to the needs of the sick.

————

19 January 1687

Today we crossed a beautiful prairie of tall grass, marching twelve leagues through land mostly level, and met with some marshy ground, which tired our horses. Here we saw several herds of buffalo and flocks of goats, turkeys, bustards, and other wild fowl. We killed four buffalo and took the best parts with us to ford a river at the edge of a wood, where the plains terminate.

Thus far we have successfully avoided the savages, who are so abundant in these parts. From a certain point of view, our little group would strike anyone but a savage as comical; some wear the remains of the clothing they brought with them from France, patched with deerskins; others have coats of old sailcloth and shoes of raw buffalo hide, quite green, which they are obliged to keep always wet, as, when dry, they harden about the feet like iron; Chuka carries the soiled and moth-eaten robes presented to him by Louis XIV in a basket on his arm, determined to display them to the chief of his people when he arrives among them on the River Colbert. In other words, this ensemble dressed in motley reminds me of those traveling troupes of actors one sometimes encounters in the countryside of France, and had our only attempt at a theatrical presentation in Fort St. Louis not been so lamentable, I would encourage them now to perform a comedy for me. For, at the end of the day we strike a peaceful lull, after setting up a rude stockade about the camp, building our fire by the bubbling waters of a brook near the edge of a grove of trees, and listening to the deep breathing of our slumbering horses and the distant howling of wolves upon the prairie. At this time, one longs for some entertainment other than the importunate attacks of savages, which we must always anticipate and guard against. But this is a dull and morose group of travelers; they speak little, only Talon sometimes sings, and few share my delight in moving toward our destiny once more.

I have given Birobel permission to return to the fort, as he is too weakened by the ailment in his stomach to proceed any further with us. Paget insisted he be allowed to go with him, but this I forbade; however, by morning today he had disappeared, too, and now the savages may double their meal.

For two entire days it has rained, and we find it best to stay where we are, since the hides of our slaughtered buffalo are so useful to cover us. We sit beneath them and watch the horses steam.

The rain having ceased, we set out today across another spacious plain, abundant with buffalo and wild fowl. Tracks made by the buffalo led in every direction, but we held northeast. By midday, we found ourselves in the midst of several large herds, some of them moving with haste, others running outright, which made us suppose they were driven by the natives. Then, as we stopped to assist one of our horses that had fallen, we saw a lone savage following some buffalo very close. I caused a horse to be unloaded immediately, which Joutel mounted in order to overtake this savage and bring him back to us.

When this creature with his pierced breast, half naked, with a wild look about him, perceived himself among our troupe, he didn't think to laugh or applaud; indeed, he concluded he was a lost man and quaked with fear, and not without reason, for Minime was for killing him. But I opposed this, for fear that by rendering ourselves odious we might endanger those left behind at the fort; and, instead, caused a fire to be built, smoked tobacco with this man, and made him presents of a knife and some fine beads to take back to his tribe, giving him to understand that we came not to hurt anyone, but to settle peace in all places.

More of his tribe have visited us this evening at our camp

inside a little wood, and to these we have made more presents. But they sneak about as though to steal our things, and this impels us to double our guard. They signify that a member of their tribe told them that we do not hurt people, and so they were come to see this curious species of humanity who does not wage war; but night draws on, and after entertaining these officious savages as best we can, I have now signaled them to withdraw, while our men hold their arms upon ready.

23 January 1687

Today we were forced northwest by another branch of the river we crossed, this one more swollen. This was a river I had forded on my previous voyage, but the recent rains have rendered this impossible. Thus, we were obliged to go up higher, sometimes crossing curious meadows and sometimes woods of very young tall trees, all of the same girth and height, which looked as though they had been planted by a gardener. The river running through the middle of these shady groves, which were also watered by some brooks of very clear water, afforded a most delightful landscape. We also met with some woods and bushes so thick that it was requisite to cut a passage through them for the horses; effecting this by marching in file with an ax in each hand, hewing left and right. This procedure fatigued us very much; but the hunters succeeded in shooting some turkeys, which eased our sufferings and assisted us in bearing our toil with more satisfaction.

GOUPIL

24 January 1687

sunlight no wind very clear   more toilsome labor through thickets and woods & across high streams   but the Sieur de La Salle refuses to admit he is lost we came to a little hill on which there was 2 hundred cottages of savages   they resemble large ovens consisting of long poles stuck in the earth and bent across the top to make a dome   but the inhabitants were all of them gone   carrying away the hides which cover these dwell-ings.

At last at a narrow bend of this river,   we cut down a tree which reached the other bank & handing our baggage from one to the other across it,   the horses swam over we camped on the other side near a beautiful pasture   but it rained again tonight   8 leagues NW

2 5 J a n u a r y   1 6 8 7

Rain again this morning,   all the streams we meet is swol-len   the rain ceasing we marched through a thick fog over places the water was up to our knees   but higher we had to cut through the bushes   all this gave us inexpressible trouble high & low, it had been much better if the Sieur de La Salle had the sense to follow the buffalo paths   who their natural instinct always leads to the parts which are easiest to pass   only 5 leagues NE

2 6 J a n u a r y   1 6 8 7

fine pasturage today easy & pleasant glades 14 leagues some stands of oak trees,   we hold steady NE,   a river we had difficulty crossing has steep banks with a descent of 40 feet, low hills nearby some timbered   many white rocks near this river with crosses & other designs cut into their sides. Father Douay very curious about this.

2 8 J a n u a r y   1 6 8 7

10 leagues NE   this morning we came to a tribe in which all the savages was sick   this was one the Sieur de La Salle had stayed with on his other voyage,   now they all had

disease many have died so virulent is the pox for these savages   but as there was so much howling & crying we could
not stay here   also nobody thought of burying the dead
they were left in loathsome & stinking piles in their cottages   with a few buffalo robes over them to be devoured
by their own dogs

this was a sad spectacle.   some of them destroyed themselves with their own knives   we took some corn beans
wheat which they had no use for   also deerskin to make
better shoes   & boats of bull hides to cross the river beside
this village   who watched us leave with moans & imprecations   some of our men took a scalp of these savages
Minime did this & some other unspeakable things,   but the
Sieur de La Salle didn't punish him,   for he only punishes
somebody when he himself feels angry or morose.

the rest of today spent marching across low hills, I could
not erase from my mind the picture of these dying savages
it reminded me of our Fort of St. Louis   each one clutching
his own naked body   utter dismay possessed them one continual crying & praying   so many heathens ushered into
eternity with no fitness whatsoever for such a change   what
has sin done look what desolation it brought into the
world,   Oh Lord I pray be my safeguard   you already
covered me in the palm of your hand   when death was
casting darts all around why did you spare me,   for some
greater affliction,

3 0 *J a n u a r y* 1 6 8 7

the 29th we marched west to avoid some ravines & low hills
then northeast again to some pools   watered the horses
then our route took us through thickets & crossing many
swollen creeks,   the last of which we camped at having
marched only 3 leagues because of this circuitous route.

today a small rain did not obstruct our march having
crossed a woods half a league in width & a marsh of the same
extent   we came to a level plain with great tracks of buf-

faloes which led to a river this was the Robek River so called
by the Sieur de La Salle   swollen & rapid we followed it to
a wide place & crossed by means of the boats of bull hides
which our horses carry   this makes it easier   then we shot
some buffaloes, one of our hunters having perceived a
buffalo on the top of an eminence fired his musket at the
animal & sent it rolling from the top to our very feet,   but
imagine our shock it sprang to its feet looked around at our
men & bounded off along the river bank, the hunter could
not stay his laughter   the bullet only stunned him we
guessed,   so no second shot was fired
　　encamped near a beautiful plain.   whilst hewing down
some bushes to entrench ourselves hearing a voice we took
up our arms   & going to the place where it was we met a
company of 15 savages who were coming toward us, we laid
down our arms & made signs for them to draw near,   this
they did & caressed us after their manner   Then we sit
down to smoke with them & the Sieur de La Salle began to
converse with them in signs and by help of some words in the
language of the Cenis which he is skillful in   he understood
that this nation was called the Hebahamos   we gave them
presents & they withdrew promising to return upon the morrow   7 leagues NE

3 1 January 1 6 8 7

today our horses being spent & hurt we are tired too   we
are giving this day & some others to rest the savages having
come this morning   they brought some bucklers or targets
made of the strongest buffalo hides   and gave us to understand that they were engaged in war toward the northwest
having seen men like us who were 10 days' journey from that
place   we supposed it was the Spaniards
　　they also said they seen a man like us who lived with a tribe
near their neighbors,   they said some *spirits* like us live
with those savages including some boys who are all skin &
bones,   the savages kick them slap their faces beat them

with sticks   these we supposed to be some boys who were kidnapped from our fort a year ago,   and the Sieur de La Salle resolved to go in that direction & find them as it was on our route regardless,

1 February 1687

visited the village of the Hebahamos where there are 50 dwellings on a hillock,   the people very stupefied at seeing us showing much fear   after they recovered from their astonishment they approached & placed their hands on our faces & bodies   and afterwards to their own faces & bodies   they gave us to understand that they conceived a friendship for us which they expressed by laying their hands on their hearts we did the same   then they brought us some sick people thinking we could cure them,   camped outside this village an arpent,   where the Sieur de La Salle proposes to spend some time

LA SALLE

3 February 1687

The Ebahamo savages, whom we have taken to calling "weepers," because at our arrival in their village they all began to weep bitterly, nonetheless have shown us great hospitality. It is their custom when they see people who come from afar to weep, because it reminds them of their distant relatives, whom they suppose to be on a long journey, from which they await their return.

They led us to the hut of their chief, where all crowded in who could fit, and commenced to touch us eagerly, thereafter touching themselves in all the places they had touched us. They gave us hung beef to eat. These people speak by carefully husbanding or repressing their breath, and at the end of a sentence or isolated word allowing it to escape with a sigh, a habit of manner which gives them an air of ennui. Furthermore, despite their hospitality, their expression is slightly contemptuous, and they never look at the person to whom they are talking, as if their speech was an act of utter condescension and proceeded from extreme fatigue.

They sleep when they want to, like dogs or cats, being often asleep in the daytime and awake nights, or vice versa, as they feel inclined. Their huts are like others we have seen, consisting of skins partially covering poles bowed across the top in a dome or circle.

Yesterday they brought me to a man they said had been shot in the back with an arrow some weeks ago, and made me to understand that the head was still in his body close to his heart. I touched his chest and felt that the arrowhead had pierced the cartilage. Because I had some of my surgical instruments with me, I proposed to these savages to remove the arrowhead, with the understanding that the operation was a dangerous one and the patient might not survive. But either they failed to understand me, or their secret design in bringing me to this person was that I might do such a thing, for with gestures they made known their eagerness for me to proceed. Accordingly, I cut open the breast and probed for the arrow, but it had gone athwart and was difficult to remove. But by cutting deeper and inserting the point of my instrument, with great difficulty I removed it; for it was very long. Finally, I sewed up the wound with a deer bone and some thread. The elders of the village begged for the arrow point. The patient seemed better at once, and they made many dances and festivities, chanting and singing in a circle, following the lead of their chief, a grotesque figure wrapped to his head in skins, with his face concealed, his long, black hair streaming over his back, and his entire body doubled over as he danced. The music came from a gourd filled with small stones, some fluted pieces of wood which they beat, and some rude flutes with two or three notes.

As a consequence of this operation, which seemed to make a great impression on these people, many sick or deformed savages approached our company asking to be cured. Minime painted his face like one of their *jugglers* or doctors, and pretended to cure some diseased braves by blowing on their chests, a procedure which had little practical result but appeared to impress the savages greatly. He made the sign of the cross over one sick child, who jumped up and exclaimed he was free of pain. Thereafter, these foolish savages commenced to following Minime around, who encouraged their attention with his antics. He danced in circles, tumbled, sang, made the sign of the cross repeatedly, and even had the audacity to mime the seizure of an epileptic in the course of his dance, a display which fortunately produced no visible effect on our party.

From these savages we have learned of some European boys being held captive by a neighboring tribe who may be the children of M. Messelet that were kidnapped from our fort some time ago. This tribe is east of here five days' journey; there is also a European adult with them who has become a chief of sorts. Accordingly, we shall march in that direction, as it isn't far off our path regardless.

The Ebahamos told us a very strange tale. They said that about fifteen or sixteen years ago, there was walking about this country a man whom they called "Bad Thing," who was small of stature and wore a beard. His features they could never see very clearly. Whenever he approached their dwellings, the inhabitants began to tremble, for he always chose one, and with a sharp knife of flint, cut his side; then, thrusting his hand in the wound, he pulled out the entrails, a piece of which he sliced off and threw into the fire. After that, he made three cuts in one of the arms and twisted the arm, but reset it afterwards. Then he placed his hands on all these wounds and they closed at once. Sometimes he would appear among them in the dress of a woman and whenever he took a notion to do it seize one of their huts and lift it up into the air, then allow it to come down with a great crash. When they asked him where he came from and where he had his home, he pointed to a rent in the earth and said his dwelling was down below.

Most of our men laughed at these stories, which, told by means of signs and some Ceni words, I translated imperfectly; but Father Douay was very taken with "Bad Thing," and said he was a demon, and explained as best he could that if they would believe in God and be Christians like ourselves, such demons would never bother them again. At this, they were pleased and nodded their heads, eager to become Christians; but my long experience with savages such as these teaches me that eagerness of this sort is a whim and passing fancy, the creature of a moment's thought. It takes a lifetime to make a savage a Christian, and even then the change may be completely reversed in an instant. On the other hand, once Christians like us become savages, there is no turning back; why this should be I cannot say.

6 February 1687

A rain which began during the night fell all day yesterday, delaying our departure until today. The Ebahamos told us that toward the east we should meet with plains, and thus shun the thickets and woods; as we left, a great many of them followed us, still begging of Minime to be cured of whatever imaginary or real ailments they possessed. Of these savages, some ten or twelve have remained with us all day, thus swelling our number and making it impossible to proceed in an orderly manner, even through the easy and pleasant glades we came to. We crossed two small rivers and came to the larger one I call La Sablonniere, after the late Marquis who accompanied me on our previous exploration of these parts. Here, we turned further east and encamped in a little wood. As the rain begain falling again, and the river was close to overflowing, we were obliged to construct a sort of scaffold to lay our powder and clothes upon, that they might not become wet.

Today we decamped to go to higher ground, since the river was still rising. Here, we made a great fire to dry us, and watched with amusement the antics of Minime and his savage followers, who dance and howl and perform all manner of specious miracles.

As the rain had stopped during the night, we rose early today and marched along the river through a vast, beautiful country, whose plains extend as far as the eye can reach. At last, we were required to cross to the other side, lest this river's course divert us too far to the south, and this we effected at a ford which Minime's savage friends pointed out; but we needed the assistance of the horses and buffalo boats, and even then some of our men were nearly carried away. On the other side, we built a fire to dry ourselves. The plains hereabouts are adorned with coppices and afford a most agreeable prospect.

Later in the morning we came to a village of about fifty inhabitants, who were astonished to see us. As soon as we arrived, Minime's savage followers began lining up the inhabitants in order to allow them to touch the white men and be blessed by them; and, while Minime, Hien, and Liotot so blessed them, the Ebahamos who had accompanied us openly plundered the homes of the inhabitants, taking their belongings as payment for the miraculous cures being effected. I dreaded lest this behavior might cause us no little trouble and strife, but I had little authority over these savages; furthermore, the inhabitants of the village thus plundered noticed how I felt and made pains to comfort me, saying that I shouldn't worry and that they were happy to see us and were glad to lose what they had for our blessing.

But as this also happened at the next tribe we came to, I was finally obliged to put a stop to it, and fired my musket in the air as a warning against such theft. For the savages who were following Minime had now doubled in number, some from this morning's village having joined the group; and immediately we came into this other place, whose inhabitants trembled to see us, the Ebahamos and others who had joined them put arrows to their chests and drew the bows back to their ears, afterwards laughing and asking them whether they were frightened. They abused and kicked some of the villagers who appeared reluctant to give up their possessions, and, in short, were not to be gainsaid without a display of force and authority. Yet, the villagers still insist that we touch and bless them, for it appears to do them good; and they say that further on they themselves would be repaid for their losses by other tribes who are very rich.

At last we came away from this place followed by still more savages, whose numbers have grown to forty or more, and whom I cannot persuade to turn back, unless I shoot a few of them; and it may come to that.

GOUPIL

10 February 1687

twice he has asked of the wretched brutes whose villages we plunder whether they ever heard of such a river as the Messipi,   but they haven't,

Today it begun to rain again it rained all day & we lost the trail such as it was,   and found ourselves in a forest through which we were forced to cut a passage for more than a league.   gradually the bushes thinned & we came to a river we could see it already overflowed its banks once & receded,   here there were many pecan trees   the river was rocky with stones & flint not easy to cross   I hope I never see another river again   that I have to wade through, they are thrown up against our path like barricades,   one after another

we came to a village & the Sieur de La Salle was at his wits' end to prevent the savages following us from plundering these people   he raves about shooting some   I say he should shoot his valet who paints his face just like a savage   I make 7 leagues east   in cold rain

1 3   F e b r u a r y   1 6 8 7

the numbers of our followers have grown so large we can no longer control them,   We are asked to breathe on their food & make the sign of the cross over every morsel they eat or drink.   we meet savages on the trail who have heard of our coming & traveled from afar to meet us, they bring us gifts of beads bags of silver bows   and those deprived of their belongings thus feel obliged to follow us in order to repair their losses, they forge ahead and rouse the tribes on our path to prepare for our coming & to give us gifts   but the Sieur de La Salle insists that they turn back & so we are at loggerheads with these followers,   he grows angry & livid & last night went away to sleep in a field apart from them.   but they came to where he was & entreated him not to be angry any longer but he pretends to be angry still, then a strange thing happened during the night some of them grew sick   this morning two of them died, the rest besought the Sieur de La Salle not to be angry   convinced that he killed them by thinking of it, they dared not go near the bodies which we caused to be buried.

but the Sieur de La Salle still pretends to be angry thinking this will drive them off   they ask him to bless them but he refuses   thus withholding the succors by which our company attracted them in the first place.

since 2 days we have made 18 leagues,   across 2 more rivers ravines low hills   ravines of red & yellow earth rivers rivers!

———

today our wretched crusade came to a village whose chief we all recognized as the Sieur d'Autray, who deserted last year from the Sieur de La Salle. this was a large village they greeted us with commotions & gifts insisting we bless them blow upon their food, they had heard of our coming they took us into one large skin tent arranged in the middle to make a huge drawing room, there we must bow down before one of their chiefs but looking up we see it is the Sieur d'Autray I was frightened when I saw it His face arms breast marked with grotesque streaks & tattoos. he didn't recognize us & seemed not to be able to speak the French language, but through the natives of the tribe he informed us he was a French king he had been sent by God to subdue these natives & teach them how to pray, whereupon he recited in French the Ave Maria the credo the 10 commandments, interposing it is a sin to break them this was all he could say in French,

when he saw Father Douay he appeared moved & con-fused a look of mortification in his eyes he rose from his seat as if in a trance falling upon his knees before him kissed the sleeve of his habit trembling, we tried to prevail upon him to come with us but this idea he strongly resisted & assuming his previous dignity stood upon a platform where his savage assistants fanned him with plumes cleansed him of sweat fumigating the dwelling with fat & some sorts of perfume unknown to us, we saw in the dwelling an ar-quebus which was broken with a flask of powder balls ramrod

he made us to understand that he had gone among this tribe upon the orders of Governor Philippe from the French fort, who we understood to be the Sieur de La Salle, but when the Sieur de La Salle stepped forward d'Autray appeared perplexed pretended not to recognize him.

a squaw in the room was his wife, she wore only a skirt her breasts had been tattooed, Father Douay asked him why he had chosen to marry a pagan & go about naked eat raw

meat with never a priest to hear his confession,   with signs
& some words our savages labored to translate his reply that
such choices were not his to make, he had gone among these
savages at the order of Monsieur Philippe.   and while
there he looked upon this woman & found her attractive, she
had given her hand a priest had performed the marriage
ceremony,   what priest we said but he pretended not to
understand.   to please his wife he allowed himself to be
tattooed in keeping with the native custom.

   we asked about the 2 boys we had heard about,   he said
they were sold to another tribe north of here   the Sieur de
La Salle resolves to go there next,   but from his answer &
the worried look on his face I think the Sieur d'Autray was
lying   maybe he ate them being a savage

   as to what the attractions of such a life as the Sieur d'Autray
leads to cause him to risk his immortal soul,   who can say
I don't want to know it   the women are not attractive
scarred with tattoos & greasy   their flirtatious manner is
repulsive.   being only women.

   this tribe is the most docile we ever met,   they never talk
together neither did we ever see a child laugh or cry   one
child who begun to cry was carried off a little distance & with
some very sharp mice teeth they began scratching it from the
shoulders to the legs,   but when the Sieur de La Salle took
them to task for this act of cruelty they said it was done to
punish the child for having wept in our presence

1 5   F e b r u a r y   1 6 8 7

the Sieur d'Autray disappeared in the night with some of his
tribe   perhaps fearing we would make him come with us,
I am glad to see him go   neither shall you make marriages
with the inhabitants of this land & defile yourselves   or
bow down to their gods who worship only the work of men's
hands wood & stone.

   we tried to purchase some horses of these savages but they

answered they had but two which they could not part with,   bartered for some collars of a sort of knots made of buffalo hides which these people use to carry their burdens

Then we proceeded on our journey but no one here has heard of the Messipi River, they say a great river lies a day ahead   but the Sieur de La Salle calls this the Maligne or the Mischievous River because on his former journey an alligator devoured one of his servants who was swimming across it,

the country here very sandy

some more of our savage followers grow ill,   they require us to bless them at every turn   and will not be satisfied with our saying no but pull upon our clothing & wail & expect the performance of miracles wherever they go
5 leagues today N

16 February 1687

having crossed a large plain we came to the bank of the very fine river called La Maligne as wide as the Seine at Rouen,
our hunters killed some buffalo also some creatures large as an indifferent cat they resemble a rat,   having a bag under their throat in which they carry their young   they feed upon nuts very fat flesh like a pig

we crossed this river with difficulty,   Joutel having to swim across it with a rope made of buffalo hides we held onto the other end.   then each man in a boat of buffalo skins held onto this rope lest he be swept away.

some of these savages following us is great thieves,   they place all their credence in dreams   their principal food is roots also spider and ant eggs worms lizards beetles salamanders serpents & vipers,   they swallow earth & wood & the dung of deer & more things I do not mention,   And preserve the bones of the snakes they eat to pulverize them & eat the powder, some fights has broken out between our men and them.

hard by here we found a place where the Sieur de La Salle
on his former journey   hid some parcels of strings of beads
in the trunks of trees   11 leagues NE

1 7 F e b r u a r y   1 6 8 7

crossed several spacious plains the grass whereof was all
burned which led the Sieur de La Salle to conclude there are
many savages hereabouts but we have not seen them
     killed some buffalo & put in a store of dry flesh,   the
savages with us very adept at killing buffalo   I have seen an
arrow pass entirely through his body & the stunned creature
walk away.
     8 leagues still NE

1 9 F e b r u a r y   1 6 8 7

today we marched 7 leagues & crossed a large river before
a storm rose up followed by thunder & rain,   which
swelled the streams & obliged us to remain where we were
     2 men deserted in the night it was Blet and Vaillant.   the
Sieur de La Salle wanted to send some men in pursuit of them
but thought better of this design as it would divide our forces
and leave us vulnerable to attack,   Hien thinks they went
to find them wives like the Sieur d'Autray.

LA SALLE

2 1 F e b r u a r y   1 6 8 7

This is a fine, curious country, diversified with small woods,
hills, and brooks swollen by the recent rain. Our path
through the forest in which the plains we crossed terminated
was favored by the buffalo as well, who had beaten it down
before us. It reminded all the men of a road to Paris, whereupon the forty or so savages who follow in our wake took up
the cry as well, corrupting the name "Paris" to *panne;* hence,

we marched through the woods as though going home, followed by a seeming group of village urchins shouting, *"Panne, panne,"* much to the amusement of our company.

22 February 1687

We traveled today over timbered hills marked with steep ravines, which gave us much trouble walking. Forded one river with some trouble, and many small creeks. My ears and temple ached all day. In the afternoon, we arrived at a village which some of the savages accompanying us had pointed the way to, but its inhabitants had all fled, leaving some fires still smoldering. Our savages were for pursuing this tribe, but I could not compass this, and we held on our course NE, much to their dismay.

24 February 1687

The natives in a village we came to today pretended not to have heard of the two French boys we had hoped to find. These savages were very suspicious and displayed their umbrage when our own native followers attempted to plunder their belongings; many began running around, several fights broke out, and finally one of our savages was murdered with the blow of an ax made of stone. As a consequence, our savages and Christians too were all for taking revenge, but this I opposed with much resolution, as the numbers of these people were superior and they would surely have massacred us all. With great difficulty, I persuaded our company to depart from that place and marched them as far as possible before setting up camp, which we enforced with stockades.

Here, the valley appears to be thickly settled with savages. We came across piles of rocks here and there, evidently placed by hand as markers. Everywhere we saw remains of villages and what appear to be cultivated fields. We crossed one river without too much difficulty.

The pain in my head lessened somewhat today due to a

bleeding, which I administered myself. But the cure fatigues me; I have great need of rest.

26 February 1687

Yesterday morning we crossed a deep ravine, preceded by a thick wood of live oak, difficult to traverse, which continued on the other side as far as the bank of a large, flowing river a league away. The undergrowth here was thick, and on both banks there were giant cottonwoods and so many wild grape-vines and bushes it was nearly impenetrable. We finally forded this river in water up the horses' shoulders, and camped on a plain beside a small tributary.

Here, we determined to rest for a day or two, while Joutel, Moranget, and several of the savages with us search about these parts and inquire of the natives whether they have heard of the two French boys who were kidnapped, though I suspect we have already passed the place where they are; or they have long ago been murdered by brutish people.

And what should I say to those men who complain that we haven't yet come to the River Messipi? They knew very well when we embarked that the journey would be arduous and long, and there would be no possibility of altering our design or turning back. We have not lacked for food on this voyage, nor have any of our men been murdered by savages, for which we should all thank the Lord; although three have deserted. Instead of complaining, they should pray for the resolution to bear up against their hardships, for by myself I have not the means by which to instill courage in timid people; and, consequently, I prefer to go off alone now and make my camp apart from the men, accompanied by only Chuka or my brother, in order not to have to listen to their grumbling.

Today our hunters killed several deer. Joutel returned, having discovered no news of the two French boys. He found three large tribes west of this place, who welcomed him with courtesy, and, having heard of the *spirits* wandering about and curing the sick, meaning us, asked him to lay his hands upon some diseased members of their tribes, and blow upon them, and make the sign of the cross, all of which he performed with great reluctance, agreeing to this only in order to avoid giving offense.

This day continued all day very fine, with abundant sunshine and warmth. Around noon, hearing a commotion by the river, I ventured down there to discover what was causing it. There, a large group of our savage retainers, assisted by Minime, Hien, and some others, who egged them on, had captured an alligator with a hook made from a buffalo bone, baited with a large piece of meat. The cord which held the hook was studded with animal bones to prevent the creature from biting through it. This creature was twelve feet long, of ferocious aspect; his captors had pulled it from the river with ropes, then put out its eyes and released it, while Minime and two or three savages, to the delight of the rest, approached and struck it blows in the mouth with some clubs. Then, as I watched, having thus tormented it, they turned it belly up and fastened some stakes to it which pressed its body right and left from head to tail, and skinned it. On its scales were thick knots of tissue. However, the beast was still not dead, for when they freed it, it ran about with half its skin torn off, while the blows they rained upon the exposed muscle and tissue caused it to howl and roar fearfully. This disconcerted me greatly, and I spoke sharp words with Minime, ordering him to kill the beast, which he didn't do at once, but offered some mocking and insulting gestures to me first. At last one of the savages killed it with a spear and commenced carving up the meat, but in my extreme vexation at this cruel entertainment, and my distress at my valet's offensive behavior, I beat Minime severely, then confined him to the camp under guard for the remainder of the day.

Today we resumed our voyage, through some open plains in a light drizzle of rain, and past some belts of live oaks. While we were marching in silence, Chuka, who was ahead of our group, of a sudden shouted out, "I am dead!" We ran up and learned that he had been bitten by a snake, which we could not find anywhere; as a consequence, fearing that the snake was poisonous, we stopped for several hours and gave him some orvietan, then applied viper's salt on the wound after scarifying it to let out the tainted blood. We bandaged the wound as best we could, and offered him to ride on one of the horses, which he refused; asserting in his pride that he could walk like the rest of us. This stoical savage then set on his way without a word, much to the admiration of our company, who, following, found it difficult to match his pace.

I was disgusted to learn this morning that Minime and his entire band of savage followers had stolen away in the night, some thirty or forty of them, taking with them our three horses, our store of grain and beans, and our boats of buffalo skins. But I am utterly tired of this business, for which it is never enough merely to place property and life in constant peril, but one must suffer the treacherous behavior of men who are always at pains to thwart the enterprise. There is too little good faith in our company to trust anyone in it, and their envy and detraction make it impossible to overcome the difficulties inseparable from operations such as this. The company was for pursuing Minime, but I refused, shaking my head and speaking not a word. Only foolish people could fail to see that turning back now to recover our losses would be paid for with the greater loss of being forced to cross difficult terrain not once but three times, and with no guarantee of success. But there was no end to the whining and impreca-

tions of these men, whom I favored with not a word, giving
the orders to pack and march with merely a stubborn nod of
my head. Later in the day, I deigned one comment; reminding them that in two or three weeks we shall come to the
Cenis, and there be able to purchase more horses.

Now we are left with thirteen men; whose reduced number at least signifies fewer able to cross my plans. They think
this makes us more vulnerable to attack, but were I speaking
with them I could point out that we still have the powder
sufficient to defend ourselves, and the good sense—if we
only knew how to use it—to divert the antagonisms of savages with soothing words and gifts. But I am resolved to
avoid savage tribes as much as possible, in order not to submit our lives to still further hazards, which we could otherwise circumvent.

As for Minime, we are fortunate to be rid of him; and I
console myself with the thought that sooner or later he will
make a meal for those savages who pretend to worship him.

GOUPIL

1 March 1687

Minime deserted with his company of savages,   I say good
riddance   his execrable behavior   now perhaps the Sieur
de La Salle will resign his indisposition to guide us,   and
abandon his reserved & haughty ways,   but he refuses even
to speak with the men   as though we were to blame for the
treachery of his valet.

they took our horses & boats when we need them the
most   in every direction the land is a marsh,   God only
knows when we shall arrive among Christians   some thick
forests we come to was dry   2 small rivers cloudy
marched 7 leagues NNE

2 M a r c h   1 6 8 7

cloudy day   little pools of water in a great thicket   nut trees here & grapes, a trail here going north   1 2 leagues NNE

3 M a r c h   1 6 8 7

rain today very light then heavy accompanied by thunder, low hills no timber   walking difficult   in a thicket of bushes we found the corpse of a panther or lion very mutilated,   forded one swollen river came to another I am sick of rivers   the Sieur de La Salle still has not spoken a word since the desertion of his valet   7 leagues NE

4 M a r c h   1 6 8 7

today as we were building rafts to cross a broad & rapid river a figure emerged from the woods behind us who we all thought was a savage,   his face all painted   but it turned out to be the Sieur de La Salle's lackey Minime who rushed to embrace his master's knees,   which prevented him from being kicked, fawning and humbling himself weeping with great demonstrations of remorse he requested to be allowed to return to the Sieur de La Salle's service,   renouncing all the while his disobedient ways & his savage acquaintances,   who he claims to have sent packing back to their tribes,   for they were plotting to murder us all Minime says but he dissuaded them he promised to return with them & become their leader if they would spare us & leave us unharmed but after they traveled 2 days he stole away from them in the night,   now he has returned to us where he belongs having rescued us all he claims he said all this speaking rapidly   with a sobbing voice clutching the Sieur de La Salle's legs   who appeared unmoved but he did not beat him.   but no one believes this ridiculous story,   now he is back with us but the only other choice is to leave him alone in this unknown country we should do that.

after this incident we set about to cross this swollen river but it was as though the return of the Sieur de La Salle's valet had cursed our enterprise,   for when the Sieur de La Salle and M. Cavelier with some others got in a raft to cross scarcely had they reached the current when it carried them off with great violence   they disappeared almost instantly, eight of us remained ashore   It was extreme anguish for us all no horses no buffalo boats & some of the men was for murdering Minime   M. Joutel prevented it,   finally later in the day we saw the Sieur de La Salle on the opposite bank with his party, we all gave a cheer   he said the raft had been arrested by a large tree which was floating in the river,   and this gave them a chance to make an effort & escape the current, one of the men sprang into the water to catch the branch of a tree & this poor lad was unable to get back to the raft, it was the younger Talon who they never saw again.   carried away by the current   making 131.

then the Sieur de La Salle advised us to construct a raft of canes larger than his,   and this we were forced to do if we wanted to cross & resume our voyage we made two rafts each to hold four persons,   Moranget Joutel Hien & I crossed I was frightened to death we went under every moment, the Sieur de La Salle sent 2 men to swim out part way & help pull the raft,   and they brought us safely in.

Those who remained on the other side Minime L'Archeveque Liotot Mousset   did not like risking this crossing but they had to do it at last when we made a show of packing up & continuing our march without them,   then they crossed but they used poles which reduced the hazard & our whole troop assembled to dry our clothes at a fire on the other side,   and here we camped having spent the entire day crossing this miserable river.

----

5 March 1687

the Sieur de La Salle leading the way   we traversed a country of very thick cane breaking it with axes,   Chuka left our
group to hunt,   being low on food   6 leagues N   why
N?   he doesn't know any more than I do

6 March 1687

no sign of Chuka he did not return   this land is all marsh
& cane.   I have never seen country so hard to walk in as
this,   light rain toward evening.
     Father Douay has a gash on his leg obtained when his raft
was carried away on the river,   it suppurates badly the
Sieur de La Salle dresses it with poultices bandages
     we saw some hills east of here & bore in that direction
to avoid this marsh,   camped on a little hillock dry fired our
pieces to signal Chuka   8 leagues E

7 March 1687

still marching east across some little hills at last Chuka came
in loaded with 3 buccaned deer & another fresh,   the Sieur
de La Salle ordered a discharge of several guns to express our
joy,   then we set to and eat on the spot being starved
and so rose refreshed to continue across some small hills &
valleys mostly N 9 leagues.

9 March 1687

now Mousset has deserted who cares   soon none will be
left but Christian savages & crazy persons,   the Sieur de La
Salle did not care to speak with us all day.   when one is
disloyal the rest are to blame
     he left in the night like the others,   plumes of smoke
from a village nearby.
     we crossed some large plains & one small river,   then a

larger river felled some trees to cross it,   camped at the
edge of a small tributary where there was some woods   12
leagues NE

speak the word & it shall not stand they shall eat every man
the flesh of his arm,   some savages we met today laughed
at the name Messipi River.   we were traveling along the
tops of some hills   to avoid the bottoms, but found a difficulty in getting down by reason of the rocks we met at the
end of them,   at last we climbed down & fording a river
heard some dogs hunting the buffaloes which was the first
buffaloes we have seen in a week.   we shot one dead to the
amazement of some savages hunting close behind creeping
from tree to tree   we made signs for them to come near &
made them to smoke,   the Sieur de La Salle reluctant to
visit their village but he thought he might obtain some horses
there,   so he went a little way with the savages to observe
the body of those people then returned & took us with him.

these savages said they were friends of the Cenis,   but
they have not heard of any great river.   we tried with them
to barter for horses but they had put their horses off a little
way where we could not see them,   for fear we would take
them except a bay we traded for some axes,

M. Joutel purchased a very fine goatskin for 4 needles used
it to make some shoes,

here the chief had a page of a book in French which was
fastened to the end of a reed.   we asked him where he got
it he said some of his people had been conducted by 3 men
like us to a camp   and these men promised to talk of peace
but on the contrary had fired and killed one of their people
which obliged them to kill these 3 men.   at this we became
afraid for our safety   supposing this was some of the men
who had deserted from the Sieur de La Salle's previous voyage,   but this chief treated us with courtesy & respect making us gifts of buffalo hides dried meat some beans   and so

we left this village & set up camp a little way off keeping
watch   having marched 8 leagues all North

LA SALLE

11 March 1687

When we attempt to learn the name of these savages they
pretend not to understand. The men and women sometimes
go about naked, and Minime claims to have seen some her-
maphrodites among them.

These people make themselves drunk by a certain smoke
for which they give all they have. They also drink a concoction which they extract from the leaves of some trees, toast-
ing them first on the fire inside a vessel which resembles a
low-necked bottle. When the leaves are toasted, they fill the
vessel with water and hold it over the fire so long until it has
boiled three times; then they pour the liquid into a bowl
made of a gourd cut in two. As soon as there is a great deal
of foam on it, they drink it as hot as they can stand, and, from
the time that they take it out of the vessel until the first drink,
they shout, "Who wants to drink?" Whereupon all the
women of the tribe are expected to stand still at once, and,
even if they are carrying a heavy load, must not move. Should
one of them stir, she is dishonored and beaten, and the men
in a great rage spill the liquid they have made onto the
ground, and spit out whatever they drank.

13 March 1687

Today on our march we attained an eminence, terminated by
a rock, at the foot whereof ran a little river bordered on its
banks with flat rocks fit for building. Climbing down, we
came to the edge of a marsh, too difficult to cross, and so
camped in this place resolving to search out the best way to
go on the morrow.

1 4   M a r c h   1 6 8 7

Owed to M. Branssac of the Seminary of Montreal	46,000 livres, to be paid in beaver skins
To the Count de Frontenac	13,623
To the Sieur Pen	34,825
To my brother, M. Cavelier	17,163
To M. Plet	11,256
To the Sieur de La Forest	5,200, to be reimbursed by preference out of Fort Frontenac
To M. Henri Cavelier	42,000
Payment for Joutel, Talon, Moranget, and the other officers	12,000
Wages for the surviving men	1,900

183,967 livres

Owed to me by the Sieur de La Forest, in the name of the Sieur de La Barre	60,000 livres
Seigniory of Lake St. Louis	19,100
Furs cached on the River Colbert	23,000

102,100 livres

Theft, mismanagement, and the scheming of the Jesuits have consumed the remainder of my property. Had I preferred gain to the honor of discovery and the King's great enterprise, I need only have stayed at Fort Frontenac, where I made more than 25,000 livres a year. As it is, the remainder can be raised in furs, not to mention pearls, buffalo robes, and other such items as we may trade on the River Colbert.

1 5   M a r c h   1 6 8 7

Last night, the rain began again, and we did not stir all day because of it; constructing huts of reeds and poles to keep us dry. Minime continues to give good service, and has done nothing offensive since returning. Even men made of wood learn to fear for their lives. The complainers and whiners who say we are lost will be surprised by the cache we come to in one or two days, in which I stored some beans and grain on my previous journey.

We have entered into the realm of spring, and now the mosquitoes plague us, leading the men to insist that we gather green wood and build fires to keep them off with the smoke; but then the smoke would plague us. In this, human beings are not unlike cats, who, hardly content to pursue their own tails, must bite them off to redeem the effort.

1 7   M a r c h   1 6 8 7

Today from an elevation above the valley of a winding river I call the River of Canoes, in respect of a journey we took on it with some canoes on our former voyage, we beheld one of the most extensive, diverse, and delightful landscapes my eyes have ever seen. The river is nearly vermillion in color, and about the width of a musket shot. In every direction, the plains are lush and green, and dotted with grazing buffalo, while small coppices of live oak and other trees afford shade and the pleasure of variety. This would be a good place for a colony, as the earth is very rich and fruit trees thrive, to say nothing of the game, which is plentiful.

France must have been like this before the Romans came; the Romans drove out the barbarians and became the Gauls, building villages and farms in valleys such as this one. Gazing down at this valley, I imagined hedgerows, walls, villages, footpaths, mills, roads, fairs, churches, commerce, sheep and cows at pasturage, cultivated fields, estates and châteaus, all the appurtenances of a thriving civilization; here a wedding feast, there some women washing clothes on a creek bank; smoke rising from the blacksmith's shop, and barges carrying livestock down the river. Then all dissolved and rose like a mist; the buffaloes returned, along with the unmowed grass and groves of trees, and the entire valley unfurled like a very carpet, untrodden by either coarse boots or slippers.

I immediately recognized the place where I had cached beans and grain last year, some two or three leagues away, and pointing it out to Minime, Liotot, Hien, and Goupil, ordered them to go there and recover it while the rest of us descended to the valley. We have agreed to meet in a day or two below, and rest in this place to replenish our food and gather strength for the journey ahead.

18 March 1687

Three days of sunshine is unprecedented here; to all appearances, the winter rains have finally exhausted themselves, and our bones will at last be given an opportunity to dry.

Instead of savages desperate for miracles, I would have preferred that poets follow us; on foot, on horseback, or up to their noses in mud. They could be our historians, and celebrate the beauty of valleys such as this.

My brother and Father Douay said Mass this morning; at the elevation of the host the sun rose; this must be a sign.

Later we heard shots from the northwest, and concluded that Minime, Goupil, and the others I had sent to retrieve the cache had killed some buffalo. Accordingly, I ordered my nephew, Moranget, along with Saget, Tessier, and the horse, to go and assist them in carrying the meat back. Then we shot some buffalo here, these animals being plentiful in these parts; and stretched the skins out to dry in order to construct some skin boats in the manner of the savages; to cross those rivers we have yet to come to. Chuka washed the robes given him by the King, and spread them out on some bushes beside the river to dry; the first time he has done this, to my knowledge. He doesn't speak of it, but by these actions he appears to anticipate the River Colbert prematurely. But we have yet to arrive among the Cenis, and our river is at least a month's journey from there. Perhaps the sunshine has touched all our heads.

20 March 1687

This morning, Goupil came from the other party and announced that the cache of grains and beans was found all rotted and spoiled. I asked him if he had seen my nephew, M. Moranget, and the others I had sent to inquire of their party. He replied with some imprudent and provocative words, saying that M. Moranget wished to see me, and this led me to believe that a disagreement has erupted among these men which requires me to settle it. Accordingly, I traveled this evening to the place where a tributary joins the River of Canoes, and where their camp is supposed to be, accompanied by Chuka and Father Douay; but found nothing except some eagles circling in the air upriver; and I had all but concluded that these men had deserted as others had, when Chuka spotted some smoke up the river, and both of us saw Minime gesturing and waving, then performing for our benefit one of his provocative mimes, with twitching motions like a puppet on a stick. Goupil was with him, a little closer to us, and appeared to be choking; then Minime disappeared. As all this happens even while I describe it, I am constrained now to put my pen aside and attend to these servants, or children, who refuse to behave in a manner appropriate to their station.

————

GOUPIL

15 March 1687

the Sieur de La Salle led our company to a ravine to avoid
the marsh but the passage all thick with vines and bushes,
nearly impossible to proceed.   then attempting to climb
the steep sides of this ravine our horse fell everything muddy
we had to distribute his load until we could attain the top the
Sieur de La Salle cursing all the way even blaspheming the
Lord,   thus are men forced to do the work of horses
only 4 leagues due north

17 March 1687

at last we came to a spacious valley marveled at its beauty
from above,   here we will rest but the Sieur de La Salle
divided our company first   to find some provisions he
stored on his last journey.   he sent me out with the disgusted party Hien Minime &c.   with space in our bundles
to carry these provisions back beans & grain,   I think hop-
ing we would not return,   and so have less mouths to feed
the loudest at that
    this land extremely fertile   grass so dewy even at midday
we wrung out our moccasins,   & so came to the spot he
indicated but could not find the cache we will search in the
morning,   sunshine all day   6 leagues NE

18 March 1687

the provisions we found was all spoiled as the Sieur de La
Salle had not protected it sufficiently from the dampness of
the earth,   but visionaries thrive on stupidity in this they
resemble scholars   unable to execute their best ideas,
    what exploration what monkey business,   the Sieur de
La Salle does not know what sort of face to put upon things
as no one thinks we shall ever see his damned river,   so he
sends us off to perish by ourselves wanting to dismiss every-

one if he could but he is stuck with us we shall all die with him,   even though he makes a great to-do about it as if we should ever come among Christian society again,   feigning to be in a rush to puff himself up   oh strange and miserable life in which we have to endure this man's foolish schemes and taste of everything disagreeable in nature & men

Hien & Minime shot some buffaloes   and smoking the meat they laid aside the marrow bones & others to roast them & eat the flesh that remains on them,   but who should ride up on our horse but the Sieur Moranget who finds fault with everything   Saget & Tessier were with him behind forced to walk.   they were come to fetch the meat back having heard our shots   right away the Sieur Moranget flew into a rage this rash & violent man   upbraiding our company with sloth for not returning sooner   though the meat on the scaffolds was not yet dry,   and seizing those portions we had placed aside and which belonged to the hunters by right,   he declared these were the property of the Sieur de La Salle he would take them in his name   and other such offensive behavior speaking insulting words to our company,

Liotot claims that the Sieur Moranget caused the death of his brother last year,   having ordered him to return to the fort on the Sieur de La Salle's previous journey,   but the poor man was murdered by savages.   but the Sieur Moranget abused Liotot for mentioning this shouting insults at the man   they could not be pacified,   but went to bed still spending their passion with words & cavils.

2 0 *M a r c h*   1 6 8 7

madness and bloody horror we are all undone   O horrible O lamentable   the floodgates of murder is opened & the horrible torrent had its way   the 19th hearing the sound of a blow I woke in the night   the Sieur Moranget spasmodic gasping   sitting up unable to speak   then Minime dispatched him with a blow from his ax,   Saget & Tessier already dead   with Hien and Liotot standing above their corpses axes in hand

I jumped from my bed expecting the same fate penetrated as I was with grief & horror at so cruel a spectacle   the Sieur Moranget's face full of blood & gore but they resolved to spare me on condition that I would comply with their wishes   & never return to France or speak of this deed and this I promised having no choice,   at dawn they set me to work with Hien dragging away the bodies   moving our camp further down the river,

we constructed some shelters of bark   after that we spent the day in uneasy alliance, more than once I feared for my life   for these men went about laughing & spitting proud of their horrible deeds   as their plans had not yet ripened they excluded me from their counsels   we feasted upon the choice parts of the buffalo retrieved from the Sieur Moranget they shot another buffalo   then today the 20th Liotot went to the Sieur de La Salle I could see their stratagems what could I do,   Liotot was to tempt him here with provocative words & news of more buffalo meat   and we awaited his arrival hidden among some thickets beside the river   at last Minime spotted him jumped up shouting dancing waving,

some eagles was in the sky because of the carrion,   I had thought to shoot one but the Sieur de La Salle fired his weapon first to bring one down then coming toward us,

I jumped up from the weeds to warn him of this plot against his life   as he was approaching with hesitation perhaps suspecting some foul design,   but the river roaring too loud for him to hear   it was midday all grew still it seemed as if the river stopped too   of a sudden I found myself grinning stupidly, staring at a rock   upriver a wind hot then cold, passed across my feet to my head then my senses grew dim I was trembling.   a foul odor   someone digging in my eye.

when I awoke from my fit I saw a face Minime's painted like a savage   he was grinning he pointed I looked off a

little ways toward the river   Father Douay and Chuka were
running toward us   then I saw the bloody remains of the
Sieur de La Salle shot through the head   they had torn off
his clothes split open his bowels & performed some other
mutilations on his body   and dragged him into some
bushes there to rot or be devoured by beasts,   without any
Christian burial   may his soul rest in peace   135

IV

QUEBEC

1688

GOUPIL
TO THE MARQUIS DE DENONVILLE,
GOVERNOR OF NEW FRANCE[1]

Château St. Louis
Quebec
3 August 1688

monsieur,

my supplications having produced no effect   as my enemies
have your ears monsieur allow me to memorialize the events
of that time we spoke of before,   and the voyage I underwent which I performed almost by myself one of the most
extraordinary voyages any man has ever performed,   a
species of miracle   having covered more than 250 leagues
across the country from our Fort of St. Louis   viz., 80
leagues to the place where the Sieur de La Salle was murdered   thence 20 leagues to the Cenis,   from the Cenis
to the Nassonis 25 leagues ENE   from the Nassonis to the
Cadodaquis 40 leagues NNE,   from the Cadodaquis to the
Cahinnios and Mentous 25,   thence to the Arkansas 60 to
the ENE.   but all of this was merely child's play as I then
walked more than 600 leagues from the River Messipi to
Quebec,   after wintering with the Chicaza   having covered by land & waterway more than 900 leagues all the

---

[1]Denonville had recently replaced Le Febvre de La Barre as Louis
XIV's Governor of Canada; the fort in which Goupil was being held
abutted one side of the Governor's château in Quebec; hence, Goupil's
return address is also the Governor's home.

distance from Mexico to Quebec across this vast continent
which no man has ever done before in their life,   for God
so ordered these things that not a hair of my head fell to the
ground without his permission,   we all looked upon ourselves as men buried alive in a remote corner of the world
where we could see & hear nothing at all   God's face
turned from us   : but I succeeded in returning to Christian
society against such afflictions as men never survive,   having been animated and sustained to the end by God and his
beloved son so that I might escape alone to tell the news,
and this is the reward for which God preserved me all this
time to be treated in this fashion,   but shall there be evil
in the city and the Lord has not done it?   it is the Lord's
doing & should be marvelous in our eyes   the affliction for
which I was preserved when my foot ever slipped his mercy
held me up,   what am I that I should be spared,   my sins
far less than deserve this affliction to be thrust into this stinking dungeon,   where he preserves me yet for my great
reward I sing hymns of praise day & night all my waking
hours holy holy holy is the Lord God almighty   and blessed
is he who comes in his name,   for which the poor wretched
prisoners here scream to knock my brains out demanding I
stop,   but my task here is the same as it ever was on my
pilgrimage to promote the good of my nation & spread the
word of God to his greater glory.   but to return to my
relation of these events,
    you asked what became of M. Cavelier & Father Douay &
the others and I tell you honestly I do not know,   I never
saw them after I left the village of the Cenis   when the
Sieur de La Salle was discovered murdered Father Douay
came up & fell to his knees   weeping at the horrible insults
the murderers had performed on our leader's body together
he & M. Cavelier mourned for the Sieur de La Salle   that
great man   and begged of their own lives too but the murderers assured them they would not be harmed,   they
wanted to bury the Sieur de La Salle but the murderers would
have none of this   but secretly among ourselves we praised

our wise commander and sung his elegy   who was constant
in adversity intrepid generous engaging dexterous skillful
capable of everything,   for 20 years had softened the fierce
temper of countless savage tribes,   his extraordinary
knowledge of arts and sciences together with an almost in-
defatigable body   only to be massacred by the hands of his
own treacherous men   whom he was wont to load with
caresses.   he died in the prime of life in the midst of his
course and labors without ever seeing their success,

together the rest of us were obliged to stifle all our resentment to these men   for we expected them to murder us at
every moment,   but I dissembled so well that they were not
very suspicious of me   and the murderers seizing upon the
effects of our company we made our way toward the village
of the Cenis   the Sieur de La Salle's valet Minime Duhaut
now assuming command he puffed himself up declaring that
every man ought to command in his turn   meaning it was
his turn,   but this officious scoundrel soon met his reward
as you shall learn,

along the way we came to a tree which the Sieur de La Salle
had carved on his previous voyage   with crosses & the arms
of France,   Minime dressed in the Sieur de La Salle's scarlet
coat with gold galloons aping his strutting ways   spit upon
this tree & set it on fire,   then strolled about abusing the
men even those of his party ordering them about as we set
up camp with so much insulting language all were enraged

but this was as much as any of us could take monsieur,
that night on my watch I noticed that the Chicaza savage Chuka was gone   leaving his bundle weapons axe behind
but having taken with him the basket containing the robes
given him by the king,   I concluded he was parted from
our company forever,   and seizing the ax which he had left
behind at the hazard of my life in a blind fury for which the
Lord God in heaven forgive me   I stole to the sleeping
figure of Minime and heavenly father planted the ax in his
brain, strange to say he neither moved nor cried out it was
like chopping a block of wood   then I noticed a quantity

2 2 1

of blood around him too great for what I had performed   the sticky effusion covered his clothes, looking
closer I saw he had been stabbed a hundred times on his
body.   thus the Lord preserved me from the sin I intended
praise his holy name   for this scoundrel had already been
murdered.

the next morning when we all awoke to find Minime's
head split open,   still dressed in his master's fine clothes
face painted like a very savage   as Chuka was gone his
things left behind his ax buried in the lackey's skull everyone
concluded that he had done this thing   & wondered where
he was if he lurked about that place   designing to murder
us all as well, in extreme distress our company hurried to the
village of the Cenis   after throwing Minime in a hole we
dug,   doing him more honor than he had done to the Sieur
de La Salle who he left to be devoured by wild beasts   and
covering it over with dirt.

finally we arrived at the village of the Cenis one of the
largest & most populous I have met with in America   at
least 20 leagues long, not that it is continuously inhabited
but in hamlets of 10 or 12 cabins each fine cabins fifty feet
high in the shape of beehives with 2 doors & holes at the top,

we found among the Cenis many things which came from
the Spaniards dollars silver spoons lace of every kind   one
savage was dressed after the Spanish fashion a little doublet
the body blue sleeves of white fustian   with very straight
breeches white worsted stockings woolen garters a broad
rimmed hat,

while we were with the Cenis Hien & Liotot determined
to return to our Fort of St. Louis,   but the women of this
tribe detained them who are not so forward as to offer themselves but will not be over difficult in complying for some
little present,   & did not grudge their time,   so these
murderers enjoyed themselves while M. Cavelier Father
Douay myself & the others fasted & prayed,   this was near
the feast of the ascension.

Then Hien went off with these savages to fight a battle,

there was a Frenchman living with these savages who had completely become a savage himself, having deserted from the Sieur de La Salle's previous expedition he recognized us, we apprised him of the Sieur de La Salle's murder, whereupon this man whose name was Ruter attached himself to the Sieur Liotot, but he was a treacherous friend as you shall see

when the savages returned with Hien having been victorious in their battle with the help of our firearms, they had killed or taken 48 men & women having slain a number of women who fled to the treetops so that many more women had perished than men. 2 of these women they brought home alive & give them to the rage & vengeance of the squaws in their own tribe who arming themselves with thick stakes sharp pointed beat these prisoners tormenting them, tore off their hair cut off their fingers & put them to other such exquisite tortures to revenge the death of their husbands & sons killed in former wars, at last they were killed with the blows of a club then cut into morsels which they obliged some slaves of that nation they had long possessed, to eat.

Then Liotot went to Hien and told him he was not for returning to Fort St. Louis, he wanted to inquire of 2 other Frenchmen also deserters in a nearby hamlet of the Messipi River & the distance to it but Hien reminded him of the dangerous consequences to them should they return to Quebec, and demanding his share of the effects they had seized from our company, Liotot refused to comply drew his pistol fired upon Hien who staggered about 4 paces back & fell down dead whereupon Ruter drew his pistol & fired upon Liotot shooting him through with 3 balls, he did not die immediately he made his confession after which Ruter put him out of his pain with a blank charge of powder against his head

monsieur I assure you these Cenis were dumfounded, having themselves so lately engaged in warfare they could not understand this ferocious enmity among companions &

its bloody result   but sat at their cabins mouths agape with undisguised horror in a consternation.   it was therefore requisite to make the best of a bad business & we gave them to understand that there had been reason for punishing these dead persons   because they had all the powder & ball and would not give any to the rest,   this excuse appearing to satisfy the Cenis.

But we were all in fear of our safety from this French savage Ruter & the other Cenis   and went to our beds that night in some cabins of these people unable to sleep soundly. then around the middle of the night I heard someone moving near my bed opening my eyes I saw a man stark naked by the light of the fire   with a bow and 2 arrows in his hand he came & sat down by my bed without saying a word.   I spoke to him he made no answer, not knowing what to think of it I laid hold of my firelock which this savage perceiving went & sat by the fire.   I followed looking steadfastly on him,   when of a sudden he spoke my name throwing his arms about and embracing me & made himself known as a man named Grollet a Frenchman who deserted from the Sieur de La Salle,   this was one of the Frenchmen said to be living in a nearby hamlet a sailor of Brittany who had so perfectly inured himself to the customs of the natives that he had become a complete savage,   naked his face & body covered with tattoos & other figures like the rest,   he had taken several wives been at the wars & killed their enemies with firelocks which had gained him reputation   but having no more powder or ball his musket grown useless he had learned to shoot with a bow & arrow.   as for religion and his immortal soul he said he was not much troubled with that,   being infatuated with the course of libertinism he had run himself into,

this man had heard of the shootings in this village, I acquainted him with the death of the Sieur de La Salle & his nephew Moranget Saget & Tessier the death of Minime the disappearance of Chuka   as for the bloody aftermath in this village in which the murderers themselves were murdered

Grollet informed me that Ruter would surely kill us all or incite the Cenis themselves to do it,   at which I resolved to take myself off that very night Grollet revealing that there was a great river some fifty leagues thence to the northeast, it turned out to be 3 times that distance   where the Cenis averred there were many natives along its banks   and believing this was the very river we were searching for   I rewarded him for his confidence and packed my bundle that very evening with as much powder & ball as I could carry   an ax knives musket cornmeal beans,   and left while it was still dark.

monsieur how can I make known to you the worries I had upon this voyage,   my tribulations my head light & dizzy my knees feeble my feet bleeding my body raw from sitting double day & night,   but God was with me in a wonderful manner bearing up my spirit carrying me along.   sometimes I was met with favors & sometimes with nothing but abuse   but the thought of going home much cheered my spirit & made my burden seem light & almost nothing at all. & many times I considered that the hearts of men are in the hands of God   & God is the very keel of creation   & his eye & his thoughts always guides us.

I departed in silence after embracing Grollet but soon unaccountably became afraid for my very life that first night,   for I felt certain that someone was following me fancying every tree or bush every shadow among the thickets with which these valleys are dotted,   to be a savage or ghost of someone murdered,   I marched to the hills east of this valley to be out of sight of the villages by dawn,   and come to a river beyond them beside which I traveled uneasy all the night for fear that Ruter or one of his Cenis was directly behind   about to plant an ax in my brain.

when dawn came I crossed the river on a sort of bridge of logs I constructed   knocking the bridge apart as I crossed, then marched to a grove of trees exhausted entrenching myself there with bushes all around and lay down to sleep in mortal fear of my safety.   for I could not stave off sleep any longer having been pressed to stay awake all the night,

sometime later I awoke to see a man bent over my bundle,   I know not whether this was the same day or I had slept the rest of that day & night, he stood with my musket in his hands silently pointing it in my direction it was Chuka   I begged him of my life on the spot trembling from head to toe   but he turned away without a word   keeping the musket   and from that day forward we traveled together Chuka hunted for our food   this stoical savage never disdaining to speak a word to me.

his only bundle was the basket containing the robes given him by King Louis, he carried that & the musket   never once did I sleep soundly at night but continued in fear of my life,   however this savage did me good service always sharing the meat he hunted constructing shelters lighting our fires.

we crossed many rivers,   I never want to see another river   constructing bridges or rafts fording the water the rains came back   through muddy sloughs thick with mosquitoes,   now the weather grew hot.   stayed with the Nassoni tribe until June, these savages attempting to dissuade us from leaving by promising us wives food provisions and representing to us the immense dangers of our journey as well from enemies who surrounded these parts as from the bad & impassable ways & the many woods & rivers.   but we were not to be moved & only asked one kindness that they would give us guides,   which we obtained with great difficulty but the guides soon turned back,   merely pointing the way to the River Messipi while mumbling their gibberish which we neither understood,

after that we met with very bad ways more rain,   then the rains stopped we passed through some pleasant country   lovely plains & meadows,   one tribe of savages we met there were the Cadodaquis   who carried us on their backs to their village making signs that this was the custom of their country & we must submit to it,   3 men carried me on their backs & shoulders and in that ridiculous equipage we reached their village.

there the women came to our cabin every night to sing a
doleful song,   these were tender & civil savages a young
boy died they shed many tears   burying him in the ground
a little ways out of the village as Christians do,   where the
chief's wife each morning went to the grave with a little
basket of parched corn ears,   the meaning of which I could
not understand.

these savages showed us in a cave the body of one of their
chiefs dead 4 years,   which had not decayed or spoiled nor
have animals eaten it,   they made us to understand by signs
that his hair continued to grow & the fingernails and toenails
to grow as well.

of the tribes we came to monsieur there is no need to
number their hairs, among others we met the Cahinnios and
Mentous   all expressed amazement that we were not killed
by the other tribes who are their enemies,   but in reality
each admitted us with courtesy in their turn,   sometimes
dancing about like a troop of devils many of their women has
their faces disfigured,   one village of savages chastised
their children by throwing water upon them without ever
beating them or giving them ill words,   this struck me very
much.

there is more trees in the country we came to.   the savages made their canoes from one piece of wood   some of
these savages eat watermelons a sort of fruit proper to
quench thirst in the heat of these parts,   the pulp of it being
no better than water,

in one tribe we were welcomed with a ceremony that
lasted all evening, they entered our cottage with a calumet
singing for about a quarter of an hour,   after that they
carried me out to a place already prepared where one of them
laid a great handful of grass upon my feet 2 others brought
fair water in an earthen dish they washed my face   I was
made to sit on a skin provided for that purpose, the elders
took their places one man planted some wooden forks in the
ground   and having laid a stick across them placing on top
a buffalo skin a goat's skin laid the pipe thereon, all this time

there was all manner of singing,   great hollow calabashes filled with stones they struck on measure   and two savages placing themselves behind me seized my shoulders muttering their incomprehensible sounds & shook & dandled me from side to side,   this motion answering to the music.   then the chief of that tribe brought 2 maids one had an otter's skin   and made them to sit down on each side of me in such a posture that they were looking upon each other their legs extended & intermixed whereupon one of the chiefs laid my own legs upon theirs so that mine lay uppermost, he tied a feather upon my head the singing continued all this time, but I drew back as if stung,   realizing these savages were marrying me to these heathen women   and pretending to be ill so as not to give offense to these people signaled the chief to allow me to withdraw back to my cottage & take my rest.   some gave tokens of dissatisfaction at this,   but we appeased them with many presents beads knives needles awls   with which they were at last satisfied but they never ceased singing all night outside our cottage with so much zeal that many were reduced to a state of utter exhaustion.

these savages provided us with guides as some of the others had.   we traveled several different ways which we could never have found by ourselves.   through very pleasant woods stately cedars   prairies where there was buffaloes in abundance,   all this time sensible of the haughty reserve of my companion Chuka   who never cared to speak a single word to me   so that I lost much sleep for fear that he would deal with me as he had Minime,

at last we met a company of savages with axes going to fetch barks of trees for their cottages   surprised to see us,   making signs for them to draw near they came caressing us presented us with some watermelons they had,   and putting off their design to fetch bark went along with us to their village, we came to a river that was between us and their village & looking over to the further side   discovered a great cross in the ground,   and some distance from it a house built after the French fashion.

you can imagine monsieur what inward joy I conceived at that emblem of my salvation I knelt down lifting my hands & eyes to heaven to return thanks to the divine goodness for conducting us so happily   Chuka knelt too,   then crossing the river in canoes with these savages we discovered the house to be empty but inside the belongings were unharmed,   as a breviary in French a Bible articles for saying the holy Mass   and we were made to understand by signs that these were left by men who came down the great river & would soon come back, I inquired how far the river was from this place, they answered it was just a ways down the river we had crossed,   from which I finally understood that these were the *Arkansas* we had come among, who have four tribes the Otsotchove the Toriman the Tonginga & the Cappa the latter live on the River Messipi the very village we had visited on our glorious voyage down that same river six years ago.

after a day in this village we made known our desire to be conducted to the Cappa,   and in short embarking on canoes we traveled down this river of the Arkansas about 4 leagues passing the other villages until we came to the fatal river so much sought after by us   called Colbert by the Sieur de La Salle Messipi by these savages   so large & dark so long the object of our search,   but I found it strange & happy that coming to this place was almost like coming home after 3 years of misery in a place no one knew,   not having departed by so much as an inch from its course in the six years since I had been there always in this place waiting   until finally I became sick of regarding it in this manner   filled with so much rapid water   I fancied it mocked me,   and turned away unable to restrain my tears.

in this village we discovered the cross & arms of France which the Sieur de La Salle had erected 6 years ago,   with a little fence of stakes about it well preserved these savages appear to treat it with great veneration.   they made us to understand that not long ago some Frenchmen had come back to this place among whom I recognized the name of the

Sieur Tonty,   who the Sieur de La Salle left in charge of his fort on the River Seignelay he came down the Messipi and traveled in these parts among the Arkansas   to discover whether the Sieur de La Salle had made any progress in establishing a colony on the river.   these natives speak the name La Salle with reverence,   they patiently await the return of the Sieur de La Salle whom they remember well in all his majesty, I thought it best for our safety to keep his death a secret,

as Chuka was anxious to return to his people after so long and circuitous a passage away,   we remained only 4 days with these Cappa who treated us like kings   feeding us in a manner each evening I shall never forget they serve up their meat in two or four large platters set before the principal guests who are seated at one end   when we ate a little these dishes were then shoved down lower & others served up in their place   in the same manner the first dishes served at the upper end & thrust down lower as others come in

at last as it was by this time the end of August   Chuka and I proceeded with great toil up the River Messipi in a canoe we purchased of the Arkansas,   against a very strong & rapid current often finding it necessary to land sometimes to travel over marshes carrying this heavy canoe where we sunk halfway up the leg   other times over burning sands which scorched our feet for by this time we had no shoes.   or else over splinters of wood which ran into the soles of our feet   in this manner arriving at last at that place whence we had first ventured into the forest to visit the Chicaza, here we saw the remains of our Fort Prud'homme,   Chuka still stoical and silent but I observed his quickened pace   his eyes fairly glittered   as we marched along that same path to the village of his people whence he had come.

these savages welcomed us with elaborate ceremony & put me into a cabin with Chuka & some other members of his family,   where they gave me very little food nevertheless expecting me to fetch wood carry burdens or loads, now & then they abused me.   in short it took me very little time to understand that these Chicazas considered me their slave   especially attached to the service of Chuka whose family used me poorly throwing mud at me or putting arrows to my chest every day saying they would kill me,   they kicked me slapped my face beat me with sticks, Chuka held back from these demonstrations regarding them without emotion   the boys idlers & roughs did this.

in this manner I was forced to dwell among these savages all that fall & winter   experiencing bitter hardship & cold smoky air treated like a dog   famine sickness thirst   with no Christian friend to comfort me thinking every hour must be my last   but you may see the wonderful power of God that my spirit did not utterly sink beneath these afflictions still the Lord upheld me,   as he wounded me with one hand so he healed me with the other.

sometimes all I had to eat was some broth in which there was boiled an old deer's hoof or ear but if I complained they answered they would break my face, soon even the most filthy trash was sweet & savory to my taste   pieces of the small guts of a deer   to the hungry soul every bitter thing is sweet.   one time Chuka killed a deer and give me some of the fawn inside her belly that was so young & tender you could eat the bones as well as the flesh   which tasted like honey to me,   but most of the time all I had was some moldy cake so dry & hard it was like little flints.

Once when I lay by the fire I removed a stick that kept the heat from me, a squaw pushed it back again   at which I looked up & she threw a handful of ashes in my eyes I thought I was blinded,   but lying down the tears run out of my eyes carrying the dirt with them,   so I could see by the time morning come.   this is the way these savages treated me.   sometimes sitting in my cottage I suddenly leaped up & ran out as if I was at home in France   forgetting where I was,   but once outside seeing nothing but wilderness woods barbarous heathens   my mind quickly returned to me,

I remembered all the time when I was with my family in

France I had a comfortable bed to lie on but instead of this now I had only a little swill to eat & then like a pig I must lay myself down on the cold ground which did not tend to cure me of the severe cramps that often tormented me

you can see by this monsieur what false lies & calumny they spread who say I became a savage with these people,   I lived with these savages 8 months & outwardly conformed to their manners having no choice though inwardly remaining a Christian,   it being said also that I lived with a savage woman without benefit of clergy as though she was my wife,   thus violating the holy bonds of matrimony, I say this is a false and scurrilous accusation   which my enemies enjoy spreading amongst Christians for the shame it affords me,   but I would never do such a thing as lie with a filthy savage, those who accuse me of murder also accuse me of these sentiments & actions in order to paint my character with any base thing they can conjure up.   as to why I arrived in Quebec in savage dress I ask you monsieur would you rather see me naked,   an insult to your esteemed person   for the clothes I wore when I began this voyage soon became rags I was forced to put on the costume of these Chicazas, but anyone can see many *patrons* & *coureurs de bois* as well who come to Quebec dressed in a similar manner   not even bothering to dress like Christians once they have the opportunity to do so, they are not thrown into prison like I was treated like a murderer when God preserved me from the most indecent temptations & iniquity as I prayed each evening for his assistance in these particulars   praying that you monsieur would have mercy upon me when I arrived here & understand my position,   and not treat me with censure and disallowance but with serious reflection on your part monsieur a person of such capacity & courage   chosen by the King to guide with firm hand our thriving colony, would embrace me and regard me with friendship,   but to return to my relation of my captivity among the Chicazas,

reduced to such misery & suffering as no man has ever endured   I began to think my life would end amongst these

savages whereupon I entreated the Lord that he would consider my low estate & show me some measure of relief,
and indeed soon the Lord answered,   for these Chicaza
began to take ill of the pox   at first a few braves who
wandered off by themselves in the wilderness to die   but
soon more of them so quickly did the disease spread   first
evincing itself by means of a rapid swelling of the body, many
died within two or three hours of the attack   some threw
themselves headlong over a ledge of 30 feet onto the rocks
below to cheat the disease by dashing their brains out,   the
chief of this tribe became ill,   and being of strong constitution lay for many days upon those robes Chuka had carried
halfway across the world to this chief sumptuous cloth velvet
satin   given him by King Louis XIV   gold & scarlet
now however reduced to rags but this did not prevent this
chief who cherished them from clinging to their tatters until
at last he expired   whereupon Chuka retrieved the gift &
soon grew sick himself,   he also lay many days on these
robes before the end, at last he evinced some tenderness
toward me   grasping my hand but saying nothing   with
a grip of such power I thought he was wont to pull me into
the afterworld with him,   and making a present of these
same robes to me I gave them to some *Natchez* braves who
passed through these parts,   these being a savage nation
with which we passed our time during our first voyage down
the Messipi   and instructing them to present them to their
chief in the name of the Sieur de La Salle and the great chief
across the waters our King Louis   and thus they departing
down the river,
      now I was free to leave as the family which was my masters
had all died   and those left in the tribe paid me no mind
so it was that when the weather grew warmer sometime
about March or April for I had long ago lost track of the day
& month,   I gathered together my miserable bundle &
taking whatever food I could find about me such as cornmeal
& dried fruit   left these wretched Chicazas who were surely
being punished for their iniquity,   and marched once more

to the River Messipi where I found a canoe   but the current being so great at this time of the year I was forced to walk.

it would be needless to relate all the troubles & hardships I met with in that long journey up this cursed river,   it was painful and tedious but the Lord bore me up   I hardly ever had food.   one day I passed between 2 bears who sat about an arpent apart, both sat & watched me but I felt no fear and after I had passed both went the same way without growling or the least umbrage,   so I thanked God for my escape who tamed the wild beasts of the forest & made them friendly to me.

for a month I marched with great toil sometimes along footpaths near the river   sometimes through marshes up to my neck afraid I would drown or find myself stuck forever in filthy mud,   but I sang hymns of praise to the Lord who guided me closer to my destination   cleaving the way through the wilderness for me,   until at last I came to the River Seignelay   much more gentle than the Messipi   as well as the country about it being much more agreeable than that about the Messipi by reason of the many fine woods & fruit,   some savages I met treated me with kindness gave me food   but I had to take care of those few belongings I still had left as these were great thieves, they were the Illinois savages   it behooves every man to watch their feet as well as their hands they could steal your very toes,   but to hasten to my conclusion,

coming at last to the fort which the Sieur de La Salle had charged the Sieur Tonty to construct on the River Seignelay,   for the first time in more than a year I arrived once more among Frenchmen & Christians,   but how can I express my joy at having come this far and being spared every hazard I passed through,   and I thought it was such in the life of every Christian who must return to God,   for how long in vain He waits for our return that we may therefore turn to him before his anger break out into a flame   & there is no remedy.

you ask why I concealed the Sieur de La Salle's death when

I met M. Tonty at this fort,   I tell you truthfully it was my duty first to give this information to the crown therefore I merely said that I left the Sieur de La Salle 10 leagues from the village of the Cenis   which is true,   also I required assistance for my journey back to Canada & feared that said assistance would be refused if information were given of the death of the Sieur de La Salle.   the story that I obtained goods from M. Tonty on the basis of a letter of credit I had from the Sieur de La Salle   which he would not have honored had he known of the Sieur de La Salle's death is malicious slander I merely begged for necessities I have no such goods about me,   nor money I arrived in Quebec with only the clothes on my back & not a bite to eat for 3 entire days   my feet bare & bleeding

as for the rest of the business monsieur you know I came by way of the River Seignelay to the lake of the Illinois thence to the lake of the Hurons & the other lakes past the great falls with some other Frenchmen who were going that way,   and took passage as soon as I arrived here on a ship for France before this unfortunate arrest prevented my departure,   in order to see the King himself as quickly as possible and sue for the relief of the colonists left behind on the Gulf of Mexico,   I beg of you monsieur to write to the King so that supplies & relief may be sent to them where they are[1]   for there is little I can do now confined to this stinking dungeon,   but I have endured much I can endure these slanders.   M. Cavelier & Father Douay have reason to be jealous of me their false accusations are designed to give a check to your inquiries and curiosities concerning their conduct,   not that they are murderers when they visited me in this dungeon even then I did not accuse them,   shocked as I was to find them here before me and their accusations of

---

[1]When word finally reached Louis XIV of the fate of La Salle and his colony, he declined to send assistance. Those left behind at Fort St. Louis in Texas were massacred by the Karankowa Indians in February of 1689.

me to my face   but I have learned that they traded on the
Sieur de La Salle's good name & credit exactly in the manner
they denounce me for doing.   a man named Boisrondet
told me this,   thus they accuse me of murdering the Sieur
de La Salle in order to assure that their own actions are not
pried into too deeply,   they say I simulate fits but it is they
who simulate piety   their base lies prove this I could never
murder a man I served for 20 years,   following him
through the worst tribulations men have ever suffered a man
I loved,   though his brain was touched he acted fearlessly,
his violation of the King's charter his illegal trading was done
from necessity,   having no choice but to rescue our enterprise,   which was always in danger of failing because of the
resentment of men he treated badly,   in like manner his
many debts his inability to plan sufficiently   caused him to
become an intrepid leader to brave misfortunes which would
have defeated lesser men,   even if he did bring these misfortunes upon his own head,   and infect all his followers
with them too.   but for this I thank him for whom the Lord
loves he chastens & scourges, before I knew what affliction
meant I was sometimes ready to wish for it.   now I see the
portion of some is to have their misfortunes by drops one
drop & then another,   but the full cup dregs & all the
wine of astonishment like a sweeping rain that leaves no
food,   did the Lord prepare to be my portion & my full
measure,   and I see now that when God calls a person to
such a life how he gains by it,   and hope I can say as David
did it is good for me to have been afflicted   for outward
things are but a shadow a blast a bubble & things of no
continuance   having learned to look beyond present troubles to measure every grief I meet in faces of the imprisoned
& free alike   and wonder how long they bore it   for out
of prison He cometh to reign when you visit a prisoner you
visit Him   when you feed the hungry take in a stranger
clothe the naked it is Him you clothe,   what? would you
turn from those whose wounds stink whose ears were bitten
off in a fury   that man with the dent in his forehead the

scurvy the pox   the poor the sick the foolish criminal,
holy holy holy is the Lord God almighty   and blessed is he
who comes in his name,

if you examine in all particulars this relation of my suffering monsieur you will find it to be true exactly as I have
set them down,   if I had the world a year ago I would
have given it for my freedom now my Lord has shown
me the vanity of such wishes,   I am your humble & obedient servant,

Pierre Goupil

AUTHOR'S NOTE

Of the primary sources used in writing this book—largely journals and letters—the following are the most important: Louis Hennepin, *A Description of Louisiana;* Chrétien Le Clercq, *First Establishment of the Faith in New France;* Pierre Margry (ed.), *Découvertes et établissements des français dans l'ouest et dans le sud de l'Amérique septentrionale* (6 vols.); Reuben Gold Thwaites (ed.), *The Jesuit Relations and Allied Documents* (especially the voyage of Marquette in volume 59); Henri Joutel, *The Last Voyage Perform'd by de la Sale* [*sic*]; Alvar Núñez Cabeza de Vaca, *The Narrative of Alvar Núñez Cabeza de Vaca* (translated by Fanny Bandelier); Bernard de Voto (ed.), *The Journals of Lewis and Clark;* Charles Preuss, *Exploring with Fremont* (the journals of Charles Preuss, translated and edited by Erwin G. Gudde and Elisabeth K. Gudde); and Richard VanDerBeets (ed.), *Held Captive by Indians* (especially the narrative of Mary Rowlandson).

Of the secondary sources, Francis Parkman's *La Salle and the Discovery of the Great West* is still the best and most useful on La Salle. I also consulted (among others) E. B. Osler, *La Salle;* Patricia Galloway (ed.), *La Salle and His Legacy;* Marshall Sprague, *So Vast and Beautiful a Land;* Robert S. Weddle, *Wilderness Manhunt;* and for information on epilepsy and religious enthusiasm, Owsei Temkin, *The Falling Sickness*, and

B. Robert Kreiser, *Miracles, Convulsions, and Ecclesiastical Politics in Early Eighteenth-Century Paris.*

Finally, I thank Frank Bergon, whose two books, *Looking Far West* (co-edited with Zeese Papanikolas) and *The Wilderness Reader,* first introduced me to the literature of early American exploration.